Blake
Allwood

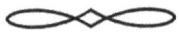

AIDEN
INSPIRED

First Edition

Aiden Inspired by Blake Allwood
www.blakeallwood.com
https://www.facebook.com/blakeallwoodnovels/
https://twitter.com/BlakeAllwood

For permissions contact: help@blakeallwood.com

Cover by Cate Ashwood.
www.cateashwooddesigns.com

*Thank you to the following
people for their assistance:*

*Kelley Lynne – Beta Reader
David Penpek – Beta Reader
Ramon Hara – Beta Reader
Dee Friloux-Editing
Lucy Lennox – Advice and Mentoring*

*A special thank you goes to all my friends
and family who supported me, I couldn't
have done it without you.*

*And special thanks
to my Husband
who tolerated me after I went down
this rabbit hole.*

PART ONE
THE
BEGINNING

Blake Allwood

Aiden

Why can't things be simple? Painting is supposed to be a mix of talent and expression with a whole lot of technique thrown in. Nowhere in my years of training have I ever heard you have to be a stupid emotional open book to reach the pinnacle of your career. Sure, some of the classics have their own spirit to them, sure you can *feel* da Vinci's work, but you can also see and feel his gift and his damned talent.

Jace was a godsend in more ways than one. She had opened her gallery to me before she even knew me that well. She marketed my paintings and even became one of my closest friends in the city, but after my last showing, she said the same thing I'd heard her say over and over again: "*Your talent is unmistakable, but you always leave your own personality out of it. If you want to go to the next level, you're going to have to give us more of yourself.*"

God help me if that woman says that to me one more time, I'll stick my head into the Hudson and be done with it!

It wasn't the first time I'd heard this. The critics have all said the same thing in one way or another and before that, my instructors had as well. I just didn't understand what they meant. What is it that's lacking?

I've won awards. I've been featured in prestigious galleries *all* across the country. I've even had art magazines write that my art is "up and coming," "someone to watch," and my favorite, "talent blooming before us." I didn't need a critic to tell me my technique was up to par, damnit, I already knew it was.

None of that mattered though, because there I was after four years of intense study, endless effort, and putting out my very best work and what did I get for it? I get to hear the same stupid critique. "Not enough of the artist's personality."

I'd already cleaned my apartment twice... ok, maybe three times, but cleaning helps to soothe me, or at least the obsessive side of me that always seems to be triggered by the critics.

Granted, "*it was one statement in an otherwise glowing review*" ... again, quoting Jace. Yet, I was still stung by the fucking comment. How can I...better yet, why would I *want* to get past this? Isn't art about divorcing yourself from your subject? Isn't it about letting others' personalities seep through? If I put myself in the paintings, wasn't I taking away from the character?

I cursed under my breath as I moved to the window. I always saved the hateful window for last, because no matter how hard I cleaned, no matter what products I used, the damned window would never be clean.

I didn't know if it was because of the hundred years of grease and grime only New York City can produce or if it was just some weird anomaly sent to torment me because no matter what I did, there were always streaks.

I was full-on scrubbing the window, the anger and frustration making me just a little concerned I may end up breaking it -- to be honest, I'm not at all sure I would have minded since the super would have to replace it with a window that could potentially be cleaned — and just as I was about to spray it again, *Dancing Queen* began blaring from my phone.

I would have ignored it, but the ring tone was my sister's. There was *only one* person in my life that knew I ignored calls and would call and harass me until I finally answered ... the ultimate dancing queen, Suzie.

"Yeah, what do you want?" I said, debating whether to hit the speakerphone button so she wouldn't interrupt my cleaning frenzy.

"You pouting?"

"Shut up, Suzie, why can't you leave me alone so I can rest in peace?"

Suzie chuckled, "You mean clean in peace?"

"That's none of your business," I retorted, and Suzie belted laughter with her huge Broadway voice. Luckily, like a reflex now, I could predict when that was coming, so I could move my phone from my ear.

When her laughter finally died down, I put the phone back to my ear and asked, "What do you want Suzie? I'm kind of busy."

"What, you've only cleaned that tiny closet you call an apartment twenty times instead of thirty?"

"Suzie, you really do need to shut up," I said, but the anger was beginning to subside. I hated that Suzie had the power to calm me even when I didn't want to be calm.

"Never, little brother," she replied.

Even though the anger was slipping out of me, I couldn't help but throw another jab. "Ha, that's the damned truth, you will never shut up."

Suzie was a master at managing me and I prepared mentally for her to do so now.

"Wow, you are definitely in a mood, aren't you? Okay, I'm coming over and we are going out."

"Suzie, no. I don't want to go out." I pleaded with her, hoping this time would be different and she'd let me brood in peace. "I'm tired and I don't want to see people tonight."

"Well, brother," she said, "you should have thought about that before you moved to one of the largest cities in the world."

"Yeah, don't remind me," I complained.

"Oh, come on, you're just pissy because of those reviews and they weren't even bad. Why do you get so upset when someone says you have ways to improve? All of us have ways to improve," she said with a sigh. "Can you imagine if I got upset with every criticism I got?"

Suzie had been recruited to do a Broadway show after she competed in *American Talent*. She had always been clear that she didn't want to be a pop music artist, so, when a Broadway producer asked her to try out for a musical, she jumped at the chance. She got the part but unfortunately, the show was a terrible bust. Luckily, her brief role had gotten her recognized enough that she was immediately cast in the role of a slutty, bisexual diva named Beta in a new musical comedy called *Gerls*. The musical was about a bunch of women who fought zombies and vampires because they were the few humans on earth who were immune to their venom.

The ridiculous plot and silly storyline had been a raving hit; so much so that it had attracted a cult following akin to *The Rocky Horror Picture Show* we used to go see in high school. Suzie loved all the attention and had blossomed in the spotlight.

I was nothing, if not her opposite ...

Where Suzie relished the spotlight, the nightlife, and the insane New York lifestyle, I seemed to languish in it.

"I'll be there at nine. Be ready and dress sexy. You need a man...or at least you need his dick," she said laughing.

I felt my face redden, as I made gagging noises. "Suzie, I told you not to talk about sex with me, it's gross."

"Little brother, how did you get to be such a prude?"

"Probably because you took all the slut," I replied. Suzie's voice blasted another laugh across the phone. This was not the first time we'd had this discussion.

Suzie was anything but a slut, but she played one so well on stage, everyone on the planet thought she was. It was funny because I knew she'd never dated anyone seriously and she was more likely than not still a virgin, although she'd deny it if a reporter ever asked. Whereas, I was a typical guy, if I wanted sex...I never hesitated to have it.

I got into the shower to wash off the smell of cleaning products, then followed my sister's directions and dressed in tight jeans -- the ones Suzie said were my *fuck me now* jeans -- and picked one of the tees I designed myself.

Seriously, I'd never admit I designed t-shirts if anyone asked. I could only imagine how the uppity

New York critics would look down their pretentious noses at me if they knew I had stooped to that. Well, screw them. Just thinking about the critics had my hand itching for another go at the streaky window.

Luckily, Suzie burst into my apartment before I could give in to the temptation, causing me to jump.

"Remind me again why I gave you a key to my apartment?" I asked, irritated by her abrupt entrance.

Suzie ignored my statement and came over pulling me into a hug. "Cause, dear brother, when you get all inspired, you try to kill yourself through starvation and dehydration. I'm the only one living in this city that is willing to keep you fed and watered!"

"Well, it might not be worth the cost," I replied as dryly as possible.

"Oh, you're going to have to get out of that funk if you're going to get laid," she said as she pulled away, winking.

"Fuck you, Suzie," I replied causing her to burst into laughter once again.

I looked over at my sister, who was taking my bad humor in good stride. Usually, I'd prefer to sit and pout, but Suzie had no tolerance for such things. She believed a gay bar was the solution to most of what ails you. Truth is, she was a typical fag hag. She swooned when she talked about all the lovely testosterone swirling around and never having to worry about anyone making a pass.

I sighed. I was a lucky guy. Not only did I have a supportive family, but I also had a sister who forced me to go out even when I just wanted to sit at home and feel sorry for myself.

"You ready to go dance with *brainless* hot men?" I said, not trying to hide my bitterness.

Suzie grinned. "Uh huh, and tonight, we are going to dance with all the hotties!"

Devin

I picked up my phone to check whether I'd gotten a call yet. Chandler, my arrogant boyf ... well, I don't guess I can call him my boyfriend ... Let's just go with boy toy...was supposed to meet me last night for dinner, or I guess more accurately, dessert.

He didn't show, which was a first. The guy was an arrogant asshole but when you lived in the middle of nowhere, your options were limited, so it is strange when a hookup date didn't show.

I chuckled at myself. I knew this was stupid. Did I even like him or was I just pissed I didn't get laid? It embarrassed me to admit, it was probably the latter. But, hell, after working the cattle and sleeping in a tent with my employees, I'd not so much as touched myself in two weeks. I was looking forward to this! Okay, I decided, I was gonna try to call him again and see.

Damn if it didn't go to messages...again. Okay, "Chan, where are you? We were supposed to meet last night, but you didn't show. You haven't returned my calls. Hey, am I missing something here? Okay, whatever is going on, call me back."

Chandler, yeah even the name was pretentious, and he, unlike the geeky fun character from *Friends*, was an ass. Unfortunately, I let it go too far but hell, he was cute. Okay. Okay, truth is the dude was hot. He was about an inch taller than me which was something since I'm six two. His body was well trimmed, although not muscular, and he always smelled like a mixture of wine and expensive cologne.

His family was all right, not what you could call happy about having a gay son, but you could tell his dad was pleased that his son was seeing a guy that owned the property next to his. That and the fact that my property was just over fifteen thousand acres probably made it easier for him to *tolerate* us.

Guessing the twink ass had probably found another toy, I stomped in frustration at my getting even remotely attached to what clearly was a whim. But it sucked because I had gotten used to him. We would spend most nights together especially after finding that the river between our two properties was usually shallow.

I decided I would rather get this over with and convinced myself that I should just drive over to his place to avoid wading through the muddy river.

I drove through the giant stone gate that announced I'd arrived at *Pandemonium Wine* which the Lafferty family bought and turned into a winery many years before I arrived here. I can't say I have warm feelings about coming over here. No one could argue that Chandler's family was *overly* friendly.

I passed a new sign someone had put up that read, *closed until further notice*. I thought that was strange, but I justified it in my head as them doing some renovations or something, so I didn't think anything of it and continued to drive toward the estate.

I hadn't had much to do with the family when I had first arrived even though I liked wine. The first few years of living there, I really didn't have time to do anything but work and after I bought the place I just bought the wines I knew and liked. Then, a couple of years after I became the ranch's official owner, old man Lafferty came over to the ranch to introduce himself—ended up that he wanted to use the river that divided us to irrigate his vines. The authorities required that he get permission from the neighboring farms before he could. Of course, I didn't mind. I signed off on the paperwork thinking that would be that.

About six months later his son Chandler showed up at my house with a case of their wine. It was good ... better than I'd thought it would be, but it wasn't just the wine that I ended up with. The man was tall, hot and willing. When he left that day, he left with a sore ass and a hickey to go with it.

I pulled up to the main house, drew in a breath and steeled myself for the break up.

I approached the door, took another deep breath and knocked. At first, it seemed no one was home but after a moment I could hear movement inside. After debating whether to just leave, I let my frustration take over and hollered out instead, "Chan, is everything okay?"

No more were the words out of my mouth than the front door was flung open and a very angry Mr. Lafferty stood in the doorway his finger pointing at me and him yelling, "No, goddammit, everything is not fine. You faggots have fucked every damned thing up."

I was in shock. I knew the old man had some issues but seriously, he'd never reacted this way. I was about to walk off the porch when Chan's sister pushed her dad back into the house and closed the door behind her.

I liked Chan's sister. She was the eldest sibling and seemed to be by far the brightest of them all. In a way, she was the family's leader and when push came to shove, she was the one who you could rely on to break down any situation.

"Have you not heard?" she asked.

"Heard what?" Perplexity caused me to shake my head. "I've been too busy with repairing fences around the ranch to hear much of anything. I just got back today after spending two whole weeks on the other side of the ranch. Why, is everything okay? Where's Chandler?"

She just looked at me and asked me to sit down on the front porch swing. "Honey, Chandler's in jail."

"What?" I asked. "Why the fuck is he in jail?"

She hesitated for a moment, and then got up telling me to stay seated. She went into the house and came back out carrying our local newspaper, *The Southeast Washington Journal.*

"Read this ..." she said handing me the paper, then she went back into the house and closed the door without saying another word.

On the front page, under his picture read: "Chandler Lafferty of Pandemonium Winery was taken into custody on Tuesday after being charged with statutory rape of an underage intern who worked at the winery. He also faces multiple allegations of sexual harassment by several workers as well. Mr. Lafferty will be held without bail until a grand jury is convened to hear his case one week from Friday."

I sat on the porch for at least another ten minutes reading the announcement over and over trying to get a grip on the information. Finally, I walked back to my car and drove home.

Aiden

The moment Suzie walked into the bar, it seemed the entire place recognized her and started chanting *"Beta! Beta! Beta!"*

Of course, being the attention whore she was, she threw open her arms and let the boys pull her onto the dance floor. As usual, I went over to the bar and ordered my signature Bud Light and sipped it while I watched my sister dance in and out of the throbbing mass of men.

Suzie was nothing if not predictable and I knew that after she had danced two songs, she would come find me and pull me into the fray.

As I sipped my beer, I was surprised by a tap on the shoulder. When I turned around, I saw Clay, a beautiful model who I knew liked to make the gay circuit.

Clay and I had dated; in fact, he was one of the longest relationships I'd ever had. We lasted about six months before Clay's need to fuck other men overcame his desire for domesticity. Luckily, he was

16

a good guy underneath the slutty exterior, and he admitted he was ready to date other guys before he cheated on me so after we broke up, we were able to remain friends.

"Hey, gorgeous, what brings the sullen artist out tonight?" Clay asked.

"My bitch of a sister drug me out," I lamented.

Clay just laughed and asked where the diva was. I pointed her out among the throng of men who surrounded her.

"She does love her gay men, doesn't she?" Clay asked with amusement.

"As long as I've known her," I sighed.

"Well we all know she would've been a better gay man than you," Clay said sarcastically.

"I can't argue with that," noticing for the first time an extremely good-looking man standing behind Clay who was beginning to become antsy.

"Who's your friend?" I asked.

Clay seemed to remember the gorgeous specimen and a smile spread across his face.

"This is Denim Freemont, a new model I met last month. Denim, this is Aiden Fisher, brooding artist." Denim tried to smile, but it ended up looking closer to a grimace.

I couldn't help but laugh, "Don't worry honey, he's all yours. Your man is safe around me."

Denim's face relaxed and the grimace shifted into a real smile that made it to his eyes.

He leaned over and said, "Then you are the only one I don't need to worry about."

I laughed again. "At least you know that."

Clay pouted, "You know I'm standing here right?"

"Ahh, honey," Denim said, "Don't be mad. You're a slut, but I worship the slutty ground you walk on."

Clay playfully elbowed the beautiful man beside him and began pulling him onto the dance floor. Denim smiled over at me and said before Clay could pull him into the fray, "Meet us for breakfast, I like the thought of having someone around who isn't trying to steal my guy."

I smiled and said, "Have Clay text me, he has my number." Then they were gone.

The beat began to filter through my peeved attitude and when my sister showed up to pull me onto the floor, I had relaxed enough to go without resistance.

By the fourth or fifth dance, I was fully engrossed in the music, but the heat had become unbearable which led to my shirt coming off and with the shirt off came the handsy men. Not that I cared that much. It never hurt to have a man -- or if experience served me correctly, several -- touching me as long as that was where it stopped.

Tonight however, one of the guys didn't seem to understand the boundaries and he almost had me exposed before I realized it.

"Whoa there," I yelled so I was heard over the music. "That needs to stay where it is."

The handsome, but way too presumptuous guy, grinned and proceeded to ignore me. Bad move because seconds later, big sis came to my rescue.

Most people had no idea how strong Suzie was, but she fell in love with weight lifting in high school so her body was like a vice grip. The poor fella didn't have time to register what had gotten ahold of him. Despite being a full foot shorter than him, she had him off the ground and almost to the door before he even knew what happened.

Suzie pointed her finger at him when she sat him down and I heard her yell, "don't touch without permission," then, like nothing had happened, she was back in the fray dancing with the beat of the music.

I couldn't help but laugh. The dude just stared after her not knowing what to do or say. I almost felt sorry for him except he was a perv who didn't know how to respect boundaries. After that, very few men touched me. Suzie always made a lasting impression on a crowd and these queens were no exception.

That evening, Suzie crashed on my couch, complaining as usual that my apartment was too small, but she had drunk too much to go home alone and my apartment was closer to the clubs than hers.

The next morning, Suzie was up way too early despite her usual hangover. She came over to my room, threw a pillow at me and said, "Let's go to the diner."

"I'm meeting Clay and his new fling in an hour," I replied.

"Oh," Suzie perked up, "Is he the tall, dark, handsome dude he was dancing with all night?"

"Yep, that's the one," I chuckled. "It seems that Denim, that's his name, was taken with me because I no longer want that kind of relationship with Clay."

Suzie laughed while holding her head. "Laughing hurts my head, Aiden, stop being funny."

"I can't help it," I smirked sarcastically, "I'm just a comedian."

"Ha," Suzie chuckled. "If that poor man thinks Clay isn't going to fuck around, he is in for a bad time."

"I think he knows what Clay is, but he seems to hope he'll change," I replied.

"Unlikely," Suzie shook her head then complained again about it hurting.

"Go take a hot shower and let the medicine kick in, then you can join us at the diner. You and Clay always got along."

"Yeah, until he crapped on my baby brother, that is."

"Suzie, we've discussed this, Clay and I both agreed we weren't working out. We had fun until it wasn't. You don't have to play overprotective sister with him."

Suzie looked at me through her bloodshot eyes and shrugged. "I know you want a relationship, Aiden, I just worry about you having your heart broken."

"I'm fine and have always had a relationship when I wanted one, but the person here that needs to be worried about is you, sis."

Suzie turned around quickly, which surprised me considering she was nursing a headache, and was in the shower before that conversation had a chance to start. I laughed out loud as she scurried away. We had discussed her lack of relationships many times and she always deflected, but I knew she was not one to play around. I just hoped when she met the right guy, he would be worth the effort.

Clay and Denim were sitting next to each other when Suzie and I walked in. I was shocked to see how close they were sitting, hands intertwined warmly, Clay leaning in as he spoke.

Clay tended to be very one-sided. He usually controlled the conversation around him and seldom let anyone else get a word in edgewise. I had to admit, I'd never seen Clay so attentive with another man. Maybe the ultimate playboy had found his match. I sure hoped so for his sake. He was a decent guy once you got below the theatrical surface.

When we approached them, Suzie took the conversation over immediately. Both men leaned back and smiled when the busty diva slipped into the seat across from them and began taking bacon off their plates.

"I have such a danged hangover," she said with a mouthful.

"Usually," Clay teased her, "that means you are queasy and aren't able to eat."

"Oh honey, I have a stomach of steel," talking with her mouth full, "it'll take more than a few too many beers to put me off food. Besides, aren't you a model? You aren't allowed to eat bacon. I'm doing you a favor."

Both Clay and Denim laughed. I sat down next to Suzie and introduced Denim to her.

"As you can see, Denim, my sister hasn't met a gay guy she doesn't know."

"Or feels comfortable stealing food from apparently," he chuckled.

Suzie swallowed then jumped right into the third degree she was famous for. "How long have you two been dating?" She asked.

"One month," Denim replied.

"Where are you from, Denim?"

"I grew up in the city."

"Are you a model too?"

"Yes," Denim nodded.

"What kind of modeling do you do?"

"I do the work I can get."

"Where did the name Denim come from?"

"My great-grandfather owned a denim factory, that is how we made our money, at least until it was sent overseas."

"So, are you rich?"

"Suzie," I chastised her, "that isn't any of your business."

"Hush, Aiden," she replied then looked back over at Denim.

"We are not rich, but I have a small trust account."

"How small?" She asked.

"Small enough I still have to work. Now my turn," Denim said turning the tables back on her. "How long have you been an actress?"

"Since she was born," I replied before she could.

The entire group laughed, including Suzie.

"He has a point. But I officially started acting in high school."

"Yeah," Denim replied, "I saw you on *American Talent*. You should have won."

"Did you vote for me?" Suzie challenged.

I just put my head into my hands. There was no stopping Suzie when she was on a roll. Nothing embarrassed her and she would ask whatever questions came to her mind.

Denim laughed and said, "Yes, actually I did vote for you every time...except once."

Suzie stopped eating mid-bacon and putting it down, pinned Denim with an intense look. "And which time did you not vote for me?" She asked incredulously.

Seeing my sister preparing to launch into her *why didn't you vote for me* tirade, I attempted to divert the conversation, but Suzie simply put her hand up in front of my face and waited for the poor man to answer.

"I didn't vote for you during the first public vote."

"And why was that?" she asked.

"Because I was sick with the flu and didn't watch the show that night."

The tension in the room cleared so quickly that both Clay and I laughed out loud.

Denim didn't seem disturbed by Suzie's reactions or questions.

"You are a cool customer, Denim." Suzie said, the interrogation apparently over, "I like that."

Denim smiled. "So, am I off the firing line?" he asked in good humor.

"Almost," Suzie said but this time she turned to Clay. "How did you two meet?" she asked.

Clay turned red in the face at the question which caused me to lean up and take notice. Clay didn't make eye contact but said, "We met online."

"Really?" both Suzie and I asked at the same time.

Denim laughed at this. "It doesn't seem to be Clay's M.O. but he is telling the truth, we met online using one of the meet-up apps. Apparently, our neighborhood slut here is ready for something more than a quick lay."

Clay's eyes got big, his face turned a brighter red and he looked like he might bolt for the door.

Despite enjoying watching Clay, who is usually too smooth for his own good, squirm with the conversation, I felt sorry for him and broke the ice by putting my hand over Clay's and saying, "I think that is great." Then I looked over at Denim and said, "Clay is a great guy, if someone is lucky enough to tie him down, they couldn't ask for a better man."

Instead of soothing Clay as I'd tried to, I could tell that that if Denim wasn't seated on the outside of the bench that Clay would've darted for the door. Clearly uncomfortable, Clay quickly turned the conversation back on me.

"So, your last exhibit was a success."

It was my turn to go red in the face. "Yeah, I guess so."

"I went to see it," Clay admitted. "I thought you captured the city beautifully."

I just smiled but decided not to let that subject become fodder for the morning conversation. I was about to shift the conversation back to the website dating app when Denim, who must have seen how uncomfortable I was, took pity on me. As if Clay had never brought up my exhibit, he began explaining how he wasn't the best at picking up guys, not really into hookups. He preferred getting to know a guy before anything happened.

"These apps were great at forcing hot men, like Clay," he said pointing his thumb at him, "to talk before fucking."

"I've never used them," I admitted. "I've thought about it a few times, but it seemed to me that it was more work than it was worth."

"Depends on what you are looking for," Denim replied. "If you want a quick one-night stand, you can go to the bar or use *Grindr* but if you are looking for something with at least a little substance, it is the best way to go."

The conversation had started the wheels turning in my head. We said our goodbyes to Clay and Denim and left the diner.

Suzie wandered back up to my apartment, evidently not done harassing me. As we walked up the many flights of stairs, I continued to think about what Denim had said about the dating site and it being a place to meet men who wanted a relationship. I *was* craving that and because the hook ups no longer appealed to me, it had been almost a year since I had been with anyone.

When we arrived in my apartment, I sat down on the small kitchen chair and Suzie sat on the sofa. I started thinking out loud and said, "I wonder if maybe the problem with my art is lack of attachment to another person. We've always had the perfect family and strong friendships, but I've never fallen in love."

Suzie looked over at me and shrugged. "I think you're over thinking all this. Critics always have to make up something to complain about, otherwise, they'd be out of a job."

Nodding, as I put my chin in my hand to prop myself up, I thought back to when I was a student at the Kansas City Art Institute. A group of friends and I were bar hopping in Kansas City's notorious Westport when I was confronted by an old woman pretending to be a psychic.

She was clearly not genuine and from the aroma that wafted off of her, I suspected she was probably homeless or, at the very least, bath adverse, but for some reason, probably because I was mostly drunk and looked like easy pickings, she squared in on me pointing her finger and yelled, "UNTIL YOU FIND TRUE LOVE, YOU'LL NEVER FIND INSPIRATION!"

Then the old woman sat back down and pretended to peer into what appeared to be a dollar-store purchased plastic crystal ball. Although she was clearly a fraud, and possibly high, I decided to give her a twenty-dollar bill simply for guessing well and forcing me to think.

"Suzie," I said with the scene still fresh in my mind. "I'm twenty-eight years old and fed up with the stand and show queens here in New York. These surface guys have long ceased to amuse me."

"You didn't seem to have a problem with them when you first got here," she challenged.

I had to agree. At first, the glitter and glamour were amazing; beautiful men seemed to lurk around every corner and my Midwestern upbringing cast me in the role of a rugged cowboy, which made it easier to find a willing partner. Sex was good, but then...it became boring.

Suzie seemed to be in her own head about things also and we sat silently going over our own thoughts when I blurted out, "I'm thinking about leaving New

York. In fact, I've been fantasizing about it for a while."

Suzie sat up and, with a concerned look on her face, asked me, "Where would you go?"

"I'm not sure," I admitted. "I'm thinking something rural or at least small-townish. You know as an artist, I could live anywhere so I've been thinking about exploring other places, somewhere that inspires me."

These thoughts had been rolling around in my head for a while, but I had yet to say them out loud. Putting them in words seemed to make them real, which truth be told, kind of scared me.

Suzie seemed to be thinking about what I'd said, and I could see the concern on her face. We had become close since we both moved to the city.

She shook her head. "I know you aren't happy here. I've seen it more and more, but I've been ignoring it, hoping it was just some funk you were in. I admit I don't want you to leave, but if you aren't happy, you really should follow your heart."

"Oh Suzie," I sighed, "I don't know. Now that I've put the thoughts into words, I'm having serious doubts about it. I have so many friends here and I don't want to move back home, that doesn't feel right either. Seriously, forget I said anything, I haven't done anything to put this thought into action so unless a miracle happens, I'll be an old man still living in this tiny apartment."

"God, I hope not," she said looking around her with disdain.

"Why do you hate my apartment so much?" I asked, after noticing her expression.

"It isn't an apartment," she said, "It's a closet. Aren't you supposed to be getting OUT of closets?" she asked with a wink.

Ignoring her clichéd closet comment, I argued, "Well, it is close to everything I do in the city: the diner we eat at, the clubs, and hell, you're here almost every weekend yourself."

"Yeah," she agreed, "but you make enough to afford a better place than this," she said giving the little place another once over.

"Ahh, but ..." I blurted out, using the same comment I had made since I moved into the place, "... small apartment, easy life."

"So you keep saying," she replied. "It isn't like you don't clean this thing repetitively. Anyway, if you had a little more space, think of how much more time you could waste with your obsession."

I stuck my tongue out at her and was going to argue that I didn't obsessively clean, but I had begun wiping down the already pristine countertop. I caught myself and both of us burst out laughing.

Devin

I drove right past my driveway and directly to an old worker's cottage my housekeeper Claire had rehabbed for herself. She'd moved there sometime before I arrived on the ranch. After the old man we worked for died, she fixed the cottage up beautifully. Claire was sitting outside in her pretty little garden when I pulled up.

When Claire saw me, she stood up, and waited for me to make it to her. When I finally did, she wrapped her arms around me and held me while I tried not to cry. When I finally got control of myself, she pulled me into the house, sat me down on her sofa and poured me two fingers of Jack.

After what felt like an eternity, the threat that I'd start crying seemed to pass. Like my mom would've done, Claire brushed my hair out of my eyes.

"I'm guessing you read the damned paper," I said, speaking for the first time since I got there.

"Yeah," she replied as she stood up and went to her little kitchen and came back with sandwiches and the rest of the bottle. She motioned for me to follow her back outside. There, we sat on her garden bench and both of us drank the remainder of the Jack.

"So, your man was a pervert." Claire said, matter of fact.

"Appears that way," I said, the whiskey turning in my stomach.

"Well, can't say I'm surprised," Claire said as she put a comforting hand on my leg.

"Why do you say that?" I asked, surprised.

Claire thought for a moment, then looked at me and said, "I had a run in with him a while back."

I sat up confused and concerned all at once. "What did he do, why didn't you tell me?"

Claire just shook her head. "Well, mostly because I took care of it and because I didn't want to hurt you."

She downed another shot of whiskey and stood to go back into the house when I stopped her by pulling her back down next to me.

"Claire did he do something to you or to the hands?"

"To me no, and if he had, he'd have been hurting a lot more than he was. But—yeah he was getting handsy with little Tom when I came into the Stables to check on him."

"Shit! Claire you should've told me."

"Maybe," she said, "but wasn't like I didn't handle it. You know a broomstick can do wonders on young men." She said trying to make light of a really bad situation.

"Damn and shit... fuck, fuck, fuck!" I said getting up and stomping around Claire's little garden.

"Honey, calm down. I told you I handled it. Besides, it looks like the law is going to fix it now anyway."

She stood up this time pulling me up with her and into a hug. "Listen to me, Devin, I ain't worried about that son of a bitch, right now, it's you I'm concerned about. After the shit you went through with that old fool we worked for, I just wanted you to find someone that made you happy."

I chuckled in bad humor. "Please don't start trying to fix me up again."

After I bought the ranch, Claire had tried to set me up with every single woman from here to Spokane. Finally, I brought home a trick I met in Walla Walla just to show her I wasn't looking for a woman. Foolishly thinking that would be the end of it, I wasn't prepared for when Claire began fixing me up with random men from Billieville, our little town. Most of the poor guys had no idea Claire had fixed them up on a damn date.

I pulled her aside after the third guy had come over for dinner and told her she had to stop. All these guys were straight and ugly as hell to boot. I assured her I didn't need help finding a man. Any normal person would've backed off, but not Claire, the conversation had opened a can of worms and she took it upon herself from that point forward to nag me about finding someone to love. And that was a daily conversation, until Chan had showed up that is.

Claire laughed, "Okay, sweetheart, I'll back off." The spunky middle-aged woman turned to go back into the house, and I heard her say under her breath, "For now, anyway."

Aiden

Suzie finally left and I pulled my easel out. I wanted to begin painting again with the hope that I could find inspiration for my next project. I always tried to have art pieces in progress. However, I usually discarded the pieces I plopped paint on while trying to find that little piece of inspiration that would lead to my next breakthrough. Unfortunately, finding that was never as easy for me as it seemed to be for others, it could often elude me for weeks and sometimes even months.

As I swirled the paint, images of the young boy I'd once been filtered into my mind. I'd always been good at drawing. My kindergarten teacher had pulled my parents aside early my first year to discuss how much more advanced my drawings were compared to the other kids. Although my elementary school years were a blur, the school's art teacher, Mrs. Buckle, had taken me under her wing and did what she could to feed my skill and challenge me to grow.

35

At the age of ten and with Mrs. Buckle's recommendation, a prestigious private art school called The Kansas City Arts Program, a collaboration of the KC Art Institute and the Kansas City, Art Museum, agreed to accept me into their program. Unfortunately, my parents were unable to afford the tuition, but I was undeterred. With the arrogance only a pre-teen can muster, I decided I could raise the money with proceeds I earned from a booth my parents rented for me at Kansas City's illustrious yet tongue-in-cheek Unplaza Art Fair.

As fate would have it, my art caught the attention of one of the fair's wealthier patrons, Ms. Margie Rosenburg. After buying three of my paintings, she happened to ask me what I intended to do with all that money.

Chuckling, I remembered the conversation. Without hesitation, I stuck out my chest and told her I intended to pay my way through the art program.

Ms. Rosenburg, who happened to also be a patron and board member of the school crossed her arms and said, "Is that so, young man?"

I nodded with all the arrogance I could muster and said, "Yep and with your purchase, I'm well on my way there."

The older lady burst out laughing. She either saw I had talent or liked my spunk, but whatever it was, she offered to pay for my tuition to attend the private school. Not knowing how to decline such a generous offer and having a son who was at that point a total pain in their behinds, my parents accepted, and I ended up attending the Arts Program from the sixth-grade until my high school graduation.

Looking back, I realize this decision had to have been difficult for my proud parents. Robert and Elizabeth Fisher were both blue-collar workers determined that their children would get the college education they both lacked. My father was a strong-willed man who spent his entire life building homes. My mother spent a few years as a hairdresser but abandoned that when my sister Suzie was born, taking on the role of housewife and mother.

Few days went by when she didn't remind us that we should always be thankful that our father worked hard and earned enough that we could have a full-time parent. "These days that is a rare gift for a child," she'd say.

As I blotted scenes on my canvas, I continued to ponder my life. I completed my degree with the Kansas City Arts Program and immediately accepted a full-ride scholarship, again with the unmistakable influence of Margie, to the Kansas City Institute of Art.

Luckily, I never had any doubt that it was the school for me. Not just because The KC Art Institute had played a huge part in my art's program, but because I already felt like I belonged there.

I looked down at the canvas in front of me and smiled. I had unconsciously painted my family. I would have to frame that one and send it to my parents. I wasn't a portrait artist. I usually reserved my work for scenes that told a story, so I seldom drew faces and I'd never painted my family before.

The painting was good though, my mom wore the yellow dress she loved when I was a child and eventually had to get rid of when I accidentally ran into her causing her to spill wine on it one Fourth of July. Of course, I only stumbled because my sister's big feet were spread out across the walkway. Dad was dressed in his typical weekend jeans and white t-shirt and Suzie was twirling in the background. All three of them were laughing. Clearly, I was missing my family for this to come out of me unbeckoned.

I let my thoughts stay on my parents. It wasn't until I was at the Art Institute that I realized just how much I was like them. My father's homes were true masterpieces. He could take the most unsavory architectural drawings and fashion them into magnificent masterpieces. Mom was not to be outdone; although she had missed the opportunities of an official culinary training, she had still mastered the art of gourmet cooking. After spending years eating among the best restaurants in New York with the most celebrated chefs, I had yet to find one Beth Fisher couldn't outcook. She was simply a magician with food and flavor.

I finished the portrait and put it aside to dry and pulled another canvas out. The light was going down indicating that I'd spent most of the day painting and thinking. I rushed over to the tiny refrigerator and made a quick sandwich which I gulped down and returned to the empty canvas. I deliberately returned my thinking to my childhood.

Of course, there was no way to think about my childhood without thinking about dad's best friend, Owen Jackson and his wife Lou-Ellen. They had kept me for two glorious weeks every summer throughout my childhood. It certainly helped that the Jacksons had a son who was my same age.

Steve Jackson and I grew up like brothers, with the shenanigans only two boys can get into when roaming completely free around wide-open spaces. I laughed to myself as I remembered the summer I made the mistake of critiquing Lou-Ellen's box mac and cheese and hotdogs.

I'd grown up with my mother's masterpieces in the kitchen, so I had the misconception that everyone cooked gourmet meals. Luckily, Lou was a good sport and instead of being offended she teased me *and* my mother throughout the rest of my childhood. Mom would turn red in the face every time Lou-Ellen would bring up my unrealistic expectations of other mothers' abilities in the kitchen.

Steve's family and those happy summers, my days in the program and the Arts Institute were all really good memories. So why had I moved away from them all?

I sat on the little chair across the room from where I worked and pondered that thought. After finishing the institute, I was quick to move to New York and all the splendor it provided. With introductions from Margie Rosenburg, I moved up the New York ladder of artistic fame quicker than most. Home was and would always be home, but the thrill of New York and the call to explore was too enticing for me to pass up.

Letting my mind shift away from my childhood, I tried to concentrate on the piece in front of me. I thought of my art along the lines of van Gogh, eking by the critic's ever-present disdain through sheer grit and determination. I had never been afraid of contrasting colors and more than one of my critics has had things to say about it. One of my favorites was, *'Fisher's art pieces require a strong sense of self to adequately appreciate.'*

That kind of criticism always makes me happy...unlike the stupid "he doesn't put himself into the painting critique." I wasn't always popular with the Institute's instructors who would criticize my choice of colors or bold brush strokes. The truth is. I secretly liked the bad boy rebel persona I developed while there. Despite our disagreement about color choices or the fact that I never hesitated to challenge a professor, I somehow graduated at the top of my class. No, they might not have always liked my work, but I was gifted enough and could defend my artistic choices powerfully enough that I survived their frustrated assessment of my work.

After leaving the Institute, I met Jace through one of Margie's contacts. Jace was a huge advocate of my work, but she also never hesitated to challenge me.

Occasionally, she would look at one of my more outlandish pieces and laugh. "You're trying to die a poor starving artist, aren't you?"

Through her tongue-in-cheek criticism, I tried to become a little more mainstream, but I wasn't willing to give much creative ground. Art was the truest expression of a person's observations of the world around them. I still felt strongly that my interpretation of those observations must never be compromised.

Of course, because I was in their faces more than not, my critics always seemed ready to point out what I lacked. Luckily, they also seemed to recognize my determination.

I loved a critique I got about an exhibit I did on Central Park. I had painted the park in extreme colors, inspired by van Gogh actually. The critics either liked it or hated it and no one was in-between.

I loved that kind of contrasting thought. My favorite critique was:

"The young artist's unapologetic grit is clearly the only reason a Midwestern country boy stood a chance in New York's sophisticated art scene. If nothing else, New Yorkers appreciate a good spit in your eye when they come across one."

Devin

After the fiasco with the idiot across the river, I decided I was better off alone. Hell, the one time since I left Seattle that I had let my guard down, I came face to face with someone who was not only a cheater, but he was also a thug.

The old man I had bought the place from, or at least bought the place from his kids, was a total piece of work. He had been married long before I came to the property and I kind of assumed he and Claire had a fling once upon a time, but he was quick to tell me a man did better when all he had to worry about was his cattle.

I didn't agree with him at the time, but damned if I don't now.

One evening while Claire and I sat out on my front porch shooting the bull and enjoying an evening breeze, I said as much to her. Before I even saw her move, she was up and pointing a finger in my face.

"I've already watched a man let himself become bitter and I'll be damned if I sit here and watch it happen again." She knelt in front of me and drew me into a hug. "Sweet boy," she said, "That was a bad man, and none of us even noticed until it was too late. You are as much a victim to his stupidity as the men who worked for him."

She pulled me back and looked me in the eyes for several moments until I could feel the tears burning the back of my eyes. "You listen to me, Devin Pierce. You don't let him win by keeping you from finding and having love. A man like that doesn't deserve to have that much influence over your life."

Then she hugged me again. I had broken several bottles of the wine the jackass had brought me, and I was about to do so with another when Claire stopped me.

"Boy," she said. "The wine ain't at fault for the man either. Don't throw that out. Open it and pour me a glass." She licked her lips and grinned, then downed the entire glass and held it out to me to refill.

"So, that's how this is gonna be then?" I said picking up her backwoodsy accent.

"Apparently," she chuckled.

"Well, in that case, let's not be shy," I said and went to get the rest of the bottles I'd put onto the back of the ATV. I had planned on taking the rest of them and dumping them on the property across the river.

I handed the open bottle to Claire and opened one myself. Claire smiled a wicked smile and we clinked the bottle necks together and proceeded to get plastered.

There were more than a few things Claire and I did that night. One of which could've landed us in jail but that was a story for another time. In our drunken stupor, Claire pulled me into my office and forced me to open a dating app.

She had seen some advertisement on TV about Christians getting together. "Surely, if they have a dating site just for Christians, they got to have one for queers …" then she hiccupped and fell onto my office chair giggling. Then she babbled on for a few minutes about whether or not she should call gay people queer. I was almost as drunk as she was but now that she had me looking at my computer, I was determined to find a site for gay men.

I pulled up *Grinder* and when I explained to her what it did, she laughed and laughed about whether I'd be able to find a gay dude lurking in one of the upper pastures. She came over pulling a chair up beside me and when we landed on *City Men to Country Men* or *CMTOCM.com*, she made me stop.

"Hey, this's perfect," she exclaimed. "Get you a city boy like you were to come live with you here on the ranch. It'll be like a war bride from when my parents were kids."

Alcohol made things seem much more logical and a better idea than they usually were. Seriously, if I had been in my right mind, I'd never have let Claire talk me into this. I suppose, even with all my brain cells floating in alcohol, I was coming to my senses because after I signed up, I got up and told Claire I didn't want a city man to come to my country... "I don't want any man. Men suck..." I remember going on in that rant for a while but Claire's face was buried in the site as she ignored me.

I lay down and fell asleep on the floor of my office. The next day, I found Claire on the cozy sofa in the living room. My head was pounding like a son of a bitch, and my back felt like I'd slept on the floor all night because, for the most part, I had.

When I came back down Claire was sitting up staring toward the kitchen. Her eyes were glassy, and it didn't appear she had moved.

"Here, drink some water and take some of these," I put the pill bottle next to her. I'll go pour us both some coffee," I said as I walked into the kitchen.

I came back out with the coffee and Claire just looked at me. "What the hell did we do?"

I laughed, "I think the question is, 'What didn't we do?'"

Claire popped two pills into her mouth then drank the entire glass of water. When she put the glass down on the coffee table she winced. "I haven't been that drunk since ..." She waited a few minutes and said, "I have never been that drunk before."

She went back into the kitchen and filled her glass again.

"You are better off skipping the coffee and drinking more water," she said. "The coffee is just going to dehydrate you more."

"Yeah, well at the moment, the heat is making my head feel less like the jackhammers inside it are about to break through."

She just laughed and winced again. After finishing the water, she lay back down on the couch and waited for the medicine to settle in. I drank my coffee while waiting with her.

After thirty minutes of neither of us moving with hopes of saving our heads from falling off our shoulders, I began to feel less queasy and a little hungry. "You hungry yet?" I asked.

"God, no!" she said, "But we should probably eat. Want me to go get something started?"

I chuckled as I watched the older woman lying with her arm across her face, knowing she wasn't moving for at least another half hour.

"No worries, I got this one," I said as I went to the kitchen. I opened a can of biscuits and tossed them into the oven as quietly as I could. I put some bacon on and then cooked some fried eggs in their grease, knowing a hearty meal would help the hangover more than anything.

When everything was done, I brought breakfast sandwiches out to Claire and placed them on the coffee table, sat on the side chair next to her again and began eating mine.

"Do you feel better now?" she asked.

"Huh?" I asked, my mouth full of food. I knew she was completely out of it or I'd have been heavily chastised for talking with my mouth full.

"Do you feel better about the SOB next door? Did the drinking help?" she asked.

I felt sorry for her as she lay on the sofa with what must have been the mother of all headaches, so I just said, "Yeah, thanks for helping me get through that...and get through all his wine."

She snickered. "We were really fucked up, Devin. I hope to god the law don't come knocking."

I laughed, "I've got a cow I need to check on. Before you talked me into drinking a case of wine, she was looking like she could drop a calf. Her mama was notorious for having breach calves, so I'd like to make sure she doesn't have the same problem."

Claire just nodded her head and tried to swallow another bite of her sandwich.

"Oh, Devin," she said wincing. "You may need to go check your computer. I think we might have set you up on a few dates last night."

I looked at her with my eyebrows askew. "*We might have set me up on a few dates?*"

She tried an innocent smile, but there was nothing innocent about it.

I went upstairs to where the computer was still open and woke it up. Sure enough, there was my profile along with a plea for a husband that Claire must have written after I fell asleep—*Rancher Looking for a Husband.*

"CLAIRE!" I yelled. "What the hell did you do?!"

Aiden

I woke up thinking about Clay and Denim. As much as I liked to think I would never stoop to a dating app, Denim's statements about relationships versus sex had hit a nerve. After getting up and eating some generic cereal Suzie had left in my cabinet, I had a quick shower, then headed to my easel to get to work. Unfortunately, the thought of the dating app steered me toward my computer rather than my easel. I opened the laptop and began surfing through different dating sites for men. Of course, there were the raunchy, sex only sites and there were the more benign sites.

I looked at a couple, like *ForeverMe*—a straight site that had created a counterpart for gay men. Mostly these sites were for regional people. If I was going to do something as stupid as join a dating site, I wanted to find something that could indulge my imagination about finding a rural place to settle.

I was about to give up when I came across a site designed especially for guys in the urban areas who wanted to find guys in the country, thus the name, *CMTOCM.com* or City Male to Country Male.

What the hell, if it ended up being a bust, at least I could meet some people and learn about different communities and whether or not they were open to gay men. I signed up, filled out my profile being honest about living in New York, but said I was an artist and therefore could travel and work. I went through my photos and found a couple of pictures of myself that I thought made me look happy and not brooding which is where maybe I was being a little dishonest. One picture was of me while I was playing on the beach at Coney Island. It was a good picture I thought because it showed I had at least a little muscle mass despite my natural skinny build.

CMTOCM had a matching bot that worked with your profile, and your likes, to pair you with the right guy. There was a lot less emphasis on locality than compatibility. The idea was to help rural guys find the right match even though they weren't able to make it into the city. I made sure I emphasized that I didn't want a hook-up but rather a relationship, so the bot knew what to look for.

I spent most of the week looking at and working with the site. The bot paired me with several different profiles, but they were either ugly as homemade sin or too old. I did reach out to a few of the men that showed up, but more often than not, they lied in their profile and were just interested in friends with benefits. After I got what had to be the dozenth dick pic, or request for mine, I decided to wait for them to make the first move instead. Seriously, if I wanted a hook-up, why the hell would I travel a thousand miles to have one?

The site still intrigued me, though, and it didn't take long before checking it became part of my daily routine. I tried to stay away from it during the day, focusing on my painting, but at night, I'd peruse.

Over the next several months, I'd look over the connections made by what I'd begun to think of as my matchmaker bot friend. I'd even sing the matchmaker song from *Fiddler* as I walked toward my computer at the end of my day.

My interest had gone from a possible match to pure curiosity. Were there really men in the country or rural communities that were out, or that I could see myself living with? The answer to that was probably not, but I enjoyed fantasizing about it anyway.

I had been asked to speak at an artist convention featured in one of the luxury high-rises in Manhattan, so I missed several days of getting online. I came home after the convention and was about to go to bed early when I decided to check out the new men the bot had sent my way.

At the top of the page, was a profile that caught my attention:

Rancher Seeks Husband

Thirty-year old, white male who lives on 15,000 acres and manages at least that many cattle, makes dating impossible. Respond only if you are looking for a spouse (not interested in playing around or mind games.) You mustn't mind living in a secluded area. Most importantly, you have to have your own life. I'm not looking for someone to cater to nor do I want to be catered to myself. I simply want a companion who can enjoy the simple life as much as I do.

The rest of the profile talked about his appearance and what he was attracted to. After rereading the profile again, I scrolled back up the page to the photos and opened the only one available. It was grainy and the person was standing without his shirt combing a horse. It didn't appear the person in the picture knew he was being photographed. Despite not having a clear look at the man, my body responded with interest. It couldn't be that I was that attracted to the guy, but I'd always loved horses and a hot man working with them always turned me on.

I couldn't help but be intrigued. Could this be serious? Did anyone ever just ask for a spouse and what about the whole 15,000 acres and cattle thing? Of course, my realistic, slightly jaded outlook made me think this was most likely someone looking for rodeo queens to play around with. I hesitated only momentarily before scrolling past the post not intending to look at it again.

Throughout the night and the following day, I couldn't seem to get the profile out of my mind. Although I still thought it was just an attempt to get someone to come out to the middle of nowhere for a hook-up, I was unable to prevent my imagination from grasping onto the idea.

Ideally, my perfect mate was someone who had their own life who could allow *me* to have *my* own life. I imagined waking up to a man having a quick snuggle maybe some morning sex then going our separate ways. I loved the idea of coming home to someone. I'd seen that kind of relationship with my parents and I had internalized that as the perfect relationship—distinctive individuals who merged into a cohesive unit.

The guys I dated tended to be either clingy, wanting to be so connected that I was suffocated, or they were so independent there was no hope of ever becoming a cohesive unit. In my imagination, I allowed the person on the site to be my perfect match.

I could almost see this mystery man and me sitting together for breakfast, each preparing for the day. Eventually, my mind began to wonder what this imaginary rancher's life would be like—hills with rivers running through them, limestone caves that you could hide in and imagine the native ancestors painting images of the bison hunts on the cave walls. The thought of 15,000 acres was almost more than I could digest, but I let my imagination roll with it, absorbing the history lessons from my childhood and the book my mom used to read to Suzie and me about Laura Ingalls Wilder living on the plains and eking a living from the earth.

I imagined the beautiful open prairie with a copse of trees tucked perfectly around rivers and natural ponds. I could almost see the wildlife with bison grazing and insects buzzing.

I put aside my doodle work and decided to paint what it would be like, what my mind's eye saw in this rancher's world who'd written this post. At first, I painted a bleak background scene—prairie with tall brush, browns with shades of rust. I painted the wind blowing the tall brown grasses. Despite the mention of cattle, I couldn't quite see them in this landscape, so I left them out. After finishing the background, I decided it was too realistic for what I wanted to show. I needed to make it more abstract. Probably more for my own sake than anyone else's, I needed the painting to be abstract so I remembered I was painting my imagination, not reality. I let it show my longing, and love for all things wild for the hope of finding someone to love me in a time and place surrounded by nature and all things natural.

So, with a wash, I changed the brown grasses to more of figurative blobs of the prairie. True to form, this new abstract naturally began to incorporate the chaos that a prairie would naturally hold. Like someone turning on a bright light in a dark room, it was at this point that inspiration hit.

The concepts I saw seemed to emanate from my soul. I began to see ... *no*, to *feel* the color—bold, but not obvious. There had to be subtlety there and I wanted that subtlety to be harshly controlled by the surrounding landscape.

When I'd finished the piece, it was a quarter of ten at night. I'd painted straight through the evening. I was a bit surprised; I had chased this kind of inspiration while working on my New York pieces, but although I thought they were good, they weren't inspired. Turning around from where I was cleaning my brushes and equipment, I looked at the painting again. I could tell it was one of my best. There were aspects of the work that screamed to the viewer to wake up and look at what was around them while other aspects simultaneously caused the viewer to yearn for simplicity. Clearly, the western landscape that had inspired me was present in the background. There were elements that alluded to possible mountains, but the colors were blurred and flowed across the canvas preventing the viewer from being able to say definitively if they were there or not.

It struck me how different it was from my recent city paintings, stark and ridged with streaks of blacks and greys. This piece was as soft, based in shades of brown with aspects of green, red and yellow.

Despite the time, I snapped a picture of the painting and sent it, without description, to Margie in Kansas City. I knew she'd give me a critical and honest opinion. It only took her 5 minutes to respond and the only thing she said was "Damn." Taking that as a sign that she felt the same way about the painting as I did, I decided to finish cleaning up and head to bed.

I tossed and turned all night. I kept having visions of prairies—some with close-up scenes of rocks with subtle wildflowers; others wide-open skies with intense landscapes. Finally, giving up on sleep, I rose and did what I knew I'd have to do if I were ever to have peace. I pulled my painting equipment back out and went to work.

I texted Suzie a message telling her that I was going to be in the throes of inspiration and that I'd likely forget to eat, sleep or do anything until it worked itself out.

I blushed remembering that I once had to be hospitalized from fatigue and dehydration after ignoring sleep, food, and hydration. As a result,

Suzie made me promise that if I felt this wave come over me that I'd let her know beforehand.

The next few weeks were a blur. Occasionally, I'd look up and Suzie would be there putting out food, juice, or water. I tried to smile at her, but more often than not, I didn't even notice her until I'd feel hungry or thirsty and see there was something there. I tried to remember to eat or drink, but to be honest, during those weeks, nothing existed for me except the wild plains.

I lost count of the number of paintings. Some of my visions needed to be on huge grand canvases which I had to call to the studio so they could be delivered and then I had to call them to come and take them away since my apartment wasn't anywhere near big enough to hold them. Occasionally, the paintings needed to be tiny, almost minuscule as I endeavored to paint a creature that spent its life hiding from predators or some small wildflower that most people never notice. All I knew is when they came to me, it was as important for me to capture them as it was for me to breathe.

Because I wasn't thinking form, technique or artistic rules, not all the paintings were abstract— some wanted to be painted in extreme reality. These realistic paintings seemed to crave the clay pigmentation of natural ochre. Yellow, purplish red and beige all seemed to want to dictate the scenes.

When I'd get done with one of these paintings, I'd stand back and I could see the realistic view forced the viewer to accept that, despite the subtle serenity, there was seldom calm while danger always lurked in the shadows. All the paintings had the common thread of harshness contrasted to the raw beauty this part of the world presented.

As I created, I felt that more than anything else, I needed to be a part of the area. I understood for the first time, what it means to be a part of my art. As I painted, I felt my soul pouring onto the canvasses. I yearned to be there, and each painting expressed that yearning.

These paintings were the parts of me I didn't know existed and with each brushstroke, I knew I would one day have to leave the city. I knew I would one day live in places that inspired me like this. As much as I was painting the scenes of the wild prairie, I was also saying goodbye to this life and opening myself to a new one.

By the time I pulled my last canvas onto the easel, I could tell I'd reached a new level as an artist. I'd painted my best and it had been about a world that couldn't be more different than the one I currently lived in. All in all, once I was done, I went back through my tally marks I had kept as canvases left my apartment and the tally came out to 32 different pieces.

I had hardly eaten, I was sleep deprived and I was happier than I'd ever been. Suzie came in as I was working on my last piece. She was no stranger to these fits of inspiration so she must have recognized that it was coming to the end.

"When you are done with this one, sleep and then call me." She turned to go, but turned back again repeating herself so she knew I heard her. "Make sure you call me before talking to anyone else. I need to talk to you about your collection," she said.

I stopped working for a moment and looked at her. What she said was confusing, but the pull of the last painting, a sweet little hummingbird dipping its long tongue into a little columbine with a Virginia Bluebell in the background, distracted me from asking her what she meant.

The little piece was small, but it was also an important piece that culminated the collection.

When I was done, I went to the cupboard, reached onto the top shelf and pulled down a bottle of *2005 Gaja Costa Russi* I had bought while touring Italy. I promised myself that I'd drink it when or if I painted something I didn't think I could have painted better.

The wine was beautiful and flowed over my tongue with a perfection that was hard to describe. I finished one glass, put the cork back in to share with Suzie later, then, shut the light off. I climbed into bed happier than I'd been in a long time and the first time in a very long time, I slept without images of prairie scenes plaguing my dreams.

When I finally woke up, I had no idea how long I'd slept or what time of day it was. There didn't seem to be a part of my body that didn't hurt and I was *starving*! I practically crawled to the kitchen and blessed Suzie's heart for the almost untouched pizza that beamed at me from the fridge.

I sat, ate and contemplated the past few weeks. Looking at the time, I guessed Suzie would still be asleep. It was nine am but she worked late nights as a Broadway performer. Practice and performing were her life and both tended to take place late into the night.

Despite this, I sent her a text that read, "You said I should call you as soon as I became human again and I think I'm close. I'm grabbing a shower then I'm all yours. Wanna grab food?"

I left to shower not expecting to hear from her until noon. When I came back 30 minutes later, however, I saw three missed calls from her as well as two texts, the first read: "Where the hell are you" and the second, "Yes, to breakfast, I'll meet you at 11 am at Vinnie's."

Vinnie's was our favorite meeting spot. Not that the food was great, in fact, we'd often laugh at how such a bad restaurant could survive with so much competition, but the coffee and bagels were good, and the crowds were small. You could talk there without having fifty strangers in your conversation.

I arrived about 5 minutes late. My achy brain-dead feeling seemed to have me in low gear. Suzie was waiting for me in our usual seat, looking annoyed. Although I tended to make Suzie annoyed, I was unsure what I could've done to upset her this time. As I sat down, she looked me over and said, "Damn, Aiden, you look like shit. Worse than usual."

"Thanks Bitch, love you, too."

She laughed and then got down to business.

"You know, I've had to be a *real* bitch to keep everyone in New York from calling you these past weeks, right?"

"Yeah," I responded, feeling a little guilty for putting so much on her. "I appreciate your playing interference. I'm guessing mom and Margie were kind of forceful, huh?"

"No, brother, you don't understand. The studio put one of your paintings up just to get a feel for the public's opinion and it seems the art word has exploded."

"What do you mean exploded?" I asked. "Why the hell did they put my painting up? I wasn't even done with the series!"

"You'll have to ask them," she said, "but Jace made me promise to have you prepped and ready to go when you came back to reality."

"Damn," I sighed. "I hate it when Jace puts my art up before its ready."

It's not like I didn't appreciate my patrons, but I liked to keep my art business as controlled as I could. In fact, I was probably more obsessed over it than I was cleaning my apartment—not that I was obsessed.

"Such is the world of business," I told myself, not that I had a clue about business. I rarely ever thought about it really, but I loved the income I made and being a ruthless saver, I liked having a nest egg that could get me by if the inspiration ever dried up.

My dad always preached. "You never know when the money flow will end, don't be a fool by blowing your earnings when the getting is good. Save first, spend later!" That was why my apartment was still the size of a closet and THAT was why the studio had my paintings before I was ready for them to be displayed.

I finished my coffee and bagel breakfast and stood to head over to the studio. Before leaving, I turned and gave Suzie a big hug which was unusual for me. "I'm not the touchy-feely type," I would tell her when she'd ask me why I hugged her like a scared cat trying to get out of the grip of a toddler.

"I'd be in much worse shape if it wasn't for you. I don't like the feeling that I've taken advantage of you, but I appreciate you more than you'll ever know."

Suzie looked at me and said, "Seeing what you just created, I was glad to be a part of it. Now, go face the music. Your world is going to change now. Be prepared for it."

Again, a bit perplexed by her words, I headed toward the studio. When I arrived, the anger struck me first, but it was quickly replaced by intrigue that the gallery already had so many of my paintings up on the wall. Hell, some of them were still wet!

When Jace, the studio owner, came around the corner, I immediately went off. "What the hell, Jace? If any of your *butches* smudged any of this, I'm going to personally rip their arms off."

Being fully accustomed to my demeanor, Jace simply smiled, "Aiden, honey you know I'm more dangerous than you. These *'butches'* as you call them, wouldn't so much as cough around any of my paintings." Noting how Jace had stated 'my' instead of 'yours', I knew I'd lost any argument before it could begin.

"Jace, why are you hanging my art up before it has had time to properly dry? And why is your door locked? I had to practically beg your receptionist to let me in. By the way, when did you get a receptionist?"

"Because, Aiden, my genius, I've already had hundreds of calls about the first piece you sent over.

And, I'm not an idiot. What people can see, but can't get to, will drive the price up and up." Jace used both hands to gesture up into the air. "Your paintings can cure on the walls as well as sitting in storage. When I have this show, I'll secure your name and mine in the history books." As usual, she ignored my question about her staff.

I gave Jace a bewildered look. "You really think these are that good?"

"My dear, these are better than that good. These are magnificent!"

Devin

When I saw the information on my profile that Claire had written in her drunken state, I was both mad and amused.

'Rancher seeks Husband'. My god, could she make me sound more desperate? I just shook my head and went downstairs to ream her for the horrible profile description.

She just shrugged and answered, "We were both drunk. I barely remember it except I kept thinking you were going to kill me."

"And you are lucky I've got a cow to tend to or I might."

She just chuckled and got up, the headache apparently held at bay for the moment.

When I came back upstairs, I sat down at my computer to answer a few emails before I went to find the wayward cow and the stupid dating site was still open on my screen. I had over a hundred messages. God help me, I knew better than opening any of them, but curiosity killed the cat, or, in my case, blinded it.

I had dick picture after dick picture in the inbox. My god, people saw the word husband and thought, you need to see my dick. Jesus Christ! It was disgusting! I deleted several until my finger got tired of hitting the delete button then I went into my account to try to delete the entire thing only to find out it was more complicated than I had time to deal with.

Claire was going to totally pay for this. I thought I should make her go through and figure out how to delete all those damn pictures and the account with it. In fact, that was a great idea. She got me into this mess, she would get me out.

I closed the screen, opened my email and responded to the requests about using my prize bull as a stud. I couldn't help but laugh at the irony between the dick pics and the stud services. Shit, now I was thinking like those pervs on there.

When I got the most important emails sent, I went downstairs and informed Claire about the site and the massive number of cocks that were now sitting in my inbox.

"You get to dispose of them," I told her, all the while the woman was laughing so hard she had tears coming out of her eyes. "Damn it, Claire," I said, knowing that under normal circumstances I'd get a scolding if not an ear twist for using such a slur. I wasn't even sure she heard the word through the laughter.

"I'm going to check on my cow, then I've got to run over to talk to Jim in the west pasture and get our bull set up for stud. And if you dare make a wisecrack, I swear I'll fire you on the spot." That just sent her into another fit of laughter, because we both knew I would never dare.

"I'll take care of it," she said as I went out.

"By taking care of it, I better not see any dick pics downloaded onto my hard drive. By god, Claire! If I do, god help me if I don't print every damn one of them and staple them to your house!"

I got on my four-wheeler and could still hear her laughing. When I got down the path a way, I let out my laughter as well. It had been a long-damned time since the old girl had laughed that hard...well, at least, while she wasn't inebriated, that is.

Aiden

The next four weeks passed quickly and Jace, as good as her word, promoted the showing as if she were displaying the early works of Claude Monet. She moved the paintings around at least 500 times. Each time complaining this piece wasn't getting the attention it needed or that piece didn't fit here but fit better there. When she was done, I was amazed that she had incorporated the smaller pieces next to larger paintings, sequenced as I'd seen them in my head. Jace was good. No, Jace was a genius when it came to placement.

The night of the showing, all of New York's art elite showed up. I was surprised to see people from Europe and the Middle East there, as well. Of course, I recognized the critics and their perpetual frowns, but I was determined to give the illusion that I didn't worry about nor care what the critics thought. In my head, I kept reciting a bastardization of an old saying "those who can do, but those who can't criticize those who can," then I'd giggle at my own sarcasm...

Despite entertaining myself with my own antics, I was shocked and a little put out by the lack of chatter that normally surrounded a gallery showing. There was always idle chitchat at a showing as well as the occasional art student who would try to demonstrate his or her knowledge by stating the obvious observation, but this gallery showing was strangely quiet. Faces were turned upward, or they were pressed close to the smaller canvases. The typical frowns and dismissal that came from the crowds I had come to expect were absent. All faces registered similar expressions. I didn't quite know how to read them. Were they intrigued, mesmerized, disgusted? Did they hate them or love them? But the lack of chatter made it impossible for me to discern. People were also sort of ignoring me. Usually, people had a million questions and although they almost always annoyed me, I was beginning to feel insecure by their absence. Were folks avoiding eye contact with me?

By the time an hour had passed, I was ready to crawl out of my skin. Jace had obviously missed the mark. People clearly hated the exhibition. I had finally pushed the boundaries too far. The fact that I had listened to the damned critics and Jace and had put my soul into this grouping, made accepting that a bit more painful than a disagreeable show might normally be. I prided myself in not needing others' approval, but in this situation, it was tough, and my pride was becoming more bruised as the evening progressed.

The crowd finally thinned out and I was waiting with anticipation for the final guest to leave so that I could go home and lick my wounds.

Just as I was about to leave, Jace skipped over and said, "I need to see you in my office as soon as the last patron leaves."

"Can this wait until tomorrow, Jace? I'm done in."

With a look of sheer shock mixed with a healthy dose of panic, Jace shook her head and said, "Absolutely *not*, decisions *must* be made tonight."

Assuming this was Jace's stubborn streak recognizing a failed show and god only knew how much she had spent, I wasn't surprised she wanted to disengage with me tonight before she went to bed. So, with growing dread, I sat next to her office in the little kitchenette and steeled myself for the inevitable.

When Jace finally showed up, she was winded.

"Come in," she ordered, and I complied.

As soon as we were both seated, she began, "You have some serious decisions to make, Aiden. Every piece has its own buyer and most of the pieces have multiple buyers. I knew this showing was going to be amazing, but seriously, Aiden, I've never seen New York speechless."

She shook her head like she was trying to wrap her mind around what she had just seen. "Aiden, you also have a buyer who wants the entire collection. They are willing to pay a handsome sum, but they insist the entire collection MUST be together."

At this, I looked up and in total shock asked, "How much are they offering?"

Jace pushed a folded piece of paper into my hand and watched me as I opened it. I couldn't quite comprehend what I was seeing. That was a lot of money. No, that was an insane amount of money. "Is this what they are willing to pay?" I asked Jace for confirmation. Mirroring my expression of shock and disbelief, she nodded.

Then she continued, "Aiden, honey I don't know how to advise you. It is possible that once we add up the offers on each piece individually, the earnings would be more, but selfishly and maybe a little naively, I would really like these pieces to stay together. What you did with this collection was a masterpiece. You will go into the history books because of it. Keeping them together could add to your legacy. What do you think?"

I stared down at the paper for several long moments unable to really comprehend the gravity of what was happening. I said aloud and as much to myself as to Jace, "Just a moment ago, I thought you were going to tell me that I couldn't show in your gallery any longer. Jace, no one said anything during the exhibition. I thought they hated it."

At this Jace's stoic persona began to crumble and she began to laugh. "My dearest, for an artist you have no grasp on the emotional reality of a crowd. No, dear Aiden, they were dumbfounded. You shocked them and amazed them into silence. A feat I never thought I'd witness myself, at least not in New York's elitist art crowd."

"Can I think about this for tonight? I don't think I can decide this now."

Jace nodded and told me she'd tally up the numbers on all the offers for the night and she'd send that to me by midmorning. "That way you'll be able to make a financial as well as emotional decision. But Aiden, your buyers are used to getting what they want when they want it. As it is, they are chomping at the bit. They will not want to wait long. So, I'll need an answer by tomorrow noon."

Jace stood up and came around her desk and gave me a huge hug. "I'm so proud of you. I'm so proud FOR you. Why don't you call your sister and have her meet you for a late-night snack? I doubt you'll get much sleep anyway. Lord knows I won't."

I slipped through the door and into the night. I decided to leave my sister alone, but instead of going home, I walked around my favorite night spots in the city. Life was surreal. It wasn't until late in the night that I realized I had forgotten to ask Jace who the buyer was or why they were willing to pay such a ludicrous amount for the collection. It probably didn't matter but I got a sick feeling when I thought the collection could be barred up in someone's home without anyone ever seeing it—without me ever being able to see them again.

As I walked, I began to figure out what I wanted to happen with the collection. The money was amazing but for the first time, I realized I felt more for this collection than I'd ever felt about my art before. I *needed* this collection to be available to the public. I *needed* it to have air as much as I *needed* air myself. I'd sell to the one collector but only if there were some basic agreements in place. It couldn't be hoarded all year... There would have to be showings...

I got back to my apartment around three in the morning and crashed on my couch dreaming about my conditions. I also thought I'd have to reserve time for my friend Margie as well as my family to come to New York to see the collection before it was cast into the wind. They had all played so much of an influence on my career as well as my personal growth that I felt an obligation to give them a chance to see this collection. To see what would likely be the *opus* of my career.

I slept until eleven in the morning. I leaned up and picking up my phone saw Jace's text with the numbers she had promised the night before.

Laughing, I realized she texted this to me at four in the morning. I guess she didn't get much sleep either.

I texted her back and said, "Call me when you get this." Within moments she was calling.

"So, did you decide what you are going to do?" she asked.

"Yeah, but Jace you may not like it."

Pausing ever so slightly, she asked, "Ok, so what won't I like?"

I launched into my prepared speech. "You know how you said this was likely my masterpiece? So, if that is the case, if this is as good as it gets, I need time to let my family and mentor see the pieces together."

"Okay," she said.

"I think I'll sell to your buyer that wants all the pieces even though their offer is a little less than the total of all the other offers. But, on one condition—they can't be hoarded...at least, occasionally, they have to be displayed in a museum or gallery."

Jace choked. "What?"

Confused, I asked her "What do you mean what?"

"Oh Aiden," she replied. "I forgot to tell you who the buyer was. He is a buyer for the Louvre in Paris. Dear one, the Louvre wants your collection! They received a hefty grant earlier this year to find, purchase, and display superior art from living artists. It is part of a new paradigm for the museum."

If I hadn't been sitting, I'd have surely fallen. "I don't understand. Last night you told me a buyer wanted my collection, but you forgot to tell me the buyer is the fucking LOUVRE?"

Chuckling, she said, "Yeah. Sorry, Aiden. I was a little overwhelmed last night."

"Ok, I rescind my requirements and add only this one. A private showing *must* be included in the introduction of the collection for my family and friends. We will be doing that in Paris!"

Jace chuckled again and said, "You damn well better include me in that friends and family."

I laughed and agreed she would be. "Jace, you know this could never have happened without you. You are my hero."

"Heroine," she corrected before hanging up.

I wasted no time in calling my parents, sister, and then Margie. The conversations left me exhausted. I was going to be in the Louvre. Little, nobody Aiden from Kansas City was going to be in the Louvre hanging on the same walls as the greatest artists who've ever lived.

I guessed I'd never fully comprehended that. I would never have considered my art good enough for that. Yet, fate had sealed this dream for me. It was only then that I remembered that this all began with my reading a guy's profile on a dating site.

Devin

I didn't realize that Claire was actually sending messages to people through the dating site until later that week when I accidentally opened it and there were messages from several men across the country. Luckily, she had deleted all the ones with dick pics but that didn't take away from the fact that she was chatting with these men while pretending to be me.

I saw red and I guess it was lucky that she wasn't around when I found the messages or I'm sure I would've said something I'd have regretted later.

It was too late to call and fuss at her. Instead, I began reading some of the comments between Claire and the other guys. As I read, I was impressed at what a tough broad she was. Or more accurately, tough ass she portrayed me as. She frankly told most of the guys they just weren't her...*my* type.

I began to enjoy the comments she sent and went downstairs to get a beer and came back up to read more of them. One man had started out well and I could tell that Claire liked him, but before long, he had deviated and started talking about all the sexual positions he preferred and Claire flat out told him that sex is important, but if you could only think with your dick, this wasn't going to work out.

That one made me laugh, but not as much as the one where a drag queen from New Jersey was chatting with her. Claire was all about her at first, which both made me happy and made me wonder what the hell she thought my type was. The queen was a total flirt and I could tell that Claire was enjoying her. As the comments became filled with innuendo, I found myself laughing so hard I was crying. I kept imagining the poor guy on the other end of the conversation. He had no idea he was chatting up a middle-aged woman.

Finally, because I too had completely and totally fallen for the queen, who incidentally was closer to Claire's age than mine, I sent him a picture of Claire and told him that she was behind all the messages.

The queen wrote me back almost immediately and told me she'd already figured out this was someone on the fix-up. I told him he should keep it up though because I wanted to find out how the two of them ended this conversation. Of course, he was in total agreement. He had clearly become attached to the old broad.

I deleted the last few messages I'd sent to him so Claire wouldn't know that I was aware of the conversation and closed out.   If reading Claire's comments as she pretended to be a gay romantic desperately looking for the right man was going to continue to be as entertaining as it had been the past few hours, I was going to sit back and enjoy the show.   In the meantime, I needed to think of something particularly nasty I could do to get back at her.   Maybe I needed to find that website they advertise on TV for 55+ and start setting a profile up for her. Now, that would be a GREAT idea.

Aiden

What was I going to answer when that inevitable question "Where did you find your inspiration?" came up?

That was a question I'd have to contemplate later, but for now, I needed to see that profile again.

Pulling my laptop to me, I opened the dating site, signed in and did a search for the profile. Despite a pretty extensive search, it had disappeared from my message board.

Apparently, once the bot thinks a person has become too popular, it does everything in its power to redirect you to someone less popular. Finally, I went back into my archived messages and found the one the bot had sent me that day.

"Rancher Seeking Husband" still came up at the top of the page. I found the link that let me contact him and pressed the comment button. The bot stepped back up with its bad attitude saying the box had reached its maximum allowance.

Shit, well that didn't help. Immediately, I thought of Steve. While I attended the Arts Institute, Steve had gone to the University of Missouri and majored in computer science. I picked up my phone and called.

Steve answered on the second ring, "Yeah," he said.

Laughing at the abrupt nature of his phone etiquette, or lack thereof, I said, "Steve, why the hell can't you just say hello like a normal person?"

Jumping right into our old argument, Steve responded like he always did, "If you wanted a normal friend, you'd have chosen someone besides me."

"Truer words were never spoken," I responded.

Steve immediately asked, "So, you normally don't call me during the day unless you need something. So, what is your command?"

"Don't be an ass," I said.

"Oh," Steve came back, "So this really is just a social call."

"Well you know it isn't, when do I ever call during the day unless I need something?"

Steve burst into laughter and said, "Ok, you got me there. How can I help?"

I told him about my showing and its success. Steve did his obligatory surprise and congratulations. All the time I knew he could care less about the whole Louvre thing. I also knew Steve might not care about the end result, but he sure as hell cared about my accomplishment. That was genuine and sincere.

"So, Steve ..." I hesitantly continued, "You see this all started with a bizarre profile on a dating site. But when I went back to try to send a message to the dude who inspired all this, the damned site refused to let me send a message, so does your hacking skills enable you to override a Nazi bot?"

When Steve finally stopped laughing, he confirmed it probably wouldn't be hard to do and likely wouldn't involve any illegal hacking.

Knowing full well I would regret it, I gave Steve the website and let him go in under my password and name. Not like Steve would ever want to go back there again even if he remembered them. Steve assured me that he'd give me a call after he'd had enough time to track down the profile and put up nude pictures of me on the site.

"You don't have any nude pictures of me, blockhead."

"I don't need them. I can Photoshop you onto some old fat dude."

"Yeah, you do that," I responded. "you do that friend. It won't matter because I have so many hot men knocking down my door these days, I'm sure a fat old version of myself would only make the men want me more."

Steve replied with a "humph, yeah right." and hung up. Within an hour, Steve called back and said he'd opened the message option back up. Of course, he tried to explain to me about making a copy of "blah, blah, blah," but seriously, I think I dozed off halfway through his description. Long story short, he didn't have to hack and there were always ways around a block like this one if you were nerdy enough to figure it out.

I thanked Steve and hung up.

I opened the email that he sent with a direct link to the messaging site so even an internet dummy like me would be able to open it without screwing it up. I had to laugh at some of the crazy shit my friend had included in the email. "Daddy needs his sugar rubbed tonight" was the headline of one. Steve was a total ass. I loved him more than ever. Finally, I opened the browser and typed a quick message to the guy explaining that his ad had inspired me, and I ended up creating a collection that not only sold for a lot, but had helped boost me up in my profession. I ended the email by saying I felt obligated to thank him for what he'd done for me.

Devin

The next month was absolutely insane. I had over seven thousand head of cattle to gather, tag and sell and I wanted to get that done before the damned rainy season started. My ranch hands were about as good as gold, however, and we were able to get the cattle separated, tag the ones I wanted to sell, check on the heifers that were pregnant and make an inventory of the year-old calves that needed to be managed the following spring. We had to call the vet out a half a dozen times because of problems we found with some of the yearlings. Either they had gotten caught up in wire and managed to escape the attention of the hands in charge of that herd or they had hurt themselves when we were rounding them up.

Several nights I didn't come home at all, rather I'd stay out on the range so we could get up the next morning early enough to get started again. Somehow, we managed to escape any rain as we worked, but I knew it was just a matter of time before the weather broke loose.

When I finally got all the stock situated, all the cattle we were selling sent to the buyers, and the two steers I processed for myself each year butchered and stored in my freezers, I came home and slept for three days straight.

Finally, Claire came in and told me sleepy time was over and I had about a thousand things to do at the homestead before the rains came. The house had been painted right after I bought it from the old man's heirs, but the soffits and gutters needed another coat. The roof of the stables had sprung a leak and even though it was a metal roof, if I didn't fix the leaks, I would find myself dealing with some much bigger problems when the interior wood started to rot.

So, I poured myself out of bed just after sunrise, got the soffits painted first, then put my attention onto the stable roof. Luckily, my ranch hands had resumed their duties and were managing the cows we'd left to pasture. It was also haying time, but this year, I decided to hire a local guy to do all my haying for me. After running the numbers which included all the mess I had when my herds weren't properly managed after the culling, I almost always lost money and stock this time of year. When I saw that I could hire the haying process out to local farmers and that doing so actually *saved* me money, I jumped on it with both feet.

I could almost my predecessor cursing under his breath. The old fool never took to having contractors on the property. If he couldn't control every damned person who stepped onto the land, he wanted nothing to do with them. Oh well, I wasn't the old man—I was the new man and this saved money and headache. Last year had been the first year I'd hired outside contractors and I'd stuck to them like glue scared they wouldn't get the highest quality hay or that they wouldn't store enough for winter, but this year, I was more confident; although, I still went over and checked their work at least once a day.

The old man's legacy had been that of a beast, everyone knew I was his protégé and if you fucked with the old man, you'd never set foot on the property again. The folks that knew him seemed to think I was the same, so, I didn't really worry too much about any of the locals trying to get one over on me.

By the time, I'd patched the roof, I was ready for a break. I'd already been down to the fields and was convinced the hay contractors were doing the job to my specifications. All the hands had done a full inventory of the stock and we seemed to be ready for a great calving season...although I said that with every finger and toe crossed. Nobody wanted to jinx a season by being too confident.

Claire left dinner for me on the table and called me to come down and eat. I knew not to keep her waiting because the woman was known to throw food away if you didn't act like you appreciated her efforts. Luckily, I had finished the roof and was just looking around for any potential holes I had missed when she called.

I came down, went to the stable bathroom and cleaned up before coming into the house.

"Where's your plate, you not going to eat with me?" I asked.

"Not tonight sweetheart," Claire said as she patted my head. "I'm headed into Billieville to get some groceries we are running low on; then, I'm going home to curl up with a romance novel I've been reading."

I just sighed and shook my head. Ever since Claire found out I was gay, she'd been trying to push her damned mushy romance novels on me, and I had finally taken the one she was shoving in my face and threw it out the front door. Of course, that got me a slap up against the back of my head, but it did get her to leave me alone about them.

I leaned over and kissed her on the cheek. "Have fun and don't forget to wear a condom," I said to her. She turned around and smiled. These were her words every time I'd gone out with the loser from the property next door.

"I wish I had a man to put a condom on. You know they say a woman in her fifties needs it more than a teenage boy," she yelled back as she walked out the door.

All I could do was moan. Yeah, note to self, don't bring up sex with a fifty-year-old woman unless you were prepared to deal with mental images of her looking for a hook-up.

When I finished eating, I got myself a glass of wine and headed up to my room. I needed to answer some emails, check my bank accounts to make sure all the money got deposited from the sale of my stock, go over my books, log the inventory and then go to sleep. I really needed the sleep part. Even though I'd done the three-days sleep stretch, my body was still tired, and I wanted nothing more than to sleep another 72 hours...like Claire would ever allow that to happen.

When I got out of the shower, I sat at my desk. As the old desktop came to life, I saw *CMTOCM* was open. Claire must have forgotten to close it. There was a message up on the screen and the picture of the author was beautiful. I looked to see where he was from and almost choked on the wine I'd just drank when I saw he was from New York. First of all, why the hell was someone from the other side of the damned country even talking to me (or Claire disguised as me) and second, why was his message up? Claire had discarded all the other guys that were not closer than a day's drive almost immediately.

I read through some of the messages and stopped short when I saw that Claire had given the guy my address. What the hell, Claire? This had gotten out of hand! I was NOT going to deal with some freak showing up from New York looking for a hook-up and harassing my men or my stock. Shit, I'd been damned lucky that son of a bitch I dated before hadn't done something horrible to my men. I closed the screen and decided I'd be having that talk with her the next morning.

Blake Allwood

PART TWO
THE MEETING

Blake Allwood

Aiden

By the time I got home, I'd decided that mailing the card was lame. Hell, this whole thing had catapulted me into fame, and I owed it to myself to close this loop and get on with the rest of my life. Besides, all the fame, parties and worrying over the profile had kept me from painting anything since the exhibition and my fingers were itching to get back to it. As I walked into my apartment, I immediately spied my last painting from the collection I had accidentally kept for myself.

I had forgotten to include it in the grouping and even accidentally threw a coat over it one night after a long evening working with Jace then didn't uncover it until the night before the show.

I decided it was fate and thought I would keep it. If I decided I didn't want it, I could always give it to my parents or Margie although all their walls were already covered with my art.

I stood back looking over the piece. It was striking—the colors were all a little too bold making them seem surreal. Of course, this was intentional. I wanted something that would end the collection with a feeling of anticipation and maybe a bit of foreboding—like stepping into an alternate reality. I knew if I decided to go that direction, Margie would have no difficulty finding a place for it. No, this one wasn't for Margie or my parents, but it almost felt like providence that I had forgotten to include it with the rest of the collection. I decided then and there that I'd keep it until I found its rightful owner.

I flipped open my laptop and went directly to *CMTOCM*. I had asked the night before if the guy felt comfortable enough to send me his address so I could mail a card and he had agreed. I quickly did a Google search of the address and found it was located in the eastern part of the state. The address was for Billieville, WA. It was just north of the Oregon border and along the Grande Ronde River. I sent a quick message to the owner of the account telling him I had a few days off and I would fly out and drop off the card, show him one of the paintings he inspired and then I'd be off. I told him I wouldn't be available to check messages after tomorrow morning.

I booked a flight to Spokane, set up a rental four-wheel drive and then set to packing.

When I got my carry-on case packed -- reminding myself I didn't need to pack an entire suitcase since I wouldn't be there long, just enough time to drop off a card -- I sent emails to Jace and my parents letting them know the address where I was going. I called Suzie to let her know I had decided to just go and get it over with, which was met with her enthusiastic approval.

Margie, my next call, was more reserved but the reaction to my decision to go was similar to my sister's, the exception being a bit of Margie's typical motherly advice.

"Don't get in the way of a good love affair darling. Those are the nuggets of fun you never forget even when you are as old as me."

I wasn't sure if it was the thought of my elderly friend having a love life or if it was the thought of her having insight into a gay man's love life that made me blush, but blush, I did. "I love you Margie," is all I could think to say before hanging up.

I met my Lyft driver in the wee hours of the morning to get to the airport with enough time for the dreaded check-in process. As I stood in the never-ending line, with shoes in hand, I asked myself what had gotten into me to cause me to jump on a plane to godforsaken eastern Washington? I doubted I could explain in words why I just needed to see this man for myself. I needed to meet him and shake his hand, or if I was honest, connect with him any way I could. I began to doubt myself again, but it was too late to back out now. I went through the line, got into my seat and passed out before the rest of the airplane loaded. As I was drifting off, I realized I was way more tired than I had thought; maybe this would be a needed vacation after all. Maybe I could get the damned card delivered and find a nice bed and breakfast in Spokane and indulge in a long massage with a Grecian-god masseuse. These were lovely dreams to start the adventure off with.

The plane landed with a hard thud, hard enough to wake me out of my deep slumber. I hadn't slept that hard in a long time. I checked my mouth to ensure there was no embarrassing drool and was pleased to see that there was none. I looked apologetically at the poor woman who had the misfortune to sit next to my zombie self during the flight and shrugged saying, I had no idea I was as tired as I was.

She smiled and patted my knee saying, "It could have been worse, you could have been a snorer." Relieved I didn't snore, I checked my body to ensure all belongings were still in the place I had put them before snoozing.

Confident I was still in one piece, I exited the plane when allowed and rushed to the bathroom to spruce up before going to the rental place to pick up my ride.

When I finally made it to the rental car pick up, I noticed for the first time the deluge that was coming down.

As I stepped up to the rental car desk, the attendant shook his head and apologized, but the SUV I'd ordered had been wrecked before it got back to the airport.

"The person had hydroplaned into a ditch," he said.

"No way to get another one in?" I asked, my frustration just beginning to bubble.

"No, sorry sir, the only thing we'll have before tomorrow morning is a Miata."

"So," I said, "you are telling me, I either have to spend the night here and wait for the vehicle I ordered, or I have to take this little sports car over Washington's rugged southeast?"

"Yes sir, that is our only option." He apologized again.

The frustration had shifted to anger and I snipped at the poor guy before I could rein it in, "I don't have any intention of paying you more than I already agreed."

"No sir, we will wave all additional fees," the clerk told him.

Not having any other option, I checked the Miata out and slipped out of the airport directly into a traffic jam only a flood can create. It took over an hour before I was able to push the car past 30 miles per hour. Within a few minutes after speeding up, I was pulled over by a cop.

"Yes officer, I am aware of how fast I was going and no, I do not believe I was speeding." The officer looked at my license, looked the car over once and let me go. I quickly remembered why I never wanted a sports car. They were an open invitation for the cops to pull you over, even in pouring rain, obviously.

Religiously keeping the speed limit and thanking god that I hadn't been pulled over again, I finally got to the town of Kennewick. Luckily, the rain had stopped. I had been driving since I left Spokane and between the rain and a headache that was now throbbing behind my left eye, I decided I'd better find a hotel room for the night and then finish my quest the next day.

I spotted a hotel called The Happy Lion and pulled into the parking lot. I checked in, went to check the room out and was moderately convinced that I was unlikely to get bedbugs from my stay and settled in for the night.

I hadn't eaten anything since leaving New York and was feeling more than a little hungry. Thanking the good spirits the rain had stopped, I spotted a twenty-four-hour McDonald's within walking distance. Preferring the walk over sitting in the cramped muscle car again, I trotted over and grabbed a value meal.

When I got back to my hotel room I fell asleep immediately, which in turn caused me to wake up rather early the next morning. Unfortunately, either the bad choice of food or the long day of travel caused the headache from the day before to magnify to a full-blown migraine. I was sure my lack of sleep was a big part of it as well. My bed ended up being lumpy, and the neighbors had obviously been deaf because I could hear their TV through the walls probably better than they could.

Grumpily, I showered, dressed and headed to the hotel lobby for some coffee and whatever they were serving for continental breakfast. The food was less than exciting, but nothing seemed more important than getting caffeine pumping through my system.

I sat down in the lobby of the hotel and after my third cup, I thought I was alive enough to get back on the road again. Blessing the universe, I checked the forecast and saw that they weren't expected to have any more rain today. Thank god for small miracles.

I typed the address into my phone and headed toward the small town called Billieville.

Well, this wasn't gonna be worth the effort if I didn't get a story out of it. I could only hope I didn't get beat up and left on a fence post to die while there.

It took an excruciating three and a half hours to get to Mountain View, a small town that sat just north and west of the even smaller Billieville. By the time I arrived, my head was splitting with pain. I stopped at the only service station I'd seen for miles and bought a bottle of Tylenol for what had to be three times the retail price and gratefully downed enough to hopefully abate a headache.

The GPS had long ceased to be of assistance, and I was forced to stop at a local restaurant and ask directions the rest of the way to the ranch.

"Are you talking about Devin Pierce's ranch?" the attendant asked.

"Yes, that's the one," I replied as pleasantly as my headache allowed me.

"Oh, there ain't no way you gonna get there today. Not after all this rain. You got to cross the *Ronde* to get there. Besides, is that you in that little sports car?"

I looked at my rental with every ounce of hatred one could muster for a Miata and said begrudgingly, "Yeah, that is what I'm driving."

I heard several folks snicker and one of the old men hollered, "You ain't NEVER gonna get there in that."

My headache was coming back full strength. I looked at my antagonizer and asked, "Why is that?"

"Cause, there are potholes bigger'n that car in the middle of that road. You gonna need a 4-wheel drive to get back to Pierce's place. Even with that, you got to wait till it ain't so damned muddy."

The old man turned his head and spit a stream of black liquid into a 2-liter bottle. I felt the continental breakfast move in my stomach. I decided it was best to leave Billie's Roadside Restaurant before I ended up making enemies of everyone there with an upchuck that I was sure would come if I saw that old man spit into that bottle again.

Getting outside in the fresh air helped settle my stomach and I looked around for someone else to advise me how to proceed but there was no one in sight. Foolishly, I decided to go as far as I could. Before the old fart had weighed in and made my stomach roll, the waitress had pointed in the direction of an old road that ran to the east of town. I decided I'd be able to get the lay of the land and then try again the next day. Maybe I could get to some civilization and hire someone with adequate road equipment to transport me to the ranch the next day.

It didn't take long before I realized what the old tobacco-stained man was referring to. The road narrowed into one lane with harrowing cliffs on either side. As I drove down into a valley nearing the river, I could hear the raging current even before I saw it.

When I arrived at a rickety old bridge, I got out of my car and looked out over the torrent of the mighty flooded river. The water was high but had not yet crested the bridge.

Knowing the rain had stopped the day before, I decided the worst of the flood was over and thought the bridge was safe enough to cross without any concern. So, slowly, I pulled the Miata onto the bridge and started to cross. As soon as I got to the middle of the bridge, the water seemed to come to life. I could physically see it rising and doing so fast enough that I was forced to gun the little car to get it off the bridge before the water crested the side. Much to my dismay, I realized the other side of the river gave way to a road of dirt that may have been gravel at one time but sure as hell wasn't any longer.

The Miata was made for pavement and smooth pavement at that. She was made to enhance a man's ego, not navigate muddy half gravel roads. I was in trouble. I knew I had to move the little car far enough to get to higher ground. The river was clearly not done rising and although it hadn't crested the bridge nor the side of her banks, it had every intention of doing so. No way could I afford to chance the bridge back to the gravel side of the river either. The river was alive, and she would take anyone who dared to challenge her to a watery grave.

I managed to coax the sports car through the mud and eventually to a rise high enough to keep it from becoming submerged in flood water. Unfortunately, as I climbed the hill, the car's tires sank deep in the mud and by the time I reached the top of the hill, the bitch of a car was unable to go any further.

I considered just packing it in and sleeping in the car for the evening, but considering where I was, I guessed I couldn't expect anyone to pass this way for many days to come—chances were no one would ever come. As much as I wasn't prepared to do so, I would have to take my chances on foot.

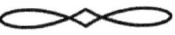

If the drive had been bad, the walk could have been a scene from *Misery*. I had no idea where I was going. The road was as much mud puddle as it was road and my tennis shoes were ill-equipped to handle the mud, or the long hike. I assumed I had tracked a mile in when I began to give up hope. I could see the road led to a tall hill. There were tracks in the dirt, but besides that, no sign of human life. It was then that I remembered this area still sported animals who viewed helpless city folk like me as dinner.

That's when the panic began to set in, "Damn. What the hell have I gotten myself into?"

I couldn't afford to be caught out in this wilderness overnight. I didn't have adequate clothing or footwear and I could tell that the area would get more than a little cold in the night.

I steeled myself to the task ahead and began walking, or more accurately sliding, through the mud. Three hours later, I had still not seen any sight of humanity. I made it to the top of the ridge, but there were only more ridges to cover. I had no choice but to continue on. It was only a few steps further that I heard the faint sound of a vehicle in the distance. I rushed back to the top of the ridge and looked out hoping to see and, if lucky, flag down the person I was hearing. To my dismay, there was nothing nor anyone around, and the sound seemed to be getting further away instead of closer.

I trudged on again, feeling sheer desperation. I was sure that this would actually be the end of me. Exhaustion coupled with anxiety began to play tricks on me. At times I thought I could hear voices in the distance only to realize it was the breeze flowing through the shrubs. Once I stumbled upon a rapid stream and thought I'd been hearing conversations.

Shortly before dusk, I crashed down onto the muddy ground and put my head in my hands. I had no tears, but I felt a need to cry nonetheless. When I heard a motor again, I brushed the thought off as another exhausted fantasy, but the sound got closer and I realized someone was really coming down the road.

Devin

I confronted Claire the next morning about the website and she had the decency to blush.

"Claire, what the hell were you thinking? You can't give our address out to random strangers on a fucking gay sex site," I said exasperatedly.

"Stop being so melodramatic, kid," Claire said. "It ain't a sex site and we both know it. That young man just wanted to send you a card. No harm no foul."

"You don't know that," I argued. "For all we know, he could be out there right now snooping around the property."

Claire burst out laughing. "He'd have to have a helicopter to pull that off."

Still exasperated, I huffed, "Claire, you know what I mean. We got lucky with that son of a bitch next door. What the hell would've happened if he'd made waves with the hands? We'd be sitting in that damned courtroom with him."

Claire's face turned ashen at that and she shook her head. "Honey, I'm sorry. I didn't think about that, but this guy seemed legit. I screened everyone I talked to."

I chuckled. "Yeah, I've been watching your conversations."

Claire looked at me surprised. "Really? You knew I was talking to those guys?"

Still smiling, I said. "Yep, I kept wondering when you were going to invite the drag queen out for a visit."

Claire blushed again, "Well, I liked him, but he said he didn't think ranch life was for him."

"Just so you know, I sent him a private message and told him he was talking to you, so that could have something to do with it."

Claire just stood with her mouth open. "I'd nail you for that, but I guess I don't really have any ground to stand on, do I?"

"That would be a hell no," I said, crossing my arms.

Claire sighed. "Did you read what the guy with the card wrote? He said you inspired him. I guess he is an artist or a musician or something like that."

"Yeah, I read it, but Claire, he could've been lying. It's time we put an end to this, don't you agree?"

Claire thought for a moment then looked up. "No, honey, I don't. You can't live your life out here alone. The old man did that, and he ended up being a bitter old beast. I care too much for you to let that happen. You need to have access to other men like yourself and if that means you use a computer site to find one, then you use a computer site to find one."

I could feel the anger rising, but one look at Claire's face and I knew this was an argument I wouldn't win. I'd just wait until later and I'd go in and disable the damned account myself then lock the computer with a password. I might not be able to win a verbal argument with her, but I could sure as hell put a stop to all the shenanigans.

Instead of continuing the conversation, I walked away. There were plenty of chores to keep me busy despite the weather we were getting outside. I learned long ago when Claire gets her jaw set like it was right now, you had better be ready for a fight because the woman could give better than she could take. I guess living with and being the housekeeper all those years for the SOB rancher either turned you into a formidable opponent or broke you. Claire had clearly never been broken.

Claire and I worked side by side the rest of the day but didn't say much. When she left for home that night, she let me know that she was going to stay home for a few days and get some work done there.

After the intensity of the past few weeks, I think all of us, Claire and I included, needed a break from one another. The rains had started, and it seemed like a good time to let that be our excuse for retreating to our corners of the ranch and taking that break.

I woke early the next morning and went to the stables to check on the horses, make sure the roof patches had held, and to take stock of the work I needed to do. The stables really needed to be mucked, but I was not in the mood. I would get that done over the next couple of days. I even yelled out, "Sorry you guys," as I threw hay and put out feed for them. I was never one to let mucking go, but Tom, my young stable boy had quit on me a couple months ago and I didn't have time to replace him with all the cattle work I had to tend to.

By afternoon, I'd finished all the chores around the place and decided I needed to take a break and check out how high the river had gotten. My phone and internet service were on the blink. No surprise there, since it did that anytime we had a huge rain or storm, or if the wind blew too hard, for that matter. I made a mental note, once again, to contact the folks who put the new services in at the winery to get something installed here. I certainly didn't mind the solitude, but I worried if one of the hands needed back-up, they'd have to ride all the way over to the homestead to get me. If it was an emergency, we'd be screwed. When the services were down, we were thrust back to a time before phones.

I pulled the ATV out and rode out to Claire's place first to check on her. There were deep ruts in the path to her place telling me she had difficulty getting home the night before. Damn it, I should've checked on her. That was the last straw! I'd definitely be putting in satellite services this month.

Claire was good, tucked in with her mushy novel and happy when I left. I rode along the ridge path to the river and it was high enough that I was concerned about the Wickerman Road Bridge. I guessed it was only a matter of time before I'd have to pay to have that replaced. The county had long abandoned the road on this side of the creek saying it was really a driveway to the ranch homestead which, to be fair, it really was. I'd get in touch with the county officials once the river receded and see if they'd go in with me to replace the bridge at least.

I rode back up the hill to avoid the low lands where the river flooded which took me to the old cattle path that ran along the top of the ridge. My heart sank when I saw a flash of color in the distance. It looked like someone was parked on Wickerman. Damn, I didn't bring anything for protection. Maybe I should go back to the house first.

I was just about to turn around when I changed my mind. If someone crossed that bridge, it was possible they were hurt or needed help. I decided to go that way and take my chances.

After topping a couple ridges, I could tell that I was seeing a little sports car in the distance and that sent my anger flying. Why the hell would someone drive that little piece of nothing onto a ranch in the middle of a storm?

By the time I got to the car, I was ready to rip the driver a new one. Lucky for whoever it was, they were nowhere to be seen. It only took a couple seconds though to see whoever drove the useless little car had gotten out and was walking up Wickerman, and in the wrong direction from the house.

The anger began to war with concern. I sure as hell didn't want some idiot to die on my property

I held down the panic as I drove along the road following the slip and slide of the footprints along the muddy road. Hell, once or twice I thought I was going to bog the ATV down in the mud.

I finally topped a hill and saw a lone figure sitting on the side of the road, exposed arms wrapped around his body. I couldn't tell if he was crying, but I could tell he had been through a rough day. He stood up and waved his arms at me and relief flowed through me. I thanked god he was still alive. It took a bit to get to him through the mud and I immediately recognized the guy from the website which made me pissed as hell. I pulled the ATV up and asked, not trying to hide my anger in any way, "Why the hell are you here?"

Aiden

It still took a while for the man on the four-wheeler to reach me, and I remained in the middle of the road, waving my arms. It was my only chance—so, I'd either be saved or run over. Thankfully, the man stopped and looked me over, head to foot, in a slow and not so positive assessment.

His anger was unmistakable. "Why the hell are you here?"

I just shrugged, "I... I'm Aiden Fisher," I said hopefully. There was no recognition in his face which told me this must not be the guy I'd come to see. Damn, if this wasn't going to be trickier than I'd planned it to be.

"I'm guessing you are the fool that drove that fancy car into the mud a few miles back?" Each word held sharp anger.

I was too exhausted to argue, so I simply nodded.

"Well, shit man! Don't just stand there, climb on the back and I'll get you settled until it dries up enough to get that pretty little toy back across the river."

Despite his words, there was nothing nice about it. He said "pretty little car" like he'd just eaten something sour.

Despite his gruff nature, I was overcome with gratitude and with my last ounce of strength, I climbed onto the back of the four-wheeler. Just being safe and no longer afraid of dying from exposure or being eaten by a bear or mountain lion, I relaxed. Despite every ounce of effort to avoid it, I fell asleep upon my angry savior's back.

The four-wheeler came to a stop much later in front of a huge home that seemed as misplaced there as any piece of architecture could be. I apologized to the guy for falling asleep on him. The stranger didn't laugh. Nor did he smile. The look on his face was disgust.

"I don't know why you came here, but you damned well better have a good explanation for being stuck on my property." At that, I looked up at the home. The property looked more like it should have been along the eastern or western seaside rather than in the wilderness of Eastern Washington State.

I shrugged, "Yeah, I've got a good excuse, but at the moment, I'm not at all sure it will make much sense."

"Try me," the stranger challenged.

"Well, damn, can we sit down somewhere before I go into it?" I had reached the end of my limits and if this crabby man was going to interrogate me, the least he could do was let me sit while I told him.

"Over there on the swing will work. You don't get to come inside my house covered in that filth. I will decide after I hear you out whether you get the barn, or you sleep on the ground."

"Let's compromise," I offered, "you call me a Lyft, or a taxi and I'll pay to get out of your hair altogether."

At this, the stranger laughed for the first time. The vast and sudden shift in his features took me off guard and I felt the immediate tug of attraction for the first time since meeting him.

"Where the hell do you think you are that a taxi could pick you up and take you out of here?"

There was a definite sense of disdain that matched the man's lack of humor.

"Listen, sir," I began, for the first time getting my back up at the man's disdain. "I'm here looking for a man who did me a huge favor. I need to say thank you, then, I am going to get the hell out of here and back to civilization."

"Since I'm the only person who lives in these parts, I'd say you somehow missed your mark a bit."

"Yeah," I agreed, "I was beginning to get that idea myself."

"You fill me in on this story of yours," the stranger offered, "and I'll see if I can help you find the man you owe gratitude to."

"Listen, I have no intention of dying out here and my story involves elements that folks in these parts might not be too keen to hear. I'm tired, but if you force me to tell my story and then have any intention of stringing me up on a tree, you need to know I'm going to fight back."

The man looked at me with a humored yet reserved look and said, "If you intend to stay here, you'll have to tell me your story, but I'll heed your warning."

I sighed, realizing there was no way out of this except to be honest. I leaned back on his swing, closed my eyes for a moment, gathered up my wits, asked a prayer that this guy wasn't a huge homophobe hillbilly and then told my story from beginning to the end.

When I was done, the man looked me in the eye and asked what this fella's name was.

I hesitated before answering. I didn't know yet if the area was friendly to gays yet and I wasn't about to throw my muse under the bus. So, I said, "Sir, I am not at liberty to share that with you. That isn't how you thank a man for helping inspire you to greatness."

At that, the man leaned back in his chair and belted out laughter that could be heard across the

valley. I had no idea why he was laughing. I had anticipated a lot of possible reactions from this man—everything from having a Bible thrown at me to a lecture about the evils of homosexuality, but laughter was not the reaction I had anticipated. I was quickly becoming uncomfortable and began to get concerned this was one of those hermits who stockpiled guns, had a militia waiting in the back 40 and would use me as shooting practice.

As I was trying to come up with a mental plan to get away and find some kind of weapon to defend myself with, the crazy guy leaned forward and said simply, "My name is Devin Pierce and what you just said was the biggest load of horse shit I've heard in years." Devin got up and pointed to the barn. "You can sleep in there and I'll figure out what the hell to do with you in the morning."

I gaped at the retreating man for several long moments before I got my wits about me. "You son of a bitch," I all but yelled. "You mean you sat there through that entire story with me thinking you were some demonic hillbilly or wigged-out militiaman and let me drone on about the real reason I came all this damned way and you are going to laugh at me and call me a liar? Devin Pierce, sir, you can go straight to hell!"

At that, I stormed toward the stable without looking back. My anger grew with every step, but as much as I'd relish the moment to hurl profanities at that horrible man, I understood there was no other option but to go to the barn. I'd wait until morning, then, I'd talk this SOB into letting me use his phone once his temper had worn off. If I couldn't get a taxi or a Lyft, then I'd hire a goddamn helicopter to haul me out of this godforsaken place. Yes, helicopters cost a fortune, but thanks to the asshole inspiring me to paint, I could now afford to rent one. Thank god, I didn't meet him before I started painting or it would've been a whole different collection.

Then, anger completely faded away when I walked into the barn. To say I was completely shocked would be the understatement of the year. This was no ordinary barn. Instead of seeing stables, I walked into a small apartment that was at least twice the size of my NYC apartment. The furnishings were clean but dated. It was clear no one had used the place in quite some time, but nonetheless, someone was maintaining it properly. I took my shoes off at the door and walked toward the other end of the room.

I immediately saw a door that indeed led to the actual stables. Through the door window, I could see it had modern horse stalls that were immaculately kept. I could only see the occasional hindquarters of a horse or two, but it was clear the stalls weren't empty. I decided after a quick clean up, I'd take the time to wander into the actual barn and meet the animals that lived there. Maybe my host was a royal ass and maybe I would always regret making this much effort to thank him, but I would at least get to spend a quality night with a few domesticated animals. That was something I missed deep in my soul. Looking into the barn, I could almost feel a horse's head under my hand and the brush of air from their nose. So, something good may actually come from the day after all.

I wandered upstairs and found a couple of small bedrooms and an equally small bath and shower. Unfortunately, I had left my bag in the back of the Miata, so I didn't have a change of clothes. Oh well, I could wash the majority of the mud out of my clothes while showering and then I could put them back on wet. It wasn't like I wasn't already wet and muddy, at least this way I'd be wet and less muddy. Hell, maybe I'd forget the horses and just climb into bed. That would make more sense anyway. I climbed into the shower and almost purred when the hot water poured over my clothes and skin. I washed my clothes first with the bar of Dial soap I found under the sink. Then I stripped, hung up the clothes where ever I could find a place and put the rest of my energy into washing myself. As a kid, I hated the smell of Dial soap, but from that point forward there would never be a smell I loved more.

While standing under the heaven-sent stream of hot water, I pondered my situation. Ever since landing in Spokane, it seemed that I had been forced to follow the beat of someone else's drum. The control and order that I craved, hell, *sought* after, seemed to elude my every effort. First, the rental car mix-up that left me in that stupid little sports car. Then the ever-present rain that led to the muddy drive to the ranch which in turn led me to get stuck on the *wrong side of the river*. That was just the beginning, being at the mercy of that beast of a rancher whose attitude did nothing to smooth out the edges of my experience thus far. Was it possible that the fates were screwing with me? Seriously, what were the chances that I'd end up being rescued by that caveman after the couple days I'd had?

It didn't matter that all those things happened— my biggest concern was that when I was off my game, I was more likely to make rash decisions and those decisions more often than not were ones I regretted.

I knew without a shadow of a doubt I'd have to watch myself around this rancher dude. Yes, he was an ass of epic proportions, but he was also a gorgeous ass. The pictures of him on *CMTOCM* were silhouettes and didn't even come close to showing how ruggedly handsome he was. The other fact remained that even though the rescue was embarrassing, he had still rescued me. Oh, boy this was an odd situation. No matter what happened, I'd finish what I had come to do, whether the redneck wanted to be thanked or not, then hopefully, I'd be on my way.

Devin

After getting back into the house, I felt bad for how I'd acted. The guy had scared me. I sure as hell didn't want anyone to get hurt and he had been more than a little stupid in driving that sports car onto the bridge during a flood then onto the dirt road. But then again, how would he know it was a dirt road if he'd never been over here.

I made another mental note to have gravel put down on the road from the bridge. I already worried about Claire coming and going on the road, and now I know it was irresponsible that I hadn't already had the gravel replaced there.

I thought about the guy and just the idea of him had me thinking about sex. The man was smaller than me, thin but muscular. I had seen that even clearer in one of the photos from his profile. Thinking of the profile, I went upstairs and woke the computer up. I knew the internet was out but if I'd left the site open, maybe I would be able to see it again.

When I opened the computer, sure enough, his profile popped up, along with the messages.

Damn, there was a new message there. He had written to let me know he was going to come out. Well, shit. If I'd looked at the damned computer, I'd have known he was coming. Now, I could understand why he thought I was a total ass. I was a total ass.

I went into my closet and pulled out some clean clothes and then grabbed a couple of towels from the dryer. Thinking the guy would want a shower, I went over to the apartment with what I hoped was a goodwill offering.

I walked into the room and the man was nowhere to be seen but I could hear movement upstairs. I should have called out as I made my way upstairs, but didn't think about it, therefore, I came face to face with a beautiful, dripping wet and really pissed off naked man.

I looked at the guy and could feel a smirk slide across my face. I could tell the man's pride had been bruised because when he saw me, he looked me straight in the eye and stood up straighter.

He didn't blink when he said stiffly, "I was looking for a towel."

I made no effort to hide the grin and said, "There aren't any in here. I brought you one and a change of clothes as well."

"That was very chivalrous of you. Hell, I bet you even take the dishes out of the sink before you pee in it."

I stopped short. "Listen, we got off to a bad start. I had a lot of nut jobs contact me from that site."

Aiden studied me for a moment before taking the clothes and towels from me.

"If you don't mind, I'm a little wet and *naked* here." I couldn't help it, just hearing him admit he was naked caused my eyes to automatically slide down his gorgeous body. When they came back up to his face I was met with mutinous eyes. The look the man held steadily on me was one of a lion who'd been backed up against the wall.

His look dared me to make a comment and I didn't dare. Instead, I said, "*Steel Magnolias* was my mom's favorite movie."

"What?" Aiden asked.

"The quote, about me being a gentleman who takes the dishes out of the sink before I pee in it... that is from *Steel Magnolias* and it was my mom's favorite movie. We used to watch it all the time. Why don't you get dressed and meet me back on the porch? Let me try this again and see if I can't improve my disposition a bit this time."

"Well that shouldn't be too hard," the guy snarked and I laughed.

"I guess I deserved that. Meet me on the porch and I promise to make it up to you. I make a mean grilled steak. I've already got them out on the counter marinating."

I could see the guy was past the mood of socializing, but instead of turning me down he said, "How about this, I'll get dressed then see what happens."

"Good enough," was my response and I left down the narrow stairway and headed out the door.

Aiden

I was still mad when I got dressed. How dare that arrogant, redneck son of a bitch walk in on me then stand there and stare at me like I was a high grade piece of meat. If I had not been so damn tired, I'd have punched him in his smug, arrogant face...or at least, I'd have told him I would punch him. Violence has never been my thing.

I figured being angry was a good thing since I was fairly sure if I hadn't been, I would already be asleep. I let the anger drive me toward the beast man's front porch ready for the next battle, but when I got there, I came up to a small table and two plates with some asparagus, a baked potato and two perfectly cooked steaks resting to the side.

When I saw the man come out of the door, I said, "I thought you said they were marinating."

"Yep, they were but the grill was hot, and I'd already had this ready for when I got back home from checking the river."

"So," I responded, "That is why you were out on the four-wheeler, rescuing city folk idiots from their own ignorance."

"Yep," affirmed Devin, "but let's steer the conversation away from that for the moment and just enjoy dinner. I'm guessing you are pretty hungry after traipsing up and down muddy ol' Wickerman Road."

I couldn't disagree, I was famished, and the look of those steaks was enough to cause me to whimper like a puppy. We sat across from each other and I didn't wait for permission before I dove into the steak. Devin watched me while I ate and then, pouring us both a glass of red wine that didn't have a label on it, Devin asked, "You weren't shitting me then, you just came here to say thank you?"

"Yep," I said between mouthfuls, "I even brought you a card. It's in the Miata back by the river."

"Speaking of Miata, what possessed you to drive that little thing down a road like Wickerman Road?"

At that, I couldn't help but laugh. "I only meant to go a short way to get the lay of the land. Then I was going to turn back, but after crossing the bridge of death, the river kicked up and tried to drown me and the Miata."

"So, do you always rent Miatas?" Devin sneered.

Feeling my ire rising again, I responded between clenched teeth, "No, the damned thing was supposed to be a 4-wheel drive. The rental company only had that piece of ego left for me to drive."

Devin laughed again, and that beautiful face bloomed once more before me. "So, now I guess you are stuck..."

"Literally and figuratively," I said. "Not only can I not move my vehicle, but I'm also stuck on a fool-hearted mission."

"Hardly," Devin spoke. "You are the only good thing to come from that horrible website. Well, you and a drag queen my housekeeper has fallen in love with."

Despite my curiosity over that last comment, I could feel my exhaustion taking over. I almost asked about the drag queen, but instead, I took another drink of the delicious, nameless wine. No more had I finished the glass, when I began to feel myself nod off.

Devin must have noticed it too and suggested that I turn in for the night. I heard myself agree and would've stood up, but it was too late. The day's events, exhaustion, a full stomach and those delicious glasses of wine had done me in and despite my best efforts, I was falling asleep at the table.

Devin

I could tell the guy was tired, but now that I had him sitting in front of me, I wanted to just keep talking to him. I didn't think about what I was doing giving an exhausted man a glass of wine that I kept refilling. By the time he got to the end of his third glass, he was toast.

I tried to rouse him and offered to help him to bed. Having lost all sense of care, Aiden stood up and headed toward the house. I didn't discourage him or shift his direction but allowed him to move where his will lead. His will led him to my living room couch.

Wouldn't be the first time someone crashed on that old couch, I thought, so I helped him remove his shoes and then tucked him into the fluff of the sofa. I covered him with my mother's old afghan and went back outside to clean up from dinner.

Aiden

The following morning, I awoke in one of the most comfortable couches I'd ever laid in. After opening my eyes, however, I had to quickly close them again. The luxurious comfort was equally met by intense ugliness. What was this horror show I was sleeping on? Slowly, I tried opening my eyes once again, but the ugly overtook me and I closed them with the conviction of keeping them closed until I could get far away from this paradox of comfort and ugly. I was pondering this contrast between comfort and eye trauma when I heard dishes clanking in the kitchen. I opened my eyes again, this time forcing myself to look away from the baby blue behemoth with gigantic man-eating flowers in mismatched and clashing colors.

What I saw made my heart stop. Devin was in the kitchen with nothing on but his boxers. The blurry pictures online had only hinted at his physique, but now that I was there in person, I noticed for the first time the incredible arms on this man. Arms had

128

always been my weak spot. Devin sported big, muscular triceps that perfectly supported beautifully rounded biceps. As I lay on the couch, I licked my lips thinking I could almost taste them.

Wait, what the hell? I quickly remembered where I was, and the way this guy had treated me upon arrival. Yes, he had gotten nicer as the night went on, but I reminded myself that I was in no place to allow my infatuations to get the best of me.

Once again, I reminded myself I was on a mission to thank this guy for helping inspire me toward my masterpiece -- as well as saving me from what would have been a tortuous death -- and then I'd make a phone call and get the hell of out of Dodge or Washington or wherever the hell I was.

Devin finished cooking breakfast and was placing it on the little kitchen table when I leaned up and asked, "According to your profile, you are too busy to have any time to be very domestic...were you just exaggerating?"

I knew I'd thrown a punch, but at that point, I wanted to make sure I kept the heat on the situation. No need getting drawn into a fling with someone like Devin ... even if those muscles were appetizing.

Unfortunately, my jab didn't get the desired reaction. Devin simply grinned and said, "No it just so happens the whole internet dating thing coincided with our annual cattle sale. I run the ranch on intervals giving me most of my fall and winter months off. That way, I can focus on enjoying life a little before the calving begins. We plan those calving events in the late spring. So, this is the beginning of the season when I've got more time on my hands than usual. Also, the ranch hands are spread out across the different parts of the ranch and they handle their part of the herd. So, no worry... I have plenty time to fix us breakfast."

I looked down around myself and asked, "How did I end up on the cloud couch from hell?"

Devin looked startled, glanced over at the couch and laughed out loud. "You fell asleep at the table last night and I didn't have it in me to carry you to the apartment."

I could feel myself blushing at the thought of him helping me to bed. "I appreciate you letting me stay the night, but I need to call my parents and get some transportation out of here."

Devin only laughed, "How do you plan on that?"

"I thought I'd call in a helicopter," I said shyly.

Devin laughed again. "Well, there are a lot of problems with your thought process. Not the least of which is we don't have phone access."

"What?" I exclaimed. "Well, surely I can do it by the internet."

Still laughing, "You really don't know much about this part of the world, do you? No phone, no internet."

"So, not even satellite?"

"Nope," Devin explained, "never wanted it. Dial-up was fine with me."

"Shit," I mumbled to myself, "you can't even look at porn on dial-up."

Clearly trying not to burst out laughing in my face, Devin said, "Well porn isn't really a necessity of mine."

"If I were living in the middle of nowhere, I'd think it'd be one of the most important parts of your life."

This finally put Devin over the edge, and he laughed with gusto. "Dude, you have an interesting insight. I was in and out of relationships over the past few years. I'd either go to them or they'd come to me, so my sexual needs have been met. Porn always made me think of machinery. I prefer a bit more romance than bump and grind."

I had often thought the same thing in regards to porn. It was fine I guessed from time to time, but for most of life's sexual needs, I knew I preferred skin to skin, lips to lips instead of just fantasizing. Despite that, I didn't want to give this guy the satisfaction that we had that in common, so I quickly said, "Well sex is mostly in the mind anyway. So, my thoughts are, watch a little porn and not have to worry about the dude the next day."

Devin cocked an eyebrow at me. Much cooler now, he apparently decided this was a good time to take his leave. "I've got a few chores to do this morning including checking on the level of the river. It has been a little over a day since we last had rain so I'm hoping she'll be calming down again. You are welcome to hang out here or you can wander around the farmstead. There is a TV in the apartment but the reception sucks. You can also watch some movies. Claire, my housekeeper, keeps a stash of movies in the apartment for when she gets stuck here or decides to stay over."

At that, Devin ran up the stairs, came back dressed, grabbed a couple canned biscuits and made breakfast sandwiches with them. He gave a stiff smile and went out the front door. I knew I'd struck some kind of chord with my host, but that couldn't be helped. I needed to get the hell out of here. I didn't want to take a chance of us *accidentally* ending up between the sheets.

I wasn't very hungry but not knowing when I'd eat again, I decided to follow Devin's lead and make a quick breakfast sandwich. After finishing, I looked around the kitchen and found that Devin hadn't made any move to clean up. I assumed maybe he'd have done it after we got done eating but I'd chased him away. So, feeling a little guilty, I decided to do the clean-up. Besides, didn't my mother always say if you don't cook, you clean? So, clean I did.

Within moments of starting in the kitchen, the familiar feeling of satisfaction I got from cleaning seeped back into my consciousness and I began to enjoy myself. The smell of cleaning products made me think of home and I slowly relaxed.

Before I knew it, I'd cleaned the entire kitchen. Feeling a little embarrassed and thinking maybe I'd shown more of my personality than I'd intended to, I decided to leave the dirty dish towel on the cabinet. Even that gesture made me uncomfortable, but I left quickly so I could prevent myself from putting it away.

I was still restless when I got to the stable apartment. I decided not to succumb to the desire to clean and instead looked through the housekeeper's movies. Just as I was halfway through, I heard the whinny of a horse and immediately decided I'd much rather be with the horses than a movie.

When I went outside the apartment's stable door, I gasped. My peek through the door last night didn't even begin to show the splendor of the stables. The exterior did nothing to give away the fact that this stable could compete with any of the prize-winning thoroughbred stables in Kentucky. I wandered around first looking at the beautiful architecture, high rafters and bright lighting from sky lights that were beautifully placed in the roof, before I noticed the horses. There were two distinct breeds. The majority were quarter horses that I was sure were used as ranch ponies. The other breed was one that I had always loved and had always been a bit intimidated by—the proud and beautiful Arabians. I couldn't help but be drawn to one very powerful looking male's stall. As I neared the stallion, he pranced nervously, and I drew back, speaking quietly and calmly.

"Ahh, there, there big guy. I'm not a threat. I'm only here to say hello and to admire your beautiful self." I stopped short of the horse's stall and said, "I'll let you get used to my presence, then you and I'll have to have a proper introduction."

Devin

I came into the stables just as my guest walked in. The look on his face was sheer joy as he took in the scope of the stables. Then, I was even more surprised when Aiden focused in on the horses. I saw and immediately recognized his love for the animals. I almost intervened when he approached the stallion, but my curiosity kept me rooted and quiet. It was one thing to love an animal it was another to know what you could and couldn't do with them. I approved when Aiden began speaking quietly to the horse and was even more impressed when he stopped and gave the animal his space.

The powerful male had little tolerance for strangers, and I was pleased to see that Aiden recognized that as well. I wondered if he knew he'd become soft and gentle when he spoke to the horses. From the look of him, I guessed it just happened naturally. That was an enduring trait that I imagined a lover would tease him about while treasuring the endearing reason to love him. Confident Aiden at least knew enough to keep himself safe with the horses I quietly left the stables and went on with my chores.

Aiden

I wanted nothing more than to touch the remarkable horse, but I knew from experience that wouldn't happen without some significant hours spent in the stables, so I reverted to lessons from Steve's family's own farm, and I began mucking out the stalls one by one. I started on the farthest end of the stable from the stallion and worked my way in. There was an empty stable where the horses could be kept while I was cleaning stalls. I moved the beauties one by one, pleased they weren't too skittish for me to work with.

Most of the horses were mares and I noticed with some appreciation that several were with foal. I guessed a ranch as large as this one could use the horses. Most of them accepted my presence well. I could tell they were used to being handled and that there were more people working with these horses than just Devin.

By the time I got to the stallion's stall, the magnificent animal was no longer showing signs of being nervous. I considered whether I was brave enough to take the guy out to muck his stall when Devin came in.

Obviously, he had read my mind because he said, "I wouldn't if I were you. He isn't one to tolerate different people. Hell, there are some days he still tries to kick my ass."

I smiled and without looking away from the horse said, "So, the two of you share similar personality traits, huh?"

Devin

I laughed because much of what Aiden had said was true. As I looked around the stables, I was shocked to see that Aiden had mucked over half the stalls. Seeing him for the first time as someone I could at least have some respect for, I said, "I didn't expect you to get your hands dirty."

Aiden smirked a bit, "No, you think I'm some city kid that hasn't ever gotten shit on my hands."

"That's true enough," I responded. Aiden had only glanced at me during our discussion so when he turned around and bumped into me I was surprised to find him so close. Looking up at me -- I was significantly taller than him -- he met my eyes for the first time and the surge of attraction coursed through me. I was rocked by the electricity in that touch and before my mind engaged, I leaned down and pulled Aiden into a kiss.

The moment seemed to last forever, and I got lost in the embrace. I was enjoying the taste of him, the

139

way he felt perfectly fitting me and pressed up against me when it occurred to me that we really didn't like each other.

Aiden pulled away first, "Fuck," he said.

"That bad?" I asked.

"No, no ... I just wasn't expect ..." he was muttering and I could tell our closeness was beginning to affect him.

"I'll be happy to muck out the rest of these stalls," he said backing away from me, "but I think I need to take a break for a minute." Aiden all but ran out of the stables, but I was spellbound from the kiss and just nodded without telling him he didn't have to muck out the rest of the stalls. Before I could get my wits about me, he was gone.

Aiden

I quickly left through the stables and headed toward a back paddock I'd seen in the distance. The ground was muddy, but I still had the mucking boots on that I'd found in one of the front stalls. I found a nice boulder sticking up out of the ground and leaned up against it, taking in the beautiful sight of the barren rolling hills around me.

I was ashamed I'd let myself get caught up in a kiss with a stranger and worse than that, a stranger I didn't even like very much. Just because he cooked me a steak and let me sleep on his couch didn't make him Prince Charming. It might make him a decent human being, but even that was still up for debate. Everything I'd seen about Devin Pierce told me he was not romance material. He was an arrogant jackass and I had no intention of getting involved with one of those. I had come here with a mission, and somehow, I had pissed off some mischievous god and gotten myself stuck in the middle of nowhere with him.

In fact, now that I knew the impact this man had on me, I needed to revisit the speech I'd already prepared, and as soon as possible, I would tell him I'm thankful. Then, if there is a god, I'd get the hell out of there or at the very least lock myself in the stable apartment where I didn't have to encounter him again.

Devin

I went over and began petting the big horse. "Alexander," I crooned, "What the hell just happened? That man is an enigma. I shouldn't be kissing him, I should be kicking his ass out to sleep on the damned porch." Alexander bumped my hand with his muzzle, seeming to agree with me.

"So, you agree, do ya? What do you know? You treated my ex like he was your long, lost friend just because he snuck apples to you behind my back. You, brother, are no better judge of character than I am!"

I pulled Alexander out of the stall and put him in the open one I used for keeping the horses when I was in muck mode. Alexander watched me intently as I mucked out the stall. When I'd thrown down fresh hay and filled his feed bucket, I went to return him to his stall. Alexander pranced when I came near in the way he did when he wanted to be ridden. That gave me a crazy idea.

"I tell you what, why don't we take our guest out for a ride? I've always thought you can get the bearing of a man while sharing the back of a horse with him."

Seeming to agree, Alexander stomped and neighed. I had Alexander saddled and harnessed when Aiden came back into the stable.

"Listen," Aiden said quickly, "I didn't come here because of your profile. I honestly thought the whole thing was a joke or was just your way of reeling in a city boy, but your profile had inspired me, and I was able to paint a series of pieces that were bought by the Louvre in Paris. I don't want a love affair, I don't want to be swept away by a mysterious man who has a beautiful stable and even more beautiful horses. My goal was only to thank you then leave. I even brought you a card." I could see that he was speaking from the heart. Maybe I had misjudged this guy after all.

For Aiden's sake, I responded with a question, "The Louvre, you say?"

"Yeah," he replied, "Your profile caused me to remember my childhood on the plains of northern Missouri. I painted scenes of rolling hills, tall grasses, wildflowers, bison, and other prairie images.

"People have told me it was my best work. Hell, it WAS my best work. I could actually feel my soul pouring into the paintings as I painted them. These paintings made me realize how much I missed the country ... it's been a hole in my heart since moving to New York that I haven't been able to fill." He looked over at Alexander and said, "I'd already planned that after the hubbub of the sale settled down, I'd start looking for property back home or somewhere similar."

I looked at Aiden for a long moment and confessed, "I understand that. When my dad died, I too craved the wild back country. I grew up in Seattle and every year the city got bigger and more and more people moved in. By the time I inherited my family's estate, I was overwhelmed by the city, overwhelmed by the fact that I no longer belonged there and that Seattle had outgrown me. So, I answered an ad for a ranch hand here."

Aiden asked, "So you started out here as a ranch hand?"

"Yep, sort of a ranch hand and assistant manager." Lost in the remembering, I replied, "I came out here when I was 22. I had dropped out of college after I lost my dad, I was angry with the world. The old man who owned the ranch was a total asshole. Even his two sons refused to talk to him any longer and most of his hands quit as soon as their contracts ended.

I, on the other hand, could match anger with anger and instead of firing me, as most people would, the old man kept me on. Over the years we became close ... well, at least as close as you could to an old fart like him, and he taught me how to run the ranch. The last two years of his life, the old man wasn't able to do much other than yell at me or his housekeeper, Claire, about not doing what we were told, but I'd gotten pretty thick skin by that time, and so, despite his fits of rage, I took over managing the ranch. Before he died, he told me he wished I'd been his son, I laughed at him and said I thanked god every day I wasn't. This amused the old geezer."

"How did you come to own it then?" Aiden asked.

"Well, that was all pretty easy—his sons wanted nothing to do with the ranch. They came to his wake, told Claire to spread his ashes around the ranch, and left. A month later, I was contacted by their attorney who said the ranch was going to be listed. They said Claire wanted me to have it so they gave me the first right to purchase. I made an offer on the place and they accepted it."

Aiden didn't miss a beat and winked at me when he said, "So you've inherited the old man's ranch *and* his disposition."

The jab shocked me, especially after the seriousness of the conversation, so much so that I couldn't come up with a witty comeback. Instead, I responded honestly, "I guess I did, but brother, you haven't been that much fun to be around either."

We both chuckled at the truth of our comments when I asked Aiden if he'd be willing to take a ride on Alexander with me.

"Alexander," Aiden replied, "That is a fitting name. Alexander the Great, I presume."

"You'd be correct, but I named him before I knew Alexander the Great was Persian, not Arabic."

Aiden eagerly agreed to the ride. Something inside me said if I hadn't offered, he would have figured out how to steal one anyway. At least this way, I could keep the city boy from being killed by the moody horse.

I rode behind Aiden and the closeness to his body was enjoyable...companionable, but it also held a threat of sexual tension I was sure we both were feeling. I distracted myself from his alluring scent by talking a bit more about my time with the old rancher or asking Aiden about his experiences with the sale to the Louvre.

I was curious about Aiden's upbringing and his years he spent with his friend's family. I was surprised to learn that Aiden's folks weren't wealthy as I'd assumed they were.

"My first impression of you was stuck up rich kid," I confessed.

Aiden took no offense to this but rather responded, "When in Rome, you become a Roman. In New York, if you are a country bumpkin from the

Midwest, they'll simply eat you alive. I'm sure I've acquired my snobbish attitude from them."

Aiden leaned back into me as we rode and talked which both sent shivers up my spine and made me feel protective of him all at the same time. "I'm glad you aren't the asshole I thought you were."

"Yeah," Devin responded, "I'm glad you aren't the snob I imagined."

The intimate conversation and his delicious scent were making me crazy. I had to do something before I began nibbling that delicious looking neck. "Hold on tight," I said, "Alexander wants to run."

Luckily, Aiden did as I instructed because the moment I let him have his head Alexander took off like a demon out of hell, which gave me the perfect excuse to put my arms around Aiden, holding him tight against me. Alexander ran across a path worn rough along the crest of the hills with mud slinging from the horse's feet as we went. Aiden yelled in exhilaration as the horse tore up the ground.

I finally had to rein Alexander in as the river came into view. We could see Aiden's rental in the distance, and he asked me if we could stop so he could get his bag. I was reluctant at first, telling him there really wasn't much room on the horse for us and his luggage. I even tried to talk Aiden into coming back on the four-wheeler.

"Trust me, I don't have much. I only brought a carry-on bag with me. I had only intended to stay for a couple of days." Not wanting to dampen the mood by arguing, I pulled Alexander toward the car.

When we arrived, Aiden slid off and rummaged through the back seat to find his bag. He reached in the bag and pulled out a small painting and handed it to me.

"See? This is one of the pieces from my collection. This is one I accidentally forgot to include in the sale."

Taking the painting from him, I examined it closer. My first opinion of the small painting was intensity of bold color, but as I looked closer, I could see that there was a beautiful surreal looking little hummingbird sipping the nectar of a red flower that was draped in blue ones. Clearly, these were supposed to be delicate spring blooms.

Aiden

I was unnerved by the amount of time Devin stared at the painting. Finally, he looked up at me and said, "This is good—very good."

I was struck once again with how people tended to go silent when observing this collection of paintings. Devin wasn't someone I assumed was cultured in the ways of art, but even he was quieted by it.

I wasn't going to lie, that caused my pride to swell a bit. I was proud of my works, but I honestly didn't quite grasp what others saw in them. I guess I was just too close to the work.

I grabbed my bag out of the back seat, and with Devin's help, swung myself back into the saddle in front of him. Devin tucked the little painting into the saddle bag without asking me if I intended to bring it back. I cringed a bit about not covering the piece with something first but if there was damage it would already be done.

We rode over to the river's edge and, although receding, the water still ran over the surface of the bridge.

"It'll be a couple more days before you can safely turn that little sprite car around and get it back on the main road," Devin said, as we rode away, "Guess you are stuck with me for a bit longer."

Not feeling nearly as put out by that as I had been this morning, I shrugged and simply said, "Guess there isn't much to be done about it, huh?"

"Nope," Devin agreed and turned the stallion back toward the homestead.

Devin

We rode quietly back to the stable. It felt great to have the horse under me and Aiden in front. As we moved, my body rubbed against his back, and I meekly tried to focus on other things. When we got back to the stable, Aiden slipped off and said, "I'll finish up the stables," and walked away with his bag in hand, clearly forgetting the painting in the saddle bag.

I unbuckled Alexander's saddle and put it and the blanket away. I came back and brushed down the now calm horse and then tucked him into his stall to eat the hay and feed I'd put there before the ride.

Aiden was whistling a tune about four stalls in. I had to admit I was more than a little impressed with the speed at which Aiden was able to muck a stall and silently thanked whoever it was that taught my guest that skill. I didn't mind mucking stalls and I did it plenty enough, but if I could put a hired hand on it, I'd do so every time. Mucking stalls was never my favorite thing to do.

I turned to leave when I remembered the painting in the saddlebag. I took it out and headed toward the apartment thinking it might be more fun to have the painting grace our evening meal together. So, I took it into the house and propped it up next to my parent's picture on the mantle.

I wasn't a clean freak. In fact, besides the basics, I usually left the cleaning to Claire. Since she had gotten up in her years, she too spent less time deep cleaning and more time just getting the basics done.

Since I bought the place, she had tried to talk me into finding someone younger. I always replied no, saying, "I don't have time to teach a filly how to wash my underwear. If you can't do it, then it doesn't need doing..." She'd always huff a bit then go on about her business. I figured she depended on the income, but I also knew she was getting too old to keep up with the chores of running a house of this size. So, I tried to clean what needed cleaning when she wasn't able to do it.

Needless to say, things had gotten a bit out of shape over the past couple of years. When I walked into the kitchen, I was taken aback by how spotless it was. I'd left the place in shambles when I walked out to avoid Aiden for a few hours. I had expected to come in to tidy up before cooking supper. As I looked around, I noticed that even the ceiling fan blades had been wiped down. The floor was clean enough to eat off of. I wondered when Aiden had found the time to clean so thoroughly. How the hell had he done all this and mucked the stalls in such a short amount of time?

I was beginning to think Aiden was some sort of magician. Then I looked over and saw the painting again and was convinced of it. No normal person could create something as beautiful as that *and* be a superman with cleaning kitchens and stables.

Aiden had apparently finished the stalls and I heard the shower running when I came into the apartment. I'd decided to bring him some iced tea for all his hard work. Of course, I knew better than going upstairs again. The image of that perfect, slim body wet and dripping from a shower had not left my mind. Aiden looked like one of the Olympic divers with perfect proportions. Even though I had thought him imbecilic at the time, I still appreciated the fine form that was blown up with pride and anger after being caught in a vulnerable position.

Now that I'd witnessed the intense work ethic as well as the beauty that came from those remarkable hands, I knew if I were ever in that situation again, it would lead to a very different outcome.

Instead of taking the chance, I left the tea on the table and went back to the house to get things ready for supper. I had put potatoes on to boil and had pork chops marinating on the counter when Aiden knocked on the front door. He came into the kitchen holding his half-full glass of iced tea with his hair still wet and looking inquisitive,

"It is amazing how much better you feel when you can use your own shampoo, huh?"

I looked over at Aiden and smiled. "You hungry?" I asked.

"More than I thought," Aiden responded. "What can I do to help?"

"Not much to do," I replied. "I'm going to make a potato salad, toss a green salad and cook the chops. Nothing New York fancy, I'm afraid."

Aiden ignored my jab and responded, "Let me toss the salad."

"Help yourself." I pointed toward the refrigerator. "Everything is in there, but it's mostly a mix of things Claire picked up before the rains came."

By the time Aiden was done putting the salad together, I had gone outside to put the chops on the grill.

Unbidden, Aiden began bringing plates out to the porch table. I flipped the chops and announced it would only be a minute until they were done.

"Do you happen to have any wine to go with the meal? With some wine this is definitely New York class, well, maybe a little rustic, but with the right cabernet ..."

I realized he had just thrown my earlier smart-ass remark back in my face so I laughed and said, "Yeah, if you go into the basement from the kitchen, there are several bottles down there, pick the one you want."

Aiden

Instead of the cobwebs and musty odors I'd expected to find, I walked into a very well organized and well stocked wine cellar. I was no wine expert, but I could tell by the design that Devin probably was.

The walls were lined with beautiful wooden shelves meant for each bottle to sit in separately; the light was recessed behind the shelves, reminding me that I once heard direct lighting wasn't good for wine. There were several wine refrigerators along a far wall, so I assumed Devin liked both chilled whites as well as reds. Unlike a normal basement, the wine cellar felt more like a man cave and I wondered why Devin didn't have a couple wingback chairs in the corner so he could come down and just sit with the incredible collection.

I was beginning to see that there were many more layers to Devin Pierce than were readily apparent on the surface. I'd have to watch my step from here on out.

I chose a white wine that was grown locally, and proudly said so on the bottle. I joined him outside, keeping my expression calm so as to not give him any satisfaction with how impressed I was with his wine setup. I knew plenty of city folk who would have died for a secret wine cellar of that caliber.

"I think this little local white would be 'fancy enough' for this feast? You okay with that?"

"I think you'll be surprised at how good that little local wine is. It was grown by my ex-boyfriend's parents that live just north of here."

I could feel my eyebrows go up at the mention of the ex-boyfriend.

Without thinking, I asked, "So, why is he an ex? Beggars can't be choosers out in the wilderness, Mr. Pierce."

Devin snickered, "Seems he was threatening the guys there with getting fired if they didn't meet certain demands. Long story short, I don't do well with sharing, and no matter how big someone's dick is, I really don't have much tolerance for someone forcing others into doing things they don't want to do."

I took a moment to let myself ponder what Devin had told me. Despite Devin's light conversation about the guy, I could sense the subject was a hard one for him. The guy had probably hurt him a lot. So instead of causing him to feel like he needed to dwell on the subject, I decided to take the bait. Smiling, I said, "So, you're a size queen then?"

Devin chuckled but didn't respond and we sat down for the meal. Devin asked me if anyone was missing me back in civilization.

"Oh yeah, I'm going to have my ass chewed by a whole list of people once I'm back to a phone. I hate that I can't at least let them know I'm ok."

"Yeah," Devin sighed, "I thought about having a satellite phone put in, but since it is usually just me, I couldn't really see the need for it. I usually crave these quiet times and I know my ranch hands also enjoy the time away from me."

"Well, if you are as big of an asshole to them as you were when I got here, I can understand why."

Devin looked at me with a serious look on his face, "And you would be thinking I'm no longer an asshole then?"

It was my turn to chuckle. "No, I think that is pretty innate from what I've seen, but once you get used to it, it isn't that difficult to tune that part out."

Devin laughed, "Well, don't you tell my hands that. I need them to respect the lion. The old man taught me that first thing. 'If you try to be friends, folks will think you are weak and walk all over you. Be friends with friends and be a manager to your hands,' he'd lecture me.

"For the most part, he was right, but I learned pretty quickly that respect should go both ways. If a hand did a good job, you shouldn't hesitate to tell him or her. I never wanted to be like the old ass that drove everyone away. Speaking of doing good, I've hired a lot of folks to muck my stalls and never found anyone faster than you. Where did you learn such a skill?"

I chewed my food contemplatively, "It's not my first time around horses, Mr. Pierce. Besides, I grew up in a family of hard workers and we were taught to take pride in doing a thorough job as much as with a finished product. Besides that, I like to clean. I've never been one to tolerate a lot of chaos in my life. I don't really depend on others to fix what I don't like seeing, so when something needs doing, I usually just go in and get it done."

"Is that why you scoured my kitchen?"

I blushed as I laughed and answered, "No, honestly, that happened while I was figuring out how not to jump you."

I had clearly startled him. "I thought you didn't want to get involved."

I looked over at Devin, losing what appetite I had left. "Yeah, I don't want to get involved and that is why my mind went to *clean everything* mode."

Devin's eyes smoked over as he returned my stare, "I don't think I'd mind getting involved with you, Aiden, you are more than you appear on the surface."

160

My hands began to sweat as I realized what he was saying. I downed the rest of my wine and let it boost my confidence before I said, "I could say the same about you, Devin, and I've pretty much come to the conclusion that as long as we are going to be stuck here alone, something is bound to happen. But, let me be clear before it does, you need to understand that I am not looking for a long-term relationship. This concerns me because in your profile, you made it clear you weren't looking for a fling, but at the moment, a fling is about the only thing I have to offer."

Devin stood up, pulled me up to meet his body and kissed me hard on the mouth.

"I'll take what I can get," he said.

I wrapped my arms around Devin's body, every nerve ending tingling just from the touch. Devin's hands burned through the back of my shirt, his breath coming quicker as he ran them down my side then pressed his cock against me. Our hips ground into each other.

Damn if he didn't fit me perfectly.

Devin all but carried me to the couch and began fumbling with the buttons on my shirt. I reached down to unbuckle his belt, but my hands were shaking too much to succeed. When my shirt was halfway open, Devin pressed his lips to my bare shoulder and kissed my neck, as if he were savoring the taste of me. Then he sucked down on my collarbone, sending electric currents down my veins into my already throbbing cock.

I sighed, and admitted, "God, I want this—I want you, Devin."

His lips slid across my neck and onto my earlobe. When he pinched the skin between his teeth, he caused every nerve ending in my body to light up.

My hands were shaking so much I gave up on undressing him completely and surrendered to his lead. My mind raced, I couldn't think, only react. When his mouth pushed at mine, my lips parted for him. My hand drifted up that beautifully rugged, unshaven face as we kissed, and Devin thrust his tongue past my lips.

He continued to savage me as he explored my body, eagerly and demanding. Before I knew it, Devin had completely unclothed me. As I lay bare upon the ugly sofa, I put my hand on Devin's chest to slow him down.

"Not fair," I panted, "I'm the only one naked!"

Devin laughed, and in a voice which was too damned controlled compared to mine, said, "I'm selfish Aiden, I take what I want." He lay on top of me, grinding his still clothed cock over me, teasing me, and stared me in the eye and said, "I don't worry about fair."

I sucked in a breath as Devin leaned down and grasped my cock in his hand. I arched into him,

162

holding back a moan as he held me, then let the sound out when he finally began to stroke me. I could feel my pulse pounding hard in my neck as I stared up at that rugged face looking back at me, my dick sliding in and out of that rough hand.

Knots tightened in my abdomen, and just as I was about to climax, Devin released me with a playful, yet cruel smirk. He began to nibble down my body, stopping at my nipples and biting just hard enough for the sensual pain to send shockwaves down my already sensitive body.

Devin let his hands work my nipples as he moved further down until his face was next to my throbbing cock. I could feel his hot breath on me as he hesitated, until I looked down at him, and the sight was almost enough to take me over the edge. With a mischievous smile, he slid his tongue down my length, and my hands clawed into the sofa. With one more glance, he took me fully into his mouth, and my own mouth snapped open with a low moan. He gave me a few quick sucks before leaning away again, leaving me trembling, again so close to climax that I could hardly take it. He was cruel, that much was certain.

Finally, Devin leaned up, pulling his shirt off to expose bulging muscles and a beautiful six pack. I wasn't usually into bodybuilder types, but seeing those perfect muscles strain as Devin stretched himself over me, sent chills down my skin. The anticipation of feeling him on my bare skin had my cock throbbing painfully.

Devin leaned back down, taking my cock back into his mouth, mercilessly drawing out every ounce of sensuality from the act. I looked down and saw his playful grin again. If I had been in my right mind, I'd have been annoyed at his arrogance.

Devin stood and jerked off his pants and underwear, standing over me fully naked now. He flipped me on top of him as he fell back onto the sofa allowing the pressure from both of our cocks to rub together. His cock was big and thick and the sensation sent me into a lust-induced stupor as I began to imagine him inside of me.

"Devin," I was out of breath, "so good—you're good at this!" the words came out as part moan part whisper.

He chuckled as he reached over my head and pulled the end table open, taking out lube and a condom. "Top or bottom?" he said, never taking his eyes off of me.

"Yes," I said.

Devin chuckled again in that low, husky way and poured lube into his hand. He used his index finger to rub gently against my ass. I moaned eagerly.

I wasn't usually emotional during sex, but damn, this man rocked me. I was desperate for him. As he moved his finger I sucked in air and all but yelled his name, and his eyes turned dark as he watched me and slipped his finger deep into my ass.

"Oh god, slow down or I'm not gonna last!"

"Been a while?" Devin asked, again with that damned smile. He was way too calm; he was making me feel like a damn virgin!

Unable to speak, I just nodded as he worked his finger in and out. As I loosened up, he slipped another finger in then a third.

"Please Devin, please..."

His eyes stayed focused on mine, but the humor had left him. He slipped the condom on and lubed himself up. He leaned over and kissed me. "Gonna make you feel good, Aiden, but I need to hear you say my name."

He pulled me up and set me on all fours. His dominance sent chills through me.

I sucked in a breath and did as he asked, "Devin, fuck me please!"

He pushed himself against me, and slowly I opened for him, and I dug my hands into the sofa through the hot intensity. Devin was so damned thick, thicker than I'd ever had so my body naturally resisted him at first. I was unable to relax and suddenly nervous.

He leaned against me and moved his hands up and down my back, soothing the knots in the muscles.

"We'll go slow, baby, just relax. Trust me baby, let me make you feel good."

Hearing him call me *baby* made me want him more. Despite the pain, I was desperate for him, and I pushed back against him, wanting all he had to give, eager to enjoy him.

I reached down to touch my own cock, but Devin grabbed my hand to keep me from jacking off. "Not yet, baby... not yet," he said.

I didn't particularly like dominant men, but damn if it didn't make me hornier for him. Despite my effort to push his cock into me, he wouldn't take me fast, and instead he let his head penetrate me but then he'd pull back out.

"Damn you, Devin, get inside me!" I all but screamed, sweat dropping from my face.

He chuckled as he moved his dick in a little more and I moaned loudly, then resorted back to begging, "Please ... please ..."

I'd only had sex with a few men that could fuck me into submission, but apparently this guy had that skill. When Devin pulled himself all the way out again I assumed he was going to tease me again but this time he surprised me by thrusting it all the way in.

I moaned loudly, crying out, "Devin, that's it, that's right. Fuck me! Fuck me hard!"

I pushed against him trying to encourage him to take me harder, but he wouldn't comply... moving at his own speed.

166

Oh god, having a man this size in me may ruin me for all other men from now on. The pleasure of being spread so wide made every nerve fire simultaneously. When he adjusted himself, he hit my prostate which caused me to see stars. My body exploded with pure ecstasy as sweat coated me.

I quaked with pleasure and Devin repositioned himself so he could hit the spot over and over.

"Harder baby, harder please ..."

Finally surrendering some of his frustrating control, Devin's hand rested on my shoulder as he began pounding into me with increasing passion. His cock felt like heaven. I needed to touch myself, couldn't stop it and when he didn't stop me, I found my cock and began to stroke myself.

"Fuck," I yelled. The second I touched my cock, I lost all control and within moments came all over Devin's sofa.

I was about to let myself fall onto the couch while Devin pulled out of me, but he surprised me by smoothly flipping me onto my back, carefully avoiding the wet spot, and began to kiss me tenderly while rubbing his beautiful body on mine.

His infuriating control seemed to return as he didn't seem to be in any hurry to come himself. Instead, he gently began touching and caressing my body stimulating and enhancing the afterglow. I was almost asleep when I felt Devin's tongue begin to re-explore the tender spots on my body. To my surprise, my dick immediately responded to the nips and a subtle lick of his tongue.

Devin

By the time I made it down to Aiden's cock, he was once again sporting a raging hard-on. I forced myself to maintain control both to tease him, but also to intensify the sensation. When I put my mouth around his cock and tasted him all sense of control left me. I went down on his throbbing cock with my tongue continuing to taste the left over cum. I sucked him deep into my mouth and slowly swallowed then continued riding the bottom of his shaft prompting it to continue to harden.

I reached over while Aiden was arching into the pleasure of the blowjob, and pulled another condom out of the drawer and began slipping it onto Aiden's willing cock. I lubed him and lowered myself onto him, wincing a bit as I stretched, but damn, he felt good.

I was happy as both a top or a bottom, but I really wanted to feel Aiden in me, I tried to ride him slowly, but I needed to feel this man inside me, so as soon as my ass became accustomed to his girth, I began riding him faster and faster. Eventually, Aiden's instincts must have taken over and his body began to writhe under mine.

"I want to pound you, Devin," he said, his eyes gleaming below me.

The thought of that sent shivers up my spine. "Yeah, Aiden, please," was all I could say. Not one for begging, but Aiden did something to me.

I lifted up and off of him as he climbed up behind me. I got onto all fours and Aiden slipped his cock back inside of me easily. The angle was perfect, and Aiden's cock seemed even bigger from this angle.

Nothing was slow or tender about how Aiden fucked me. He slipped his cock roughly into my ass. Hell, even I'd gone slowly at first, but he was merciless. All I could do was moan and call his name prompting him to fuck me harder and harder. I'd been holding out for too long and felt myself coming up on the climax all too fast.

I began to see stars behind my eyes. My toes curled into the sofa and I pressed back against him eagerly.

"I'm coming, Aiden!"

Aiden purred into my ear, and tugged at some of my stray hair, "Yes, baby, come for me."

I'd never been with a man as vocal as Aiden, but it turned me on even more and I did as he asked and spewed all over the place where he'd come earlier.

Aiden pulled out of me just as I finished and to my surprise, I felt him come all over my back. I didn't move for a moment, maybe couldn't, as I caught my breath, then shakily stood and hobbled to the guest bath for a towel. Aiden dabbed his mess off my back and then handed the towel back to me to dry up our mess on the couch. I collapsed back into the sofa with a spent sigh, and he joined me, resting his head on the crook of my shoulder where it fit perfectly. I tossed a quilt over us and didn't question it when we both fell asleep, deeply immersed in the afterglow of our lovemaking.

Throughout the night I would feel him stir and kiss the crown on his head to settle him back down, and in turn, he would plant a kiss on my chest or neck, wherever he could reach, before we'd drift off again.

We eventually moved to my bedroom and when morning finally dawned, we showered and wandered down to the kitchen to feed our ravishing sex-induced hunger.

"It's been awhile since I had sex that good. Damned, if it doesn't make you hungry though," I said.

Aiden just nodded and followed me into the kitchen.

After such passion, neither of us seemed happy going too long without the touch of the other.

Eventually, we ended up in the oversized swing. Aiden leaned into me snuggling and I reached over to brush my hand across his chin feeling the soft skin against my callouses.

"You are so beautiful," I said.

He blinked at me and smiled. Without responding, he leaned over and kissed me then melted back into my side.

We both dozed slightly with bellies full and sexual needs satiated.

Unfortunately, living on a ranch ensured there were always chores to be done, and having sent all the extra ranch hands home after the sale of our fall stock, I was the only one there to do them. So, reluctantly, I pulled myself away and told Aiden that I had to do the morning chores. Aiden just smiled and said he'd clean up the supper and breakfast dishes and then he'd come to find me to see about that turn in the hay. He was so cute, I laughed as I left feeling lighter than I had in years. I whistled an old tune I remembered from my youth as I went into the stables to feed and water the horses.

Aiden

I picked up the dishes from the night before and carried everything into the kitchen. At this point, I realized for the first time that there were no dogs. How could there be no dogs? Normally, I'd have tossed the scraps over the side of the porch for the outside dogs to eat ... such was the natural way of farm life.

One of the first things I planned to do when I got back to the country was to get dogs. In fact, I'd fantasized more than once how fun it would be to set up a place for unwanted dogs. I would have to ask Devin about the dog situation. It seemed to me a few dogs could go a long way in helping round up cattle, but since I'd never actually used cattle dogs, I was not one to judge such things.

I hummed as I cleaned. Within no time the kitchen was put back to order so I turned my attention to the night on the ugly couch. Luckily, I found some fabric cleaner under the sink and went to make things right in there as well. That baby may be ugly, but god help me, she would *not* be dirty, at least not while I was around.

Devin

As I went through the morning chores, my mind cycled through delightful memories of sex the night before. I was getting horny just thinking about seeing Aiden's beautiful body. Then my mind turned to the memories of past relationships and their horrible endings. I had dated a lot of men starting at the young age of 16 when I came out after falling for a football jock who had been my best friend all the way up until this last piece of shit who was surely headed to prison.

"Men are jackasses," I muttered to myself, causing Alexander to shimmy away from me. "Sorry big guy, I wasn't talking about you, but it does seem that there were more men who were bad than good, don't you agree?" Alexander just ignored me and continued eating the sweet feed I'd just dumped into his trough.

I went back to thinking and left Alexander to his meal. I have certainly had my fair share of losers.

175

But losers or not, I was a man who loves sex with another man. God help me, I didn't have the time or the interest in playing the games necessary for chasing down another loser sex toy. Unfortunately, *Grindr* didn't yield much in the backwoods where I was. Signing up for *CMTOCM* had been a drunken mistake but I'll admit, the thought of having someone come to me was certainly appealing.

Sex was the farthest thing from my mind when I'd pulled up beside Aiden the day before. I was pissed. Royally pissed that I'd created a profile and that Claire had kept it active long enough that one of the losers who'd been talking to her found us. I was so angry and not just at him, Claire certainly had a talking to coming her way as well, if it wasn't for her, Aiden would've never come this way. I was a bit surprised I didn't punch him first, ask questions later, but when I'd seen him, the poor man was wiped out. By the time we got back to the house and Aiden had changed – not to mention that very nice peek at his body -- my temper had settled from raging boil to low simmer.

I had to admit that the fact Aiden had held his own was pretty damn sexy. I was used to people giving me a wide berth when I tossed my temper at them, but this guy was not afraid of me nor of giving me back *what for* when I deserved it. I could also admit I sort of deserved it.

It hadn't escaped my attention that somehow, I had the real deal here. No loser, no slacked off, lazy city boy, but a man who not only didn't mind work, but clearly liked doing it—a man who enjoyed being around horses, someone who had a gift with his hands and on top of all that, he had been inspired by my stupid profile. So much so that he came all this way to thank me. Who did that?

I knew I was a difficult lover. I considered myself lucky that the things I liked usually satisfied my partners. But the truth is I really didn't give a damn. Granted, I would *never* take advantage of a guy and unlike the loser I dated last, any man I took to bed would damn well be more than willing, but once there, I had my way of doing things. More than once, I'd left a man in a lurch because he wanted to lead the way in the bedroom.

Last night when Aiden had taken control, I was surprised that not only had it not irked me, but rather sent me into a level of ecstasy that I'd seldom felt before. I could tell Aiden had enjoyed my willful lovemaking, but he had held his own there as well, giving us both pleasure and leaving me in a state of bewildered happiness.

What was going on with this man? Well, despite what Aiden said, I could tell there was interest on his part and by god, I was going to find out how far that interest went. Even more important, I was going to have sex with him again and again. I was going to have that man on me as much as possible before that river receded and the inevitable time for parting came.

By the time I returned home from my chores, the place was spick and span. Not only had the kitchen been put to rights, but Aiden had cleaned the old sofa and every other surface on the first floor as well. Aiden's painting that I'd quickly shoved onto the mantle was now sitting beautifully on a side table, embedded between two old-fashioned lamps.

I couldn't help but wonder if Aiden even knew he seemed to be putting things in order everywhere he went. I just shook my head and guessed it was so natural to the man that he didn't even realize it.

There was no sign of Aiden, so I assumed he'd gone back to the apartment. I went upstairs to get a quick shower before getting things ready for the evening and was surprised to find Aiden lying on the bed asleep. My god, the man was beautiful. I could tell he hadn't intentionally lain down, but rather had probably crashed there in the middle of putting the bedroom back together. Clearly, when this guy needed sleep, it came over him with a vengeance. I'd seen puppies do that but never a grown man. It was something else I was finding endearing. I slipped into the bathroom and undressed there so as not to disturb Aiden and quietly turned the shower on.

Aiden

I woke up in time to see Devin step into the bathroom. When I heard the shower come on, I smiled. What a great way to wake up.

I stripped on my way to the bathroom and slid in behind Devin. I slipped my arms around his waist and leaned up against him.

"I thought you were asleep," he said.

"Apparently, I was." I pressed my cock up against him and said, "I'm not asleep now, though ..."

Devin began lathering soap across my body giving extra attention to my cock, which caused me to giggle. Despite the playful gesture, I felt myself becoming hard under his slick touch. As the shower rinsed us off, I bent down on my knees to take Devin's cock into my mouth. The water fell off of his chest and onto me as I sucked him. Devin watched me as I took him just to the point of finishing and then backed off, just like he'd done to me last night. Licking my way back up his rock-hard chest, I rubbed my teeth over his nipples then took his mouth with my own.

I broke away from him with a grin and leaned over to encourage him to enter me. He took the bait, closing the distance in the spacious shower and gave my ass a wet slap. He loosened me up with his fingers again, and I came undone from his familiar touch. He replaced his fingers with his cock, the leftover soap acting as lube. As he fucked me, he leaned in to kiss me lightly on the mouth, then the neck.

I hissed in a quick breath and then moaned with pleasure as Devin thrust inside while holding me close. Devin bent over to kiss me again splattering sweet, loving pecks across my neck then sticking his tongue into my ear. I could feel myself humming with pleasure.

I was completely malleable below Devin as he continued pounding my ass. He choreographed the experience so that we would both come at the same time. I couldn't help but cry louder and become more vocal every time Devin thrust his cock into my prostate. Just as Devin climaxed, he buried his cock's bulk into my G-spot causing me to ejaculate hard against the shower tiles.

I was staring up at him when he said, "Had I not known better I'd say it had been a while since you'd come."

I woke first, untangled myself from Devin without waking him up then went back into the bathroom for a real shower this time. Night had fallen at some point, but I had no idea what time it was, nor did I really care. For the most part, my mind was firmly on the fact that I had never made love in such a fashion before. I was sure, I had already begun having feelings for this guy and it was unlikely I would ever overcome these feelings since I doubted I'd ever have sex like that with another man, as long as I lived. Was I falling in love with him? No, I was not feeling love but a definite feeling of satiated relaxation. Something about that man filled voids I didn't even know I had.

I finished my shower, dried off and slipped downstairs trying to avoid waking my handsome lover. I guessed several hours had passed since my stomach was growling with hunger. I again perused Devin's refrigerator and found a variety of cheeses pulled them out and decided I'd go back into the wine cellar to see if I could find the no-name red Devin had served the first night I was there.

By the time I returned to the kitchen, Devin was leaning against the counter eating the cheese.

"I see you are helping yourself to my wine cellar. You know I have the right to take the cost of that wine out of your thieving ass."

Playing along, I gasped and handed the wine to Devin and said, "Oh please, kind sir, please don't turn me in. It's just my lover has a huge cock and that cock drains all the blood from his brain and I was afraid if I didn't find sustenance for him, he'd lose consciousness."

Laughing, Devin said, "Well, in that case, I can't begrudge an old woman sustenance for her lover."

I pretended to be offended. "Old woman, my ass! Here, don't eat all that cheese before I've had some. Why don't you open the wine before I bang you over the head with it?"

Devin chuckled again and did as he was told. We cuddled as we ate cheese and drank the wine standing up.

Devin bent down and kissed me on the ear, "Wanna watch a movie or something?"

"Hmm...or something, but I'd like a moment just to be in your arms first," I replied.

"Sounds good to me, let's go back out to the swing. I like to sit out there and listen to the insects."

I followed Devin outside, wine glass in hand. Once settled in the swing, I leaned back against his chest.

"Devin, I never intended to make love to you. I thought we'd have a roll in the hay, but I never intended it to be..." I drifted off, not having the right words.

"Never intending on it being special," Devin finished. "Yeah," he continued, "I didn't expect it either, but have you ever thought this whole thing seems surreal?"

Devin leaned up so I could turn to see him. "I mean, I get drunk, set a crazy profile up on a gay dating site, which incidentally, I've never done before, and you see my profile then have some out of body experience where you paint so well that the Louvre purchases your entire collection. Then you come looking for me, get put into a Miata that gets stuck on my side of the river JUST as the river floods her banks. We seem to be in a *Twilight Zone* event here."

I took a moment to respond. "I hadn't thought of it quite that way."

Before I knew what was coming out of my mouth, I asked, "Devin, I've been granted a special showing of my collection at the Louvre as part of their agreement for me to sell to them. I'm able to invite my family and friends to see the collection before anyone else does. Would you consider going with me as my date?"

Devin looked at me genuinely shocked. "You want me to be your date to your own private showing at the Louvre?"

"Yeah," I said, beginning to like the idea of it more now that I'd invited him, "I'd really like you to come. You are my muse after all, it only seems fair."

Devin pulled me around so he could get a better look at me. "Aiden, we are in a strange bubble at the moment, I'm under no false impression that that bubble won't eventually burst. Are you sure you want to bring that much reality into our ... whatever this is?"

I was taken aback by this comment. In fact, I was more than a little wounded by it.

I pulled away, trying not to be a drama queen, but still needing the space. I stood up, breaking physical contact. "Devin, you are probably right, in fact, we probably should put the brakes on this now before reality hits. It's best if we don't get too deep and just end up with hurt feelings once the river recedes. I'm getting a little tired; I think I'll sleep in the apartment tonight."

Devin, seeing he'd hit a nerve, tried to patch things up and replied, "No, Aiden I didn't mean that, we can still enjoy each other until reality hits, but we both know there is no future between us." Those words hit me even harder than the ones before. I felt the knot in my stomach before I felt the burning tears behind my eyes.

Anger and pride mixed to give me the resolve to walk away before my inner queen betrayed me. "You are right, Devin. That is exactly why I'm going to sleep alone tonight and until the river recedes. We need to put an end to this before we ... before *I* get too attached."

Devin

I almost went to the apartment several times before finally deciding Aiden had been smart to end it then. It was stupid to keep things going when there was no future in this.

So, instead of going after Aiden, which is what my heart wanted, I listened to my head instead...to the part of me who'd been hurt by men in the past...the part that didn't trust in anyone and who didn't believe in love anymore.

Aiden

I felt tears falling despite my resolve not to cry. I had grown up with a dad that told me keeping tears in was a sure way to die of cancer, so I didn't have the same issues most guys did with crying. Keeping them at bay, however, was more pride than being manly. I had clearly let myself have feelings for that hateful man and he had turned out to be exactly what I thought he would be. Fuck the fact that he could make love like a god, fuck the fact that I had already admitted to myself that I had feelings for him and fuck the fact that given just a little more time, I could probably fall for him. The fact was that Devin Pierce was an asshole, and that he would always be an asshole. I had to remember that, no matter what my heart said.

I fell asleep in the wee hours of the morning and had a fitful sleep that was plagued with images of ecstasy mixed with images of Devin pointing and laughing at me.

Devin

I didn't sleep at all. Instead, I tossed and turned, got up, threw a few things across my room, went back to bed, cursed and finally in the early hours of the morning realized that I had *already* developed feelings. No matter what, I was going to be hurt when Aiden left. It wasn't until that moment that I realized the look I'd seen on Aiden's face as he left. He wasn't just angry or upset; my words had also hurt him.

Aiden

Sleep did little to alleviate my temper. I got up, determined to get through the day without any more run-ins with the man of the house. As soon as I was dressed, I headed straight to the stables. The stalls had been mucked the day before, but there was always work to be done, so I found the curry comb and set to work on the nearest mare. As I combed, I tried to soothe the mare by talking to her in soft tones. "You are a beautiful one, you are," I said combing then nuzzling her. When I was done, I repeated the process on the next mare and so on. By the time I heard the woman's voice, I was completely embedded in the work and the beautiful horses I was combing. At first, I ignored her thinking maybe it was just my imagination, but when she came into the stable and demanded to know who I was, she was much more difficult to ignore.

Turning away from the mare that was half-combed, I saw a middle-aged woman who had her hair pulled back in a tight bun. Small strings of hair had pulled free, showing that although this woman was a force to be reckoned with, she certainly didn't mind a little imperfection.

"I'm Aiden Fisher, and who are you?" Realizing I sounded harsh, I said, "I'm sorry, I'm Aiden Fisher. I wasn't expecting to see anyone else here."

I could tell the woman was sizing me up. Ignoring my questions, she asked, "Are you the one who cleaned up in the main house?"

Sheepishly, I replied, "Yes, Ma'am, I was upset with Devin and when I'm upset, I clean. I didn't mean to step on anyone's toes." The woman looked me up then down again, humphed, and then walked into the main house. As she walked away, I heard her say something about not letting another *man* screw with Devin as she walked away.

I wasn't sure what to make of her, but if she was able to get to the ranch, there was a good chance that I'd be able to get out and that was something to look forward to. I thought about going to the main house to figure out what was going on, but decided I was better off letting Devin and the woman hash things out before I got in the middle of it. So, I turned back to the chore of combing out the beautiful mare in front of me.

This beauty was clearly a young mare. I assumed she was one of Alexander's as I could tell she was probably a mixture of Arabian and quarter horse. I

190

wondered why Devin wasn't more concerned about pedigree.

As I thought about it, it could be a safe subject to ask about in the future. As my temper cooled, I believed Devin had been very right about putting up the stops. Yes, it had hurt my feelings, but it was better to have them hurt in the beginning than after I'd fallen in love with him. As I combed and sweet-talked the beautiful princess, she reveled under my attention.

Horses were so similar to humans. They loved attention, craved company and were suckers for sweet talkers. Although my experiences with horses were limited to my summers on the farm, I had learned that Arabians were proud, high strung beauties that could be dangerous if not handled carefully. Quarter horses were pretty much your best bet for beginners. For the most part, they were easy-going and tended to be happy working in a field or traipsing along a riverside trail.

One summer, Steve and I had worked a short job at a stable close to his farm where there was a man who owned several thoroughbreds. These horses were magnificent but demanded a great deal of time and effort on the part of the owner. Although sitting atop a tall thoroughbred was a thrilling experience, I would choose the quarter horse any day. As far as the Arabian is concerned, they were also brilliant horses.

I just wasn't quite sure I was trained well enough to handle that breed without assistance.

After finishing with the pretty young filly, I put the comb down and headed toward the house. Now that there were more people on the ranch than just Devin, I knocked instead of just entering. "Come in," was the reaction. It was the woman, not Devin who had called out.

I removed my boots while on the porch and walked into the house anxious to learn more about the roads and my chances of getting out of this situation.

"Did you get to speak with Devin?" I asked.

"She did," Devin replied as he walked into the room from the back hallway.

"So, are the roads clear?"

This time the woman replied, coming in from the kitchen. "No, not the main road. I came up from my homestead which the river doesn't separate from the ranch house. I don't usually come up when it's raining cause my rheumatism tends to act up and I figure when the river is up, Devin can use some alone time." She stood with her hands on her hips and asked, "So, what is your hurry to leave, young man?"

I looked over at her and replied, "I haven't spoken to my family and I'm sure they are concerned about where I've disappeared to. I also need to get back and handle matters at home."

The lady seemed to be ok with my excuse and, although still quite cold toward me, she turned to leave.

Apparently, everyone in this part of the world was an ass. I also turned to leave when Devin said, "Wait. Let me introduce you before you leave. Claire, I believe you and Aiden have spoken so you already know his name is Aiden." Then, he looked over at me, "This is my housekeeper, Claire."

Clearly, the woman didn't want me to be there, but I decided to take the higher ground and said, "It is a pleasure to meet you, Ma'am."

For a moment, I was sure she was going to say something hateful, but instead, she looked at me and said, "I hope you are better than the last one," and turned toward the kitchen.

I stood rooted to the spot not knowing whether to laugh at the look on Devin's face or to be offended. Either way, it didn't matter as I was headed out of the area as soon as the situation made it possible.

So, with that thought firmly in my mind, I said, "Ok, well that about sums that up," and I turned to leave.

Devin came up behind me as I walked back onto the porch and sat on the swing to put my work boots back on. "Don't mind all that, she saw me at my worst since my parents died. I wasn't that attached to the guy, but he did a number on both of us. She will warm up to you, just give it a little time."

I looked over at Devin and said, "There isn't going to be time, Devin. You, yourself, said last night that we need to be keeping things real here. I'm biding my time for the river to go down then I'm headed out. I'm sure Ms. Claire is a good person, but it doesn't really make much difference to me whether she is or isn't."

I finished with the boots and stood to go.

"Wait," Devin said in a commanding tone, but this time with more desperation than he probably intended. "I didn't really mean that last night. I wasn't really saying that we shouldn't see where things go, I just wanted to make sure you understood that I wouldn't be offended if you decide you really don't want me to go to your opening."

"I don't invite people to big-ticket events usually reserved for family and friends lightly, Devin. You are a very important part of the process that led to this opening and, as such, it would be fun to have you there—whether as a friend or a lover makes no difference. The inspiration is what I'm thankful for. That is why I came here in the first place."

I walked off the porch before Devin had a chance to make a comment. I could tell he was watching me as I walked toward the stables, and before I got out of hearing range, he asked, "What are you doing in there?"

I turned again to face Devin and squinting into the morning sun, said, "I'm combing down the mares. I can't just sit around staring at your walls, Devin, and I know Claire won't be too happy with me underfoot. So, unless you feel like rescuing me again when I get lost traipsing around your ranch, I'm gonna keep myself busy with the stuff I know how to do. Is that ok with you, Mr. Pierce?"

Devin turned and walked away without responding.

Devin

I didn't reply, but rather turned and walked back into the house thinking, "Well, what the hell do I do about all this?"

Claire was never cold to anyone, so I was shocked that she had been with Aiden. Hell, she was the reason he was even on the ranch, for god's sake—another thing we needed to clear the air about. The only thing I could do was confront her and find out what was up. So, I walked into the house and did just that.

"Claire, what do you have against this guy?"

"I don't know," she sighed and sat down at the table. "When I walked into the apartment and saw it had been used, I was curious who was here. So, I walked into the stables and heard him speak before I saw him. I immediately thought this was your ex who'd come back. I don't even know why I'd think that, but I did and when I called to him, he must not have heard me because he didn't respond. This really ticked me off so when I walked closer, I demanded he tell me why he was here. When he walked around the filly, I could see it was not your ex but some other guy. You'd think that would dampen my temper, but it riled it up instead, so I kind of laid into him. Then I was embarrassed, so I walked into the house. I expected him to follow, but when he didn't, that riled me up even more."

I'd been party to her anger more than once, so I knew to let it work itself out or I could be a recipient of her anger as well.

She continued, "Unfortunately, when he came in, I let my inner bitch rule my attitude. Devin, I guess I still have some unresolved issues with that ass of a man you dated. I'll go talk to the boy and straighten things out."

"Wait a moment before you do," I requested. "I like this guy, probably more than I should after just a couple days together, but he feels different than the other men I've dated. He feels...right somehow."

Claire stared at me for a moment, shook her head and said, "Well, damned if I be or damned if I'm not. So, you are telling me, the first guy you've felt this about and I go and make an enemy of him before I've had a chance to even meet him."

I just looked at her, helpless to help the situation.

"Well, shit," she said, and marched out the kitchen door toward the stables without saying another word.

Aiden

"Young man," she said when she saw me combing down another mare, "Can I talk to you a minute?"

I sighed, not hiding the fact that I'd prefer not to have another unwarranted confrontation with what I had already dubbed as the Wicked Bitch of the West. Claire persisted despite my cold shoulder.

"I know you probably would prefer to avoid me, but I need to apologize to you. Can we start again?"

"I'm sure we can't do anything but improve it." I retorted. Claire looked at me and the expression on her face surprised me as it looked as if she was pleased with my smart-ass remark.

"As Devin said, I'm Claire—Claire McDane, Devin's housekeeper. When I heard you this morning, I thought you must be Devin's ex, returned to create havoc. I let my feelings for that ass of a man color my thoughts about you and that ain't fair.

So, I'm here to apologize for that and to try to get to know you proper," she said.

I sighed again, letting the anger and frustration with her unfair reaction toward me slip away.

"I heard he was a total ass. Devin filled me in on the criminal charges against him. I'm sure that would make anyone a bit leery."

"He was a doozy, that one. Guess we still have some shit to work through. Unfortunately, you were the one who got the brunt of it."

"Well, let's let that go," I said, still working on the mare. "As Devin told you, I'm Aiden and I'm from New York. I came here to tell him thanks for his inspiration, but I guess you already know that since I was really corresponding with you on that site." Claire blushed a bit. "I didn't mean to be here more than a few minutes, but I ended up stuck on the wrong side of the river. So, I'm an uninvited guest and I can't do much about it."

Claire must have heard the frustration in my voice. "So, are you upset about being stuck or upset about being stuck with Devin?"

I stopped combing the mare and squinted at Claire. "Well, if you've met the man, you'd know I'm upset about being stuck, but *more* upset by being stuck with *him*."

Claire laughed in spite of herself. "Yes, our boy can be a bit of a knucklehead. Of course, he learned that from the master of knuckleheads." Her face clouded, then quickly cleared.

"Well," she continued, "I am more than thankful for the wonderful job you did with the house. I haven't been able to get down deep for too long. I hate to see the house not in tiptop shape, but I'm afraid my days of crawling on the floor to clean baseboards or swinging from ladders to remove cobwebs are over."

I could see the frustration in her face and felt sorry for the woman who clearly took great pride in the place. "I clean when I need to put my mind in order; and being stuck here with no phone, internet and with a man as beautiful and frustrating as your Devin is...well, I was thankful the house was here to clean."

Claire looked at the horses and said, "Devin told me you were not only good with house chores, but that you mucked the stalls also. If I didn't already know you were a painter, I'd be trying to get him to hire you as one of his hands that I could steal from time to time for housework."

I laughed and turned back to the mare. "If I weren't already gainfully employed, I'd probably take him up on the invitation. I've really missed horses since living in the city. The only ones we have in New York are usually under very intimidating police officers or tortured to pull tourists in carriages through Central Park. They aren't really the kind of horses that you can love on, at least not without being severely chastised by their owners."

Claire smiled and said, "Despite our beginnings, Aiden, I think I'm going to like you." She turned to leave, then turned back saying, "I am going to put some lunch together, I'm guessing neither of you have had breakfast and now that all the drama is over, I think you both could use a little food." She turned to leave and without waiting to see if I was interested, she called back, "I'll call you when the food is done, I'll be able to learn a bit more about you while we're eating, too."

I chuckled as the powerhouse of a woman walked out of the stables. Lord knows I was used to strong women. I had always been surrounded by them and had come to really appreciate when I ran across a good one. Claire would be an interesting person to get to know, but as I told Devin earlier, I was pretty sure my time here would be too limited for me to get to know anyone well. At least, having her here would keep the gasoline-fed fire between Devin and myself banked to a simmer. That was something I could be happy for at least.

I spent the rest of the morning combing down the beautiful horses in the stables. Knowing that Alexander was Devin's horse, and having learned over the years that a relationship like theirs was best left alone, I settled with giving him a little hay through the gate and petting his muzzle. I left his combing for Devin to do.

I went into the apartment to clean up before lunch and had just finished my shower when I heard Claire call out my name. I combed my hair and finished buttoning my shirt before heading over to the house. Claire set the table on the front porch and the food she prepared was better described as brunch than lunch. There were scrambled eggs, bacon, and sausage on one side of the table and what appeared to be a casserole made with hash browns on the other.

"How many people are joining us?" I asked as I came up to the table.

"When Claire apologizes, she does it with food," Devin chuckled.

"I can see that," I replied. "Good thing I'm starving then."

That clearly pleased Claire as she walked out of the house with a pitcher of orange juice in one hand and another hand with a carafe carrying the earthy scents of coffee.

Despite the fact that the morning had been brisk, I'd forgotten to drink my coffee, which was a shocker as that was usually what I went for first thing when I woke up. I'd been so keen on working with the horses and avoiding Devin -- and therefore the house -- that I'd completely forgotten about coffee.

Now that I saw the carafe, my head jolted with a little pang that indicated I was about to develop a caffeine-deprived headache.

"Bless you, I forgot to have coffee this morning," I said as Claire sat the pitcher and carafe down.

"I've always believed that working men need two things above all else," she said, "a good breakfast accompanied by a strong cup of coffee."

"Oh, Miss Claire," I sighed, "I think I might just need to marry you."

Claire laughed, "Like you could keep up with a woman like me," she responded.

The banter was amusing so I continued to play along. "Alas, you are correct, I could never meet your needs, however I could be very fulfilling in other areas...for example, how do you feel about shopping?"

Claire and Devin both laughed. "You got the wrong woman for that skill," Devin jumped into the conversation. "She complains for a week about having to shop on a Saturday."

"Ahh," Claire retorted, "There is a big difference between going into Billieville and buying food for a bunch of lug nuts like you and the farm hands and going girl shopping. Aiden dear, it has been so long since I bought myself a new outfit that I wouldn't even know how."

I feigned shock and in my best Southern Belle voice said, "My dear, you are entitled to a day of retail therapy from time to time. You must put your foot down and keep this slave driver from keeping you from the things all women are entitled to—you included!"

At that, we both looked at Devin with disapproving looks, which immediately put him on the defensive. "I don't keep her from shopping," Devin responded defensively. "I didn't even know she liked to shop. I thought she *hated* shopping."

I just shook my head then put my hand on Claire's. "My dear," I said, "It is a fact that some gay men, albeit few, lack the shopping gene. Unfortunately, when they have this genetic flaw, they resemble our straight counterparts. You *must* stand up and demand your female rights. my dear. From this day forward, let's make him promise to give you one paid day every month to go shopping for yourself!"

Claire sighed, "It isn't so simple Aiden dear," she said. "I've been surrounded by men for so long without anyone who appreciates the joys of a new outfit that I would be stuck by myself, on the long trip to a town with real shops and where is the fun in that?"

Devin looked at Claire like he was seeing her for the first time. "You never even mentioned that you were interested in such things."

"Would you have gone with me, Devin?" she asked.

"Well, no, not *me* but I'd have tried to find someone to go with you."

"Now, there is a lad," she said. Looking then at me, she continued, "You see, Devin may lack that gene for shopping, but he knows how to make an old lady feel special."

I smiled, recognizing the real love between the two. With that, I said, "Excuse my manners, but I'm going to dig in. I'm starving and I need to kick this headache before it gets a mind of its own." I dug into the casserole which I topped with the yummy eggs.

The food was delicious and I could taste her expertise. There was a woman who knew how to cook for lots of men. The flavors were there, the food was hearty, and there was plenty of it.

"You eat as much as you want, Aiden. Nothing makes my heart happier than a hungry young man appreciating my food," she said and poured coffee in my mug.

We ate companionably, getting to know each other and enjoying each other's company. After we finished eating, Devin left to check on the cattle and I stayed with Claire to help. "What do you need doing, Miss Claire? I'm all yours."

Instead of waving me off, she seemed to understand that, like her, I needed to be busy, so she put me to work on different parts of the house that needed attention that she was unable to give. She had me dusting fan blades, sweeping under furniture, washing down baseboards and so on. When I'd finish a task, she'd have another one waiting for me.

I was about to head upstairs when Claire told me it was time for a break and so we both headed to the porch with a glass of iced tea in hand.

"Son," Claire said. "I haven't gotten a full day of cleaning done like that since the old man died."

"Felt good, didn't it?" I replied.

"Oh, like peeling a fresh peach," she said.

We both were sitting quietly on the porch, enjoying the relaxing moment and feeling of accomplishment when Devin walked up.

"So, I've been working my ass off, and the two of you have been sitting on the porch drinking iced tea and cackling like a couple hens."

I cocked an eyebrow, about to lay into him, when Claire stepped up to the conversation with, "Why Devin, you know I'm only here to look pretty, son. Why do you persist in complaining about what you pay me for?"

I realized this was a private joke between them, but getting into the banter, I added, "And here I am sitting on your front porch improving your property value and I'm doing it for free." Claire grinned and nodded approval at my quick-witted, smart-assed response.

"I don't know what I'm going to do with the two of you," Devin sighed and walked toward the door.

"You'll be taking your shoes off, for one thing," I said, before I could stop myself.

"And, is this not my own floor I'd be walking on?" he asked.

"Yes, yes, it is *your* floor for sure, Mr. Pierce," I answered, "but it is *my* back that hurts from cleaning it."

"Ahh, well, if that be the case, then maybe we could find a way to remedy that later," then Devin looked over at Claire who seemed a bit too smug with my chastisement and added, "once Claire leaves, that is."

Claire's eyes grew big despite herself and I had to muffle a laugh, then, for Claire's benefit, I added, "Now, only an arrogant man like yourself would ever think *that* would be adequate payment for a hard day's work."

Claire burst into laughter, "This one, dear boy," pointing at me while addressing Devin, "this one is a keeper." She jumped up, laughing while walking back into the kitchen to begin working on supper.

Devin watched her go inside and slid onto the swing next to me. "You stink," I said, scooting away from him.

"Yep, that is the way of the ranch," Devin said. "Pulling a stupid cow out of a mud hole she should have had the sense to stay out of, can make a man stink." With that, Devin scooted closer to me and laid a mushy kiss on my mouth.

"So," I said, "*after* you get your shower, which I hope is happening sooner than later, tell me more about what you had in mind about payment for these cleaning services."

Devin laughed and replied, "I thought we had put that behind us."

"Well, sir," I continued, "You were the one who brought it up. I just thought I'd get a better picture of what you had in mind."

Devin, completely disregarding his muddy, smelly self, reached over and took my chin into his hand and pulled me to his mouth. He kissed me deeply and passionately, then slowly pulled himself away and said, "Does that answer your question?"

My head was still spinning from the kiss and it took a moment to respond. Smiling in his smug, arrogant way, Devin stood up and started walking toward the house.

"Devin," I had regained my composure, "Sex is all well and good, but a real gentleman would be offering to massage my back, feet, or shoulders after getting a free day of work out of me."

Obviously, having heard the conversation between us, Claire could be heard once again cackling in the kitchen. "You've really made her day," Devin said, not too happily.

"She's made mine as well. It is really nice to have an ally where you are concerned," I retorted.

Devin just shook his head and walked inside, but not before he remembered to remove his muddy boots.

After he was gone, I went into the kitchen to help Claire with dinner. We both chuckled at Devin's expense. "He took them boots off, didn't he," Claire whispered.

"Yep," I nodded proudly.

"Do you know how many wars I've had with that boy and the old man before him trying to get them to take those damned boots off before they walk in? Hell, I even went on strike one week. They changed for a while but were right back at it in less than a month. My hat is off to you if you can get him to take those boots off."

"I wouldn't be cleaning the same floor every day if that is what you are thinking. I'd rather shoot 'em than do that," I replied.

"Oh boy!" Claire cackled. "Yes child, you are an old woman's dream come true." I put my arm around Claire and side hugged her.

"So, what needs doing?"

"Nothing," Claire said, putting her hands on her waist and turning toward the food. "I turned the leftover breakfast casserole into cheesy egg potatoes, and I steamed some broccoli. That will go nicely with my meatloaf."

Wistfully, Claire looked at the meatloaf and commented more to herself than me, "I haven't made a meatloaf in so long, but with you tackling the big chores, I had time to pull it off. I think this is one of my better ones too."

"Dang Claire, if I lived here, I'd be the size of a bus within a month," I responded as I looked at the food.

"That'd be unlikely, son," Claire chuckled. "When calving time comes around, whatever fat you've stored during the winter would quickly be gone. That is our busy time and it is all-hands-on-deck. I tend to put on ten pounds when we slow down and that used to worry me silly, but after a few years on the ranch, learning it don't stay on long, I stopped worrying and just go ahead and enjoy the food as it comes."

"Is that why Devin is in such good shape?" I asked sheepishly.

The older lady looked at me and a slow deliberate grin crossed her face, "So you've noticed that, have you?"

"It is kinda hard not to," I replied.

Claire burst into laughter, "I suppose that's true, the men do beef up while working here. It's some tough work on the ranch and the hours are long and backbreaking. I wouldn't wish this life on anyone, but once it's in your blood, it is there to stay. Now," she changed the subject, "help me get this stuff out on the porch. It's gonna start raining more and more and we better take advantage of the reprieve and eat out on the porch before it starts getting chilly."

As I picked up the cheesy egg and potato casserole in one hand and bowl of steamed broccoli in the other, Claire grabbed her meatloaf with two potholders she already had on her hands. She called out as we walked past the stairs,

"Devin, we are setting the table, come on down when you are ready."

"Yes Ma'am," was his response.

By the time the table was set, Devin showed up freshly showered and smelling a lot better than when he'd gone upstairs. He had his shirt in his hand but hadn't put it on yet and he had not combed his hair.

When he noticed me looking at him, he said, "We all learn fast that when Claire says it's time to eat, you don't waste time getting to the table. More than once she threw everything in the trash because we dilly-dallied too long. When you're hungry, you don't dilly dally!"

Claire beamed and said, "And you'll also know, I don't tolerate a man at my table that isn't fully dressed."

"No, Ma'am," he said, and quickly pulled his shirt on over his head.

I looked at Claire with a new level of respect. She might not be able to get them to take their boots off at the door, but she sure knew how to command respect at the dinner table.

We all sat down to a mellow evening, each chatting about the parts of our day, Claire asked me questions about my life in New York, but the conversation always seemed to drift back to the ranch and what needed doing. I suspected if I were to stay there long, my life in New York would quickly become a distant memory.

Devin

I noticed Aiden had drifted off and asked, "You seem to be in another place, where did you go, Aiden?"

Aiden came back to reality and smiled, "I was just thinking about how easy it is to let this life take over your existence. There is always something that needs doing, isn't there?"

Both Claire and I nodded in agreement.

"Yes," Claire said, "But you have time for other things, too. Mrs. Jennings, who was married to the old man when I arrived, loved needlepoint. She and I used to clean and cook in the mornings and by noon, she'd disappear into her quiet space, as she called it, and do up her masterpieces."

I was shocked by this revelation and asked, "Where was her quiet space? Didn't she have two boys?"

"Oh yeah," Claire replied, "But everyone knew when Mrs. Jennings went into her quiet place, you

213

had better be bleeding when you went in, else you could be when you came out."

Claire laughed sadly at the memory. "Anyway, the room behind the stairs is where she'd work. It is full of stuff now, not really big enough to be a bedroom, the old man started using it as a storage place after she died. Unfortunately, he seemed to want to eradicate all traces of her. Guess we all mourn in different ways. Anyway, she loved the space because it had natural light she'd say. I guess it does... It'd catch the morning light all the way into the early evening. I always thought it'd just make it hot in there, but she never seemed to care about that."

Aiden had been listening with quite a bit of interest to the conversation. "Do you mind if I see the room after supper maybe?"

"Sure, I guess," I replied, "but don't get your hopes up, it is really just a junk room."

I could tell Claire was playing her cards just as she meant to. She'd already taken a shine to Aiden and knew he'd be thinking about where he'd fit into the whole scheme of things on the ranch. I'd never thought of the back room as anything special, but maybe the old room might have some appeal to the artist in him.

"I tell you boys what, I'll clean up the dishes, while Devin, you show Aiden the room. It warms my heart to think someone would look at that space again after all these years."

Before anyone could respond, she was up clearing the dishes off the table. I forked up the last piece of meatloaf just in time for my plate to be whisked away.

"Well, that was abrupt," I said, after Claire disappeared into the house.

"Nah, she's trying to convince me she wants me to stay on. That's okay let's play along," Aiden chuckled.

So, I walked with Aiden into the old storage room behind the stairs. I couldn't remember the last time I'd been in there. It had been well over a year at least. The door stuck and had to be jerked and lifted before it would open. "I'm not sure what you are expecting, but it probably isn't what you are going to find," I said grimly.

When the door finally gave, Aiden stepped into the room and smiled. "Claire knows what she's about, yes, this is a mess, but if you look, even though it is evening and the sun is well past this area, you can still get good light. An artist could still be working even in this light. In fact, this is about 100% better than my apartment and about the same size at that."

"So, what you are saying is you could see yourself painting in here?"

Suspicious, Aiden looked at me and frowned. "No, I didn't say I could see *myself* here, but I can see why this Julia thought it was a perfect room for a studio or quiet space. Do you really need all this stuff?" Aiden asked.

"No, none of this is mine. It all belonged to the old man or his family."

"Why don't you get rid of it?" Aiden asked.

"Never needed the space, I guess." I looked at Aiden and could tell he'd like to see the room without the clutter. So, it gave me an idea.

"I tell you what? I have time tomorrow before I have to go repair a fence that got washed out by the flood. If you'd like, we could empty this stuff out in the morning. What we need to keep can be put in the shed and what needs to go can get put into the truck to haul off when the river recedes."

"Sure," Aiden replied, apparently mystified that such an amazing space was left to collect dust. When we came out of the room, Claire was walking out of the kitchen, drying her hands on the apron she had on.

"Well, Aiden, what did you think of the space?" she asked.

"It is hard to tell with all the stuff in it, but the light is definitely good, so Devin and I are going to clean it out tomorrow morning, then I'll have a better opinion of it."

She smiled and reached behind her to undo the apron string. "Ok, well I'm done for the night. Devin, I'll be in around eleven tomorrow morning, so you are on your own for breakfast. If you get that room cleaned out before I get here, I'll help Aiden clean it up while you are off playing with your cows."

I cocked a friendly eyebrow and said under my breath, "Play with my cows, humph," going with the old standing joke.

She hugged Aiden as she headed for her old four-wheel drive Ford F-250. "It has been fun getting to know you today. I promise not to jump on you first thing tomorrow like I did today."

"Cause that can wait until afternoon?" Aiden asked.

"Well said, young man," then she patted him on the cheek.

"Y'all get some sleep," she added. "You'll need to get an early start on that room if you want to be done by noon."

She climbed into her truck, cranked it, and it bellowed like it had glass mufflers. I laughed at the shock Aiden had from hearing Claire's muscle truck.

"Don't think for one minute you've got that one figured out," I said, gesturing toward Claire. "She is more than meets the eye." I turned and watched as Claire bumped down the half-road, half-trail toward her place on the far side of the ranch.

"You care a lot about her, don't you?"

I looked back over to Aiden and sighed. "You have to understand that Claire is all the family I have and, although she has a sister and brother that still live in Billieville, they don't see each other much.

The old man's two kids were practically raised by Claire, but they too have drifted away and refuse to come back to the ranch even to visit her, so I guess, in a way, I'm her family as well."

"Well, for what it's worth, I think you are lucky to have each other. I've got great people in my life too—sometime ask me about Margie. I guess in a way, she's my Claire, although in more of a CEO-of-a-top-company-who-collects-priceless-art sort of way."

We sat in the swing, my arm resting comfortably behind Aiden.

"So," Aiden said, "things ended kinda strange last night, huh?"

"Yep," I agreed, not adding anything more to the conversation, but just rocking back and forth in the swing.

"Ok, well, if you'd rather not talk about it...," and he started to rise.

"I want to talk about it," I said, "but I'm also really enjoying just being here with you."

Aiden looked over at me, apparently taking what I said as the truth and slid back against my arm. A couple moments later, Aiden snuggled into me, laying his head on my shoulder.

The breeze came off the rolling hills, warm and smelling of the earth. Birds sang in the nearby trees and distant calls from the cows pastured around the home echoed off the landscape.

We sat like that for about an hour when Aiden leaned up and said, "It is getting cold, I think I'm going to turn in and get that rest as Claire suggested."

Without saying a word, I leaned over and gently kissed Aiden on the mouth. "Why don't we turn in together?"

Aiden looked at me sadly and looked out over the paddock and pasture to his right. "I don't know, Devin, I would like that very much, but I can't afford a broken heart. Isn't it smarter to keep things platonic between us?"

I chuckled at that, "I think it might be a bit late for a platonic relationship between us, Aiden."

"You know what I mean," Aiden huffed.

"Yes, it would be smarter and likely to lead to less heartache for both of us, but I have seriously never wanted a man as much as I want you. I'd rather regret loving on you tonight than regret letting the opportunity slip away." I kissed Aiden's neck and shoulder where the skin was visible around his shirt.

"It is a bad idea, a really bad idea," was all Aiden said before he kissed me, pulling me up on my feet and both of us climbed the stairs to my room.

I began unbuttoning Aiden's shirt and as I did so, I let my mouth move down to savor each new piece of exposed skin.   Once Aiden's shirt had been unbuttoned and removed, I reached up and pulled my own button-down shirt off without making any effort to unbutton it.

Aiden laughed, "So that is your trick! I wondered how you undressed so quickly last time. My eyes must have been closed when you pulled that stunt."

I smiled but didn't bother to respond. Instead, I began removing Aiden's pants and just as I'd done with Aiden's shirt, I slowly kissed each part of his skin that became exposed all the way down to his feet which I kissed after taking off his socks.

Aiden

I wasn't usually a foot fetish guy, but seeing Devin kiss the arches of my feet sent tingles down to my quickly growing cock. After Devin had removed every article of my clothing except for my briefs, he rose up to remove his own pants—which he did unceremoniously and with ease. I began to wonder how often this man must have done this to be so practiced. Fully unclothed, Devin began nibbling my neck and ears—this time, much more passionately than when he was removing my clothing. I moaned with pleasure as the beautiful man worked his way down my body licking, nipping and devouring me.

I had expected Devin to switch from foreplay to sex but he surprised me. When he reached into his bedside table, instead of a condom, he pulled out massage oil and remote control, he pushed a button and soft music with waves in the background immediately began playing from discrete places around the room.

Devin returned the remote to the drawer after asking me if the music was okay. Still rather surprised, I nodded.

"You were right you know," Devin said then, "when a man goes out of his way to clean another man's house, the very least he could do is repay him with a massage."

My eyebrow went up as Devin put the lotion in his hands and began massaging my feet. Oh god, I immediately turned to putty. There was nothing more relaxing than having your feet massaged—especially if you've been on them all day. Devin moved up my calves and onto my thigh carefully missing my man parts which were standing at full attention as they had since the moment Devin started removing my clothing.

He moved up my stomach, chest and then the front of my shoulders and arms. When he got to my hands, he slowly worked them, getting the muscles in between each finger. I had my eyes closed enjoying the incredible and unexpected experience.

Devin came up and kissed me, then asked, "Are you ready to turn over?" I nodded, still not quite sure what to expect. Devin reached down and pulled my underwear off as I turned onto my stomach.

Ok, I thought, here is where it gets interesting. But despite my expectation, Devin started massaging my shoulders and worked my muscles in a way that would make a warrior purr like a kitten. Devin seemed to know every part of my body and how to make each part sing and then relax.

He skipped over my buttocks but massaged my legs and calves before moving back up to my ass, this time, giving them the attention, they needed.

I had to admit, I'd never had a butt massage before and the pleasure surprised me. Devin worked his thumbs over my pelvis area first, then he drew his fingers down and into the muscles, massaging as he went. I couldn't help but moan in pleasure as the man's hands worked miracles along my tired, strained muscles.

Just as I was about to drift off in ecstasy, Devin began to massage my hole, although seriously relaxed, I felt myself slowly getting harder. Devin slowly moved the oiled fingers in and out of my hole, relaxing what would normally be taught.

Devin wrapped his arm under my waist and lifted me effortlessly onto my knees, and still using those amazing hands, Devin spread me wide and stuck his tongue into my ass, rediscovering the parts of me that his finger had just explored.

I was completely at Devin's mercy and the feel of Devin exploring in my ass was nothing less than ecstasy. I moaned louder and louder as Devin's amazing tongue continued to massage me. Then with practiced skill, Devin slipped on a condom I didn't even realize he had pulled out and using the massage oil as lube, he easily slipped his large cock into me. I was so desperate to feel Devin's cock inside of me that when it finally happened, it was pure relief that was quickly replaced with an intense desire for Devin to ride me and to ride me hard.

Despite my begging him, he refused to comply, instead, he continued to the slow penetration as he had massaged me, slowly, methodically and with intense control. Finally, he pulled his cock out of me and whispered, "I want to see your face while I fuck you."

I nodded weakly and turned over on my back.

Devin slowly lifted my legs and positioned himself between them, then he leaned down over me and said, "You make me want to give you pleasure, you make me want to make love in a way I've never loved another man. Thank you for that, Aiden."

An unwelcome burst of feeling surged through my heart at his confession. Even though all the warning signals went off in my head, in that moment, nothing I could've done would've stopped my heart from falling for this beautiful man and attentive lover.

Devin kissed me intensely, then slipped once again into me and continued to ride me slowly, giving us both pleasure while we stared into each other's eyes.

The intensity of being fucked slowly eventually took its toll on me and again, I began to beg Devin to fuck me harder.

Devin's smirk returned as he said, "As you wish," this time he thrust his cock fully into me then out and in again picking up speed until he was banging against my ass. My eyes rolled back, and my mouth gaped, unable to keep my moans back any longer.

As Devin picked up speed and intensity, I began to call his name. Devin readjusted so his cock was hitting my prostate and I came without even touching myself.

Then he pulled his cock out, tossed the condom away and crawled up to my face half fucking my mouth half jacking off. Devin poured himself into my mouth as he sighed with pleasure and my heart felt like it would burst. He came so much, I was afraid I was going to choke but I managed to swallow it all before he bent down to kiss me.

"If you'd have kissed me any sooner, we'd have been cum swapping mister." Devin only laughed a deep throaty laugh and then snuggled in beside me. "You are an amazing lover, Devin," I said before drifting off into afterglow sleep.

I woke up shortly after with a towel on my belly to soak up the mess, but Devin was nowhere to be seen. I made sure I was well wiped off then went downstairs to find Devin sitting on his porch swing just as I'd left him the night before. Remembering last night, I hesitated, afraid there would be a repeat argument. I almost turned around to go back upstairs. Instead, I went out the door and looked at Devin long and hard.

"You're upset, aren't you?" I asked.

"No, and yeah, I guess," he replied.

"Wanna talk about it?"

"No and yeah...I don't know, Aiden," Devin replied again.

I sat next to him on the swing and nuzzled into him. "It's a lot for me to process also. It's okay though, right?"

"Is it ok?" Devin asked, pulling away and looking me in the eye. "I'm beginning to have feelings for you," Devin began. "Aiden, I've never been in love before, I don't know how someone is supposed to handle this, especially knowing that you are going away."

I sat still, unable to say anything for several minutes. The revelation that Devin could have developed feelings for me so quickly was like cold water being splashed on me on a hot day. On one hand, it was a shock to the entire system and on the other, it was refreshing and exhilarating.

Finally, I sighed and responded, "I don't think anyone really knows what the future holds, but if it helps any, I have pretty strong feelings for you, too. We really only have two options, I guess. One is to stop making love with each other, which we don't seem too good at doing, or two, to ride the wave and see where it leads us. Besides, didn't Tennyson say 'tis better to have loved and lost than to never have loved at all'?"

Devin looked at me impressed. "You know Tennyson..." it was a statement not a question and he looked out over the pasture before he continued. "Yes, it's probably true, but losing someone I love is something I've already encountered several times. I'm not that keen on doing it again."

"No, I guess not." I looked at him sadly, "I'll have to let you take the lead here Devin. I already said I think what we did tonight was a bad idea, but oh, was it not one of the best bad ideas I've ever experienced."

Devin laughed. "It was pretty nice," he agreed.

"So, what is it to be, Mr. Pierce? Shall we continue to throw caution to the wind or pull back and wait for the waters to recede?"

Just at that moment, rain began to patter around us. "Hmm," Devin said, "I think that must be a sign."

"So," I asked, "What is that sign telling you to do?"

"It is telling me to make love to you as many times as I can before the river recedes."

"Then by all means," I agreed, "let's go take advantage of the signs."

Unlike the first night of lovemaking, we spent the hours snuggling and kissing each other. I loved the way Devin's muscles felt as I touched him. I learned if I tickled him on the ribs his laughter would display his incredible six-pack. I couldn't remember a time when I enjoyed a man as much as I enjoyed Devin and knowing it would soon come to an end caused me to cherish the time we were together that much more. We finally fell asleep early in the morning and didn't wake until long after the sun rose.

Devin

We came down in our underwear, unsure of whether or not we might get caught by Claire so, better safe than sorry, we both agreed. I put some coffee on and Aiden found some frozen cinnamon rolls in the freezer and put them in the toaster oven to cook.

While those were cooking, we continued cuddling on the couch in the living room. We were lying together when it popped into my head to ask Aiden what he'd do if he'd have bought this place. "How would you artsy it up?" I asked.

"Well, some paint would help, and I'd recover this sofa as soon as I could get someone to do it."

I tickled Aiden and then razzed him, "What have you got against my sofa?"

Aiden just shook his head, "For starters, she is butt ugly."

I interrupted, "*Your* butt isn't ugly."

"Hmm," Aiden replied. "Devin, you are not without style, you know this thing is ugly."

"Yeah," I begrudgingly admitted, "but it is the most comfortable sofa I've ever sat on."

"On that, we both agree," Aiden said.

"What color would you paint the walls?" I asked.

"Something simple and a bit neutral but with a little color...something light. The old wood floors, mantle, and staircase are masterpieces in and of themselves; you need to paint the walls so they complement those."

"I really haven't done much to this part of the house since I bought it. I guess, I always thought I'd eventually get married and that he would want to be a part of the decision-making."

"Oh, there is no doubt of that," Aiden replied. "I don't know any gay men that don't move into a home and totally rearrange it. Hell, even you rearranged the upstairs bedroom. I'm guessing you took a wall down to build that master suite up there. That isn't the traditional turn-of-the century work."

I laughed at Aiden's astute observation. "You are correct, of course—on both counts," I said.

The bell on the toaster oven went off and Aiden stood to go into the kitchen. "If someone like you came into my life, Aiden," I said, "I'd give them anything they wanted."

Aiden smiled at me, stood, then leaned over and kissed me. "You say that now, but I watched my parents who are the most attached, loving couple in the world and they definitely had their wars over the way things go in their home. It was through their cooperation that beauty occurred. Hell, look at how good I turned out." Then Aiden slipped away from me and scurried into the kitchen, me close on his heels.

When I caught him, I tickled him and kissed him as he squirmed to get out of my reach. I held him tight and whispered in his ear, "I admit, I like how you turned out." Aiden turned in my arms and we embraced in a long, delicious kiss.

After we finished the cinnamon rolls and coffee, we slipped on some work clothes and set to work emptying out my storage room. The stuff in the room was random—almost like it was put there instead of being put in the trash where it belonged.

Nothing was redeemable other than a couple of old chairs and a few other odds and ends that appeared to have been in the room before it was used for storage.

Working side by side was almost as enjoyable as the sex had been. We both seemed to enjoy the other's company and as the last piece of junk was taken out of the room and tossed into the back of the old pickup, we both seemed to regret that the project had ended. It had only taken us a few hours to take the stuff out of the room and Aiden assured me that he felt he should wait for Claire before cleaning up. Something about the way she described the room made him think she needed to be a part of bringing it back.

Dusty and grimy, we grabbed a quick drink in the kitchen before going into the stables to feed, and hay the horses.

"How often do you muck these stalls?" Aiden asked.

"Depends on the time of year, I like to let everyone pasture during the day when I have my hands here, but when they are gone, I try to keep them stalled. There are mountain lions and coyotes, as well as a few bears that'd do some damage to a horse if not properly seen after. So, I muck at least twice a week, when I don't have them on pasture."

"Maybe I can help you muck again tomorrow if you want me to," Aiden offered cheerfully.

"I always want help mucking stalls, Aiden, *always*!" I responded with as much expression as I could.

This made Aiden laugh. "You remind me of Steve, but at least you like the horses, just not the poo."

"Steve sounds like a well-balanced man, how long have you known him? More importantly, is he an ex-boyfriend?"

Aiden burst into laughter at the question. "First, no, Steve has never been a boyfriend, more like an overbearing, demanding brother, and second, since we were little. My dad and Steve's dad are best buds from high school. We grew up together. Heck, if it wasn't for him, I'd never have found your contact information. He had to go negotiate a few background computer things, so I could send you a message. You had such an overwhelming response to your profile that the computer restricted your access information, so we owe Steve for this whole mess and mix-up."

"I'll be sure to thank him when I see him...or cuss him out—depending on how things turn out."

Aiden laughed at the comment.

Claire arrived as he and I were finishing with the horses. Her old truck was literally covered in mud.

"Looks like you had a hard time getting here," I said.

"Well aren't you the observant one," she said temperamentally.

"Hey, you said you weren't going to be an ass this morning," I complained.

"No," she responded, "I said I wouldn't be an ass to Aiden." She looked over at Aiden and then walked over and patted his cheek, "Good morning, good-looking, hope you slept well," she said.

"I did," Aiden answered, then snickered as Claire turned her scowl back onto Devin.

"The trail up here is sheer mud. I would've turned back if I hadn't wanted to spend some more time with this handsome young buck here." She pointed over at Aiden. "When are you going to put some gravel down, so I don't have to go off-roading just to get to work?" She continued to glare at me.

"I'll get right on that, Claire, meanwhile, you could stay here," I argued.

"And listen to the two of you go at it all night? I'd rather crawl home on all fours."

Aiden smothered a smile and turned to go toward the apartment, "I'm going to head up to the bathroom and brush my teeth, the two of you appear to need some time to yourselves," he said and disappeared before either of us could react.

"You fallen for him yet?" Claire asked.

"You know damned well that I have," I replied.

"Well, that is probably bad for both of us. He ain't keen on staying yet, but I've got some tricks up my sleeve. You best be off and get your chores done. Do you want me to pack you a lunch?" she asked.

"Well, if you are going to kick me out of my own home then, yeah, I'll probably need something between now and supper," I retorted.

"You better take ol' Alex up with you. That rain last night didn't last long but it did a good job making the whole place slick with mud," she advised.

"Did you get by the river?" I asked.

"Yep, swollen again, but not as bad as it was before."

"Maybe we'll get another rain storm tonight," I said hopefully.

"Maybe," Claire responded, "maybe ..."

We both looked toward the apartment, then Claire turned toward the house and I went out to the barn to saddle Alexander.

Aiden

When I came into the house, I saw that Claire had put a sack lunch together for Devin and left it sitting on the countertop. "Is Devin leaving to fix the fence?" I asked.

"Yep, he's saddling Alex now. Too muddy for the four-wheeler," she replied.

"Should I offer to go with him?"

Claire looked over at him, "I wouldn't, at least not today. I know my Devin and the man needs his alone time, even when he don't know he needs it. If he don't get it, he can become a bear. No one wants to deal with Devin the bear," she chuckled.

I had experience with Devin the bear and nodded my agreement. "All the better," I said. "Maybe we can get that old room put together before he gets home. You were right, the light in there is pretty amazing."

Claire looked over at me with a sad smile on her face and said, "Julia loved that room. It broke my heart when the old man filled it with garbage.

Nothing to be done about it though, he was set on blocking everything about her—even his old heart."

I leaned on the table and asked her, "Were you and the old man ever a thing?"

Claire sighed, "Aiden, dear boy, that is a long story. Maybe I'll tell it to you while we are cleaning, but the short answer is 'sort of'."

Devin came in through the kitchen door and got a hateful look from both me and Claire for not removing his boots. "I'm just coming in to tell you I'm leaving and to get that sack lunch."

Claire reached over and grabbed the sack and handed it to Devin. She kissed him on the cheek and said, "Now be gone with you, it's my turn to spend some time with Aiden. You two will have plenty of time to play between the sheets after I'm gone."

Devin shook his head as he left, "I know when I've lost an argument before it even starts, Claire," he said, and she just chuckled.

Claire and I went to work immediately. When Claire came into the room, she stood silently for a moment. I wasn't quite sure if she was going to cry or not. In the end, she did wipe a tear away but apparently like me, she dealt with her emotions by cleaning.

We started in the far corner. Claire cleaned the furniture first then moved to the windows and window seals. I dug deeper and cleaned the walls and ceiling, pulling down cobwebs and washing the entire room with hot water, vinegar, and soap.

As we toiled, I prodded her story from her. "So, how did you end up here and more importantly, if the old man was as hateful as you and Devin portray him as, why did you stay?"

Claire sighed again and said, "It is a long story, but considering all the cleaning we need to do, I'll tell you.

"My dad drove me over to the ranch when I had just turned twenty years old. The owner, Jim, eyed me dubiously, like I was some kind of rabid thief," Claire chuckled, "but his wife Julia took to me quickly. It was only a matter of time before we were close as sisters.

"Jim and Julia were madly in love and being a young woman who loved all things romantic, I enjoyed watching their relationship grow. I helped Julia with daily chores, but mostly I kept an eye on her two boys." Claire grinned at the memory.

"Things were good until Julia got cancer and passed away. Everything went to shit after that." Claire sat down on the chair, sadness and frustration rolling off her.

She took a long sigh and looked out the window. "As the life drained out of that incredible woman, so did the light on this ranch. Before she died, I promised Julia that I would stay and take care of Jim and the boys.

"As time went by, Jim and I grew closer. We would confide in each other the way only two people who've experienced the loss of a shared loved one could. Eventually, Jim expressed his love for me, but even though I felt the same toward him, I couldn't get past the feeling that it was somehow betraying Julia, so I told him it was wrong—that I wouldn't allow myself to feel that way."

The sadness in Claire's face was painful to watch. She looked down at her hands as she continued, "Jim seemed to hate me after that. Whatever feelings we had developed after losing Julia turned sour, and he became a bitter old man that chased everyone away including his own sons. As soon as they could, they left, and I rarely ever saw them after that."

Claire turned to me now, and looking me in the eye said, "I don't want you to think I regret my life," then she turned away again and stared out of the window, "but I do regret all those years that could have been filled with the same type of love I saw between Jim and Julia."

Claire blew her nose on a clean rag she had brought with her into the room. She looked around the room then and sighed, "I guess being in this room has brought out my need to confess."

After that admission, Claire seemed to be lost in thought, so we worked quietly for a while.

Finally, my curiosity got the better of me and I asked, "So, when did Devin come on the scene?"

Claire answered without looking, "Well, that was by necessity. The years flew by and the old man was beginning to show signs of his age. It was apparent that the ranch was going to go under if he didn't get help, so I helped him write up and put out an ad for an assistant manager. This is when Devin showed up." As she spoke, the sadness that had settled on her face was slowly replaced by a smile.

"Devin told me he grew up in Seattle, so how did a city boy function on a ranch like this one?" I asked.

Claire chuckled, "It wasn't an easy transition for him, I can assure you. Devin was as green as any young city boy could be, but he carried himself with a sense of pride. You could see the silver spoon sticking out of his mouth," she winked at me before saying, "although he worked hard to hide it. In fact, he worked hard in general. He clearly didn't want to be treated special. Even under the tyrannical direction of the old man, he never broke. When he screwed up, he simply straightened his back and fixed what he had done wrong.

"In over thirty years, I'd not seen the hard heart of the old man soften for anyone or anything—until Devin, that is. Despite himself, the old man was clearly impressed with the boy. No amount of hateful attacks or unjustified criticism would break Devin. The old man's words seemed to roll off the boy like water off a duck's back. He seemed to have a knack for separating the old man's hateful remarks for the valuable insight a man with that many years' experience could impart.

"I, too, was intrigued by Devin and over time, my admiration for his tenacity began to shift to caring. One night, Devin confided in me that he'd lost both of his parents. His mom had died when he was young and like the old man here, the loss of his mom had hardened his father's heart. However, unlike the old man's sons, Devin's mom had taught him to recognize the love behind the hurt, so Devin had learned to ignore the bad and glean only from the good.

"The same lesson seemed to work with him and the old man. As time went on, Jim leaned on Devin more and more. In the end, I believed that Devin had filled a void in the old man's heart. Some -- although not enough -- of the ice fell away and Devin became part of our family."

"Devin told me you were part of his buying this place. How did all that happen?" I asked, not thinking that could be conceived as nosey.

Claire went on with the story clearly not offended by my question. "The boys wanted nothing to do with the ranch after they grew up, so after Jim died, I told them about Devin and how he had been the only person in all the years since Julia's death that even remotely melted the heart of the old man. I told them that if they could and if he wanted it, the ranch should belong to him. In the end, I told them, "He is the only person who can bring back the joy your mama gave to this old ranch." The boys agreed to sell to Devin if he expressed interest and as fate would have it, he did, and they sold the property to him as I had requested.

She looked at me a moment then said, "I'm going to share another bit of information with you that Devin doesn't know and I prefer he not learn of it— at least not yet. The old man left enough money to keep me comfortable for the remainder of my years along with the little bungalow down at the edge of the ranch. I didn't share that I'd inherited money with Devin because I wanted to stay on the ranch and watch him turn it back into a place of beauty, so, maybe unfairly, I pretended to be poor, so he'd feel obliged to keep me on."

I could tell that she was blushing a little, so I said something to help, "Hey," I put my hands in the air, "I'd have done the same thing!"

"Well, she laughed, "as the years passed, I have come to regret my decision to stay on as a housekeeper. My body has begun to betray me, keeping this big, old home clean has become more and more of a challenge. One day when my back felt like it was going to split apart, I decided I'd had enough and finally told Devin it was time to find another housekeeper, but displaying a temper reminiscent of the old man, he denied me and made some statement about fillies and underwear."

She stomped her foot then reliving the frustration as if it had just happened, "I figured god was punishing me for my deceit, so I didn't argue with the boy about it. There was some good that came from the conversation though. Following that talk, Devin began picking up after himself and I figured the future husband of Devin Pierce would appreciate any training in housework that I could impart, so I decided to stay on for as long as my body would let me."

With that, Claire stood up, reached into the old bucket and grabbed a washcloth and began washing the walls where I had left off.

"So, you don't need the work, but Devin thinks you do."

She nodded and returned to her work.

"Claire, you need to come clean. Devin doesn't need you breaking your back—especially when he can't take the time to remove his old work boots before coming into the house."

Claire laughed again, "He isn't that bad to work for, you know. The two boys and the old man were much more work than him. As I said, he does try to clean up after himself now that he knows my back hurts."

"Like hell," I said. Claire looked surprised at my reaction which had surprised me too and we both laughed out loud at my reaction.

"Can you tell me about how you dealt with Devin's sexuality? That had to be difficult for you and what about the old man?"

Claire shrugged, "I doubt the old man ever knew, but after his death, Devin brought a man home after I tried fixing him up with some of the women in town. I was surprised at first that Devin swung toward men, but he never made much of the issue, so I didn't either. After a while, it wasn't something I even thought that much about."

Again, she shrugged, but then continued in a conspiratorial whisper, "One thing I did notice though, is how much I didn't like any of the men Devin brought home. They were not the kind of men who would do very well as the husband of a rancher." She straightened up again and said more matter of fact. "In fact, most of them weren't anyone you'd think of as husband material at all. The last one was really a piece of work. He found that one on the property next to this one."

She shook her head as she remembered, "I came into the barn one day and found him harassing one of the lads that cleaned out the stables. I figured I'd been around for a long time and if I got fired for confronting the son of a bitch, it would be a blessing, so I didn't even hesitate. I grabbed myself a broom and walloped the miscreant over the head with it. I told him to leave the ranch hands alone and that if he couldn't settle with a man as good as Devin, then he should just move on.

"Of course, the arrogant little shit threatened to have my job. I still think it is a miracle I didn't hit him again. I fully intended to tell Devin about the boy, but I knew it'd hurt him and that was the last thing I wanted to do. So, I decided to put off telling him for a week or so to see if Devin would dump the ass himself.

"As fate would have it, the law seemed to take care of the problem for me—unfortunately, not without Devin feeling the pain. One night, Devin came to my home all upset. I'd read the papers, so I knew what was coming." Claire shook her head at the memory.

"That was an awful night, Aiden. I think right then, Devin began to lose hope, and I'll be honest with you, I felt a little fear. I've seen the worst that can happen when a man loses hope. I put my arms around Devin and tried to console him. He tried not to cry, but I could see he needed to. That night, he asked me why he picked such awful men and why he couldn't just find a regular, honest and good guy who wants to settle down. I hugged him tighter reminding him that I was no judge of character. I'd fallen for the worst possible man and had spent a life of punishment as a result.

"Understanding what I meant, he hugged me back and we sat in my little garden for a while feeling sorry for ourselves. Finally, I told Devin that it wasn't all his fault. 'You can't find gold in a place where it doesn't exist. If you have a hankering for gold, you have to go to a goldmine'." She snickered at her joke. "You know he was totally confused, so I explained. 'In other words, you got to go somewhere else to find a good man, clearly, there ain't none here!' We both laughed a bit at the truth of that.

"I followed Devin back to the big house to make sure he got back ok. When we got here, I saw Devin had been breaking bottles of wine the idiot had brought over. I told him not to waste good wine and so he and I drank it all. That was the night we found that website *City Men to Country Men*. Of course, we were both hammered when we found it.

"When he sobered up, he didn't want anything to do with it, but I just pretended like I was him and went through the site until I found you." She looked out the window and a smile crossed her face. "Well, you and deLisha. She is a drag queen I found. We've become close, but she isn't the kind Devin would be looking for.

"Anyway, Devin was proper mad at me when I gave you this address. He was afraid you'd be some perv who'd harassed his men like that last one did, but I showed him what you wrote and then, as fate would have it, here you are."

It took a moment for me to grasp what Claire was insinuating. "Claire, don't you get the wrong idea, I like Devin, but I live in New York. I only came out here to thank him for being my muse. If it hadn't been for that blasted, swollen river, I'd have already been long gone."

Claire just smiled and patted my cheek and said, "We don't always control our destiny, dear boy, now do we?" She walked around the room ignoring my pouting and sighed a happy sigh.

"Young man," she exclaimed. "I do believe we've brought this room back to life." I stopped pouting long enough to look at the finished product and smiled.

"I'll be damned, Claire, I was so wrapped up in your story, I didn't notice we had finished the work."

I turned in a circle and when I glanced at Claire, I could feel the wheels turning in my head, I might not have wanted to admit it, but the room spoke to the artist in me. Even as I turned, I could see myself in the space.

Yeah, it needed paint and personalizing, but how could any artist resist this kind of light and warmth?

Shocking me, Claire leaned over and kissed me on the cheek. "Thank you for helping me bring this back to life."

She wiped another tear from her cheek as she turned and took in the room herself.

"Let's get cleaned up and get supper started. It is almost half past five and that boy will be back any moment, and if I know Devin as I think I do, that little sack lunch will be long gone by the time he gets back. Why don't you run and get cleaned up, I've got a casserole in the freezer that I put aside for occasions like this."

I did as she instructed and went to the apartment and took a shower and changed into some of the clothes Devin brought over when I first arrived. Remembering the uncomfortable encounter where Devin caught me completely naked, wet and rather angry, now made me chuckle.

Just a few days later, not only had Devin seen me naked, he'd probed every part of my body that could be probed.

I sat on the little bed in the room and thought about Claire's story. I wasn't an idiot, I knew she had disclosed the story to draw me further into their world and to probably scare me about the consequences of letting love go but I didn't have much choice. How was I going to live on a ranch in the middle of nowhere, no internet, phone or other modern amenities I was used to? Even if Devin were to lose his mind and ask me to.

Even though her story might not have changed the outcome, I knew I'd take her with me for the rest of my life, just as I knew I'd never forget Devin Pierce either.

After getting dressed, I walked over to the house just as Devin was arriving back from the fence repair.

"Did you get it fixed?" I asked.

"Yeah, at least for now. I need to move the fence another few feet in front of the wash but that can wait until the guys are back to work. How about you, did you get the room finished?"

"Yep," I replied, "all clean and ready for some paint and fix-up. You have a really nice room there, Devin. It is a shame it was neglected all this time. Claire also told me about her life in the process. She has been through some sad stuff."

Devin mirrored my look of sadness, "Yeah, I don't know all of it, but I do know the old man made her life pretty miserable. I don't really understand why she stuck around all these years."

I came over and put my arms around Devin's neck, "One day, you should ask her. It would be good for her to tell you," then I kissed him on the mouth and continued walking toward the house.

"Go get cleaned up, I'll help Claire finish the meal. I think she's heating up a frozen casserole or something."

Devin's eyes got big and a smile came across his face, "Is it her hamburger casserole? She makes the best hamburger casserole, but we don't get it very often. She says it's only for special occasions."

I laughed at the eager boyish look on Devin's face. "I'm not sure, but the sooner you're ready the sooner you'll find out."

Devin turned to sprint the rest of the way to the house, but stopped at the door and removed his boots, which gave me a hearty chuckle.

Before he disappeared into the house, I yelled, "That's a good boy, might even earn you some dessert,"

Devin turned slowly around and winked a naughty wink at me, then dashed into the house. That man is randy all the time, I thought with a smile.

I followed closely behind him and walked into the kitchen just as Claire was standing up. I caught her before she could mask the feelings she'd been having, and I was able to see that our talk had drudged up some pretty strong memories.

"Remembering can really suck sometimes, can't it?" I asked.

She smiled a sad smile at me and nodded. "But," she said, "there's always a need for the remembering...you young people need to remember that. You got to take the good with the bad and that goes for memories as well as life."

I nodded in agreement as Claire walked over to the sink to wash her hands. "What do you need me to do for dinner?" I asked.

"Not much, just set the table while I pull the casserole out of the oven."

250

"Is this your hamburger casserole?" I asked.

Claire smiled, "So, you must have run into Devin on your way in. I thought I heard him. The boy sounds like a herd of elephants sometimes. Yep, it is the famous hamburger casserole. I still don't know why they make such a fuss about it, but they all seem to love it. I keep one frozen in the freezer for when I don't feel like cooking, and go figure, that is their favorite thing I make." She chuckled, but her smile didn't hide her pride.

"You go set the table. I think we'll use the porch again tonight. I just love these late summer evenings. When Devin comes down, I'll have him go pick us out one of those fancy wines of his."

I agreed that would be a great idea and hurried off to set the table.

Devin was down in a matter of minutes, the casserole seemed to have a motivating effect on him. Devin disappeared down the stairs and came back up with one of the unnamed bottles.

When I saw the bottle, I asked, "What are those? They are delicious."

Both Claire and Devin chuckled at the question. "This is our homemade brew. We made it from some grapes we found down by the river. Julia must have planted them down there before she passed away."

"Well, you should make more of it," I replied. "It is one of the best wines I've ever had."

"Maybe we should," Devin looked over at Claire who was smiling like she was keeping a secret.

"Why am I getting the feeling that the two of you aren't sharing everything you know about this wine?"

With that statement, both Claire and Devin burst into laughter. "Now I know something is up. Wanna fill me in?"

The two looked at one another as if to determine if they should share their secret. "I think he can be trusted," she said to Devin.

"I don't know," Devin said, "he looks like a law-abiding citizen to me...not sure he won't call the sheriff if we tell."

I cocked an eyebrow at Devin which caused him to burst into another bout of laughter. "Okay, okay, we'll spill the beans, but you have to swear not to breathe one word of this to anyone."

I didn't respond but kept the cocked eyebrow glare on Devin which Claire thought was wonderful and laughed more than she had before.

"Oh, I do like this boy," she said between laughs.

"Well, I told you about my ex, right?" Devin asked. "How he had cheated on me by sexually harassing every man that worked at his winery?"

"Yeah," I replied.

"Well," Devin continued, "the asshole had squirreled away a secret stash of the best wine they ever made for himself. In fact, he told his parents that he'd sold the wine and spent the money. What really happened was that he hid the wine in a cellar the family never used because it tended to have rattlesnakes in it during the hot summer days. I'm not sure what possessed him to tell me this, other than maybe he wanted to brag to someone about his unethical and selfish behavior, but he did. While he was confessing, he pointed in the general direction of the cellar, so I had an idea where it was hidden.

"When he got in trouble with the allegations, the judge put him in jail with no bond for a few days until a preliminary hearing could happen. I also knew all the workers had disappeared since they were all part of the case against him, so on the night I found out, I went over to Claire's for comfort and we got lit on Jack Daniels. We began talking about his sorry ass and Claire suggested we needed a way to hit him in the balls."

"Which I meant literally," she interrupted. Devin laughed and continued.

"Yeah, she meant literally, but I told her I had a better plan and filled her in on the barrel of expensive wine he kept hidden."

"Again," Claire interrupted. "So, you know we had to steal it right?"

"Of course, you did," I replied in the affirmative as if they had no choice.

"Of course, we did," Claire replied.

"We got on the 4-wheeler and drove over to where the river separates the two properties, then, we both waded across the river which was not very deep at that time and up to the winery. Claire was the lookout because we figured her bungalow wasn't very far away from the winery and she could make up some excuse about looking for her dog if someone found her, while I snuck around trying to find the cellar.

"Luckily, we weren't in the security camera's view which we didn't think of at the time—it could have been pretty rough on us if we had. Of course, the asswipe must have known if the cameras could see him hide the barrel, his parents would be able to figure out his scheme. Anyway, I walked right up to the hidden cellar and with a little lock pick, I was able to get it open in no time. I shined a little flashlight to make sure there were no reptilian surprises waiting for me and when I saw it was empty, I slipped down and grabbed the barrel. The ass had even made it easy to steal by forgetting to remove the ramp and pulley-leverage system he'd used to steal it in the first place. Without it, we'd never have succeeded as the barrel weighed way more than I could lift by myself."

Again, Claire chimed in, "And I sure as hell wasn't going to lift the damned thing."

Continuing, Devin smiled, "I brought it up and rolled it toward Claire. Here is when things got

254

interesting; Claire was standing about 50 yards away from me and just slightly downhill. I turned to close the cellar doors and return the lock when I heard Claire scream. When I turned back around, the barrel which had to weigh about 600 pounds was headed straight toward her. I ran toward the barrel and was able to change the direction just in time to miss her."

"I was so scared," she said, "that and my mind was still befuddled from all the Jack we'd drank before coming on the adventure."

"We were lucky, that is for damned sure," Devin shook his head.

"But," Claire continued, "This is where our luck really came into play. Devin had knocked the barrel off its course of squashing me and back toward the river.

"Now this wasn't a steep climb really, but it was just enough to have the barrel headed down the hill toward the river. We were both sure it was going to hit a boulder and burst open spilling all the wine. So, we decided to take our losses and run."

Devin nodded as Claire finished talking and said, "I went back up and finished securing the cellar and lock, then we both high-tailed it out of there before someone came to check out why Claire had screamed. By the time we got to the river, the barrel was nowhere to be seen. There were lights on in the winery, so we couldn't risk being out there any longer. We quickly waded across the river and headed toward the 4-wheeler and straight back to the ranch house."

Claire took the story back up, "We were both a bit rattled not only that I almost got squashed by 600 pounds of wine, but because we almost got caught in the process. It also didn't take much imagination to figure out who had the four-wheeler either. I'm sure they heard that as we left."

Claire looked back over to Devin and said, "You tell the rest," then she giggled and said, "Here is why I believe in karma young man," and pointed back to Devin.

Devin laughed at himself and picked the story back up. "The next day, I was looking for a cow that had disappeared—when they do that, you can almost guarantee they are giving birth. I found her down by the river downstream from the heist that occurred the night before. She had given birth to the prettiest little calf, and guess what I found washed ashore, *right next to them?*"

"You are shitting me," I exclaimed.

"Nope, it was the barrel, sitting right there just as pretty as you please."

The second Devin finished speaking, Claire burst into a round of laughter. "Whoo Hoo!" she said. "Not only was it next to his newborn calf, but it was about a mile closer to the ranch house."

Devin nodded and laughed, too. "I ran to the house, grabbed a piece of plywood and put Claire on the back of the four-wheeler."

Claire interrupted again, "He refused to tell me where we were going."

"I wanted it to be a surprise," he said.

"But when I saw that barrel lying next to that baby calf, I laughed until I cried, I laughed so hard I was afraid I was going to wet myself."

"We were able to get the barrel onto the four-wheeler just the two of us by parking the thing just a little downhill of where the barrel sat and placing the plywood between it and the four-wheeler."

"I think it was that and a little superman adrenaline," Claire added.

"How we did that without any of the hands seeing us, I still don't know, but we managed to get the damned thing into the stable apartment and close all the window blinds, so no one could see in."

Devin chimed back in, "Over the next few days, we bottled the wine in these nondescript bottles."

Claire stood up and walked over to the edge of the porch and pointed out toward the end of the stairs. "Do you see those two half-barrel pots down there?" she asked me.

"Yeah," I said mystified by the story and the two capers I was beginning to love even more.

"We hid the evidence there. Devin cut the barrel in half and I planted those flowers in them."

Claire burst into another fit of laughter. Then, she took the bottle and poured all three of us a full glass of the wine. "Bottoms up," she said.

And each of us took a long, enjoyable drink. "Damn," I said, "I do believe that tastes better now than it did before! So, I have a question," I began.

"Yes," Claire and Devin said together.

"Is this the same night you created your *CMTOCM* profile?" I asked

Both Claire and Devin burst into a fit of laughter over the comment.

"Yep," Claire said laughing again, "It was a full night."

"Wow," I said, "You two should get drunk more often."

We laughed the evening away drinking bottle after bottle of wine. The two of them taking my advice and getting drunk enough that Claire had to sleep on the sofa.

"Y'all don't be doing the rabbit dance up there," she said drunkenly, "I don't wanna be traumatized for the rest of my life." Then, she fell into a deep sleep.

"Unlikely she'll remember anything tomorrow morning except the hangover that is headed her way."

"That is very true," I agreed and gave Devin a sloppy drunk kiss.

"Damn," Devin said, "Am I the only one here that can hold his drink?"

I hiccupped then laughed out loud, "Apparently so," I said slurring my speech.

Devin picked me up and carried me upstairs, which I found to be exceptionally funny.

He put me down on the bed and was about to get up when I said, "Mr. Pierce, I hope you take advantage of me," I slurred.

"I would, but I'm willing to bet you are asleep in less than five minutes," Devin replied soberly.

Offended, I leaned up on my elbows, "I will not, hiccup, hiccup," and laughed again.

Devin

I undressed Aiden which was hard to do with him constantly trying to kiss me and pawing at my own clothing. Finally, with most of his clothes removed, I gave up and went into the bathroom to brush my teeth and get ready for bed. When I returned, Aiden was out for the count. I smiled to myself, then sat on a chair and stared at the beautiful man lying in my bed.

I knew I was a goner, there was no falling left to do—I had completely and utterly fallen for Aiden. But, the question was, had Aiden fallen in love with me? It didn't appear that he had. There was no doubt Aiden enjoyed making love with me and the man fit me better than any man I'd ever had sex with, but there had to be more; but no way I sized this up, could I see Aiden giving up his life in New York to live on a ranch in one of the most remote areas of the country.

I buttoned my shirt up again and slipped down past Claire and out into the night. At first, I thought about sitting in the swing, but decided I'd be better off going for a walk. As I walked, my half-inebriated mind became more and more convinced that Aiden and I were doomed from the start. I circled around the house at least three times, putting myself into a tizzy. Finally, exhaustion and alcohol did their work and I lay down on a half-used bale of hay and dozed off.

When I woke up the next morning, my attitude was less than stellar, although I didn't have a full-on hang-over, the lack of sleep and dehydration along with my decision that Aiden was not for me, had done their work on my nerves.

I walked back into the house seeing Claire already in the kitchen treating her hangover with a cocktail of juices, aspirin and a little whiskey. Aiden stumbled down the stairs head in hand and headed for the kitchen when he bumped into me. "How can you be up so early? I can't see anything except the pain... red pain..."

I didn't laugh as I would have in any other state of mind, but instead said in a hateful voice, "Anyone who'd drink that much deserves what he gets the next morning," and I headed up the stairs to the bedroom.

Aiden

"What's got into him?" I asked Claire through slanted eyes.

"Who knows? Who cares?" she asked. "Here, down this, it'll help."

"Ugh," I said but swallowed the concoction, gagged a little and then grabbed my head again. "That was the worst thing I've ever tasted in all my life," I said.

"Yep, but it works," she replied and downed hers, gagging only once. We sat at the kitchen table and held our heads in our hands as we waited for the headache to clear. Slowly, life came back to us and Claire got up and poured each of us a glass of water.

"Here, drink this. The more water you get in you, the quicker this will blow over."

I nodded then winced as I picked up the water and drank it slowly as not to cause myself to become sick.

Devin came back down just as we were finishing the first glass of water.

"The two of you are pathetic," he said again with a considerable amount of venom.

"What the hell has crawled up inside of you, Devin Pierce?" Claire demanded.

"I just don't think it's healthy for two grown adults to drink so much they end up with hangovers, that's what."

"If I remember correctly," I chimed in, "You were matching us drink for drink."

"But, you'll notice I don't have a hangover now, do I?"

Neither Claire nor I really cared much about whatever it was that Devin was spouting on about—each still nursing our headaches—so seeing that he was getting nowhere, Devin stomped outside and into the stables.

"Well, I'm glad he's gone," Claire said.

"Yeah, me too," I agreed. "I gotta go pee, then I'll go see if I can work up enough strength to go help him out."

"You drink another glass of water before you go out there or you'll be no use to anyone, you hear?" Claire stood back up to fill both of our glasses.

I went to the bathroom then returned just in time to see Devin come back from the stables with a look of pure anger on his face. He walked into the kitchen, and spotting Claire, unleased his anger on her. He was yelling nonsense at her about drinking and being irresponsible. Each word he yelled straightened her back just a little bit more until he had finished. I stepped in and confronted Devin before he could launch into another tirade.

"You have no right to talk to her like that. You have no right to talk to anyone like that." The anger I was feeling had pushed the headache aside.

Claire looked over at me and said, "Trust me, son. I've been on the other end of this kind of treatment plenty enough to take care of myself. Devin Pierce, you can take your smelly attitude and whatever has caused you to get into a tizzy and shove it up your ass. I'm headed home, and you can clean your own damned house from now on for all I care."

Claire stomped out of the house, got into her truck and was gone.

I stared at Devin long and hard, waiting for him to say the first word.

Devin turned to me and shrugged. "I'm sorry. I...I'm sorry," and he sat down at the kitchen table.

"You damned well should be! I have never seen anyone speak to someone they care about like that! What the hell is wrong with you?"

"I'm an idiot," he replied. "I swore I'd never let that woman go through that again, and now I'll be damned if she didn't at my own doing. I'll go up later when she gets done being angry with me and make amends."

I continued staring at Devin in disgust.

"Aiden, sit down. Let me explain what happened."

"No," I replied. "I'm going to walk to Claire's house and see if I can help her out."

Devin shook his head and said, "You can't walk, it's over three miles."

"I'd rather walk three miles than be with you right now," I snapped.

Devin pointed out toward the driveway, "Take the truck," he said. "The keys are in the ignition. Just follow the path until it ends. You'll see her bungalow when you get there."

I left Devin sitting at the kitchen table.

I arrived at the little cottage at the end of the road and was immediately impressed by how adorable it was. Claire had painted it in pastel colors and there were flowers planted everywhere. She even had a little kitchen garden over to the right of the cottage. She had certainly created quite the home. I went to her front door and knocked, but there was no answer. I started to go around to the back when I heard her crying.

"Claire," I yelled. "It's Aiden, let me in so we can trash talk Devin."

I heard her laugh a bit through the tears and she said, "Aiden, I really need to be alone right now."

"No, you don't," I argued, "that is the last thing you need right now."

Claire came to the door with tears streaming down her cheeks. "You are right. I don't need to be alone. I thought the days of being yelled at were over. Devin has never done anything like that before. Damn him for making me feel this way again."

"Damn him all to hell and back," I agreed and put my arms around Claire and held her in the doorway.

Finally, Claire said, "Come on in, no use standing in the doorway."

We walked into the room and again I was impressed with how perfectly designed the little cottage was. It had a natural open-concept feel to it and her furniture and appliances were updated and cute.

"How long have you lived here?" I asked.

Wiping away the remaining tears, Claire responded, "For about 15 years," she said. "I moved down here when the boys left and Jim had a few of his employees who were good with carpentry come to help me remodel it. It had been vacant for a while before I moved in, but I gave him the ultimatum that he'd either fix it up or I'd move to town."

"It is really cute, but the appliances are newer than 15 years," I said looking around the place.

"Oh, yeah. I got the house in the will so when the old man died, I had the place renovated again, but more to my standards. Do you want a tour?" she asked. "I don't get many visitors out in the middle of nowhere."

"If you're up to it, yeah, I would,"

She smiled, put her arm around me and took me around the house showing what all she'd done to the place. As we talked, her mood lifted. When she'd shown me around, she poured us both some water and demanded that I drink.

"We both still have this hangover to deal with," she said. I took the glass, my stomach much more solid than it had been before Devin went nuts, and drank my fill.

"What the hell got into Devin?" I asked.

"Most certainly, it has to do with you," she said. "This is not a man who deals well with things not under his control. In that way, he is like the old man. Unfortunately, today I saw more similarities than I have before. That will have to be snuffed out immediately or else our boy will find himself out here alone. I won't be living through that kind of experience again."

"Yeah, me neither," I agreed.

"I'm not going to defend him, Aiden, but you have to see he is in love with you, right?"

I stared at my empty glass. "We haven't been around each other enough to be in love yet, Claire," I replied.

"That is bullshit and you know it. Are *you* in love with him?" she asked.

I hesitated for a long moment and then responded, "No, I don't think I am," I lied. "It has been so fast and overwhelming. When I first arrived, Devin was nasty and hateful, but I understood why. He thought I was here to mess with his life. That I was some wacko queen. But, today, that was another level of mean. I can't get that image out of my mind," I concluded.

"No, I'd expect not," she said, "but let me ask you this. Did you have feelings for him before you saw him throw this morning's temper tantrum?"

I looked at her not wanting to admit the truth. "I guess we both know that I was beginning to feel things for him. But I've never led him on, Claire. I was honest from the moment we met that I was only here until the river receded. I am still *only* here until the river recedes and then, when it does, feelings or not, I'm leaving."

Claire looked over at me sadly and then looked down into her still half-empty glass of water.

"I think both he and I knew this, but it doesn't mean we weren't hoping. I've never met someone who fits with us so well and so quickly as you have, Aiden. I think you and Devin could have a good chance with love if circumstances were just a little different."

I stood up, refilled my water at her faucet and came back to the table. "Let's talk about something else. I'm still woozy and these serious thoughts are making my head throb again."

Claire nodded and stood up to get some medicine for me to take. "Here, take these," she said, "this will help with that."

We carried on a conversation while I helped Claire with various chores throughout the house. We had some dry toast, unable to stomach anything with more substance.

Late in the afternoon, we heard Devin's ATV coming up the old lane. "He'll be coming to make amends," Claire said.

"Just like the old man used to do?" I asked.

Claire looked at me and shook her head, "No, the old man *never* apologized. He'd happily throw everything, everyone, away before he'd admit his wrongdoing. Devin did wrong, but don't ever confuse him with that old jerk. Devin is three times the better man than Jim."

I sighed, "But we are still going to give him hell, right?"

"You damned well better believe it," she said laughing.

"Aiden, why don't you go out back and grab that bucket we were using earlier for the flowers. I'd like to face Devin first by myself. If you could water the pansies in the back by the garden again, I'm sure by the time you are done, I'll have had my say."

I left as she'd asked. I heard Devin knock on the door as I went out, but I was unable to hear the conversation between the two. That was for the best, I thought. It was a conversation that belonged between them. She needed to stand up for herself, and he needed to make amends. The two loved each other like family—hell, they were family, and this needed mending before it became a real issue.

I re-watered the pansies as Claire had asked me to, then I turned the bucket over and sat on it, staring out over the pretty pasture that was framed so well by Claire's flowers. I was just thinking I'd love to have my paints to capture this view when Devin walked out of the back door and sat on the ground next to me.

Devin

I heard the truck start as Aiden left for Claire's place. I put my head into my hands and allowed myself to cry. Even the mix of no sleep, a small hangover, and feeling like I was losing the only man I'd ever loved didn't excuse my outburst. The old man's bad attitude must have rubbed off on me.

I went about the chores for the day feeling more and more like the ass I'd displayed earlier in the day. I knew the two of them needed time and space and I didn't want to interrupt that. I'd done enough already.

I felt miserable and I knew if I didn't make amends, I could lose them both. So, after I finished the chores, which took most of the day, I got to the real work.

I went to the refrigerator and pulled out the ingredients to one of Claire's recipes she had taught me in the past. I threw the ingredients together and popped it into the oven. I knew as I did so, this would, from this point on, be the meal I think of as the apology casserole. While the casserole was cooking, I headed upstairs for a shower.

When I came down, the casserole was just finishing. I pulled it out of the oven and put it in the case Claire used to keep food warm when we were working out on the ranch and couldn't get back in time to eat.

I sighed as I got into the ATV and started the engine. Time to go eat crow ...

When I came in, Claire was sitting at the kitchen table by herself. "Before you ask, he is out back watering some flowers for me. You can talk to him after I've had my say."

I just nodded and sat down across from her. Claire stared at me for a long moment, then said, "You are like family to me, Devin, and you already know that. There isn't much I wouldn't do for you, but let's get this straight once and for all. I'll not be living with another man like Jim. If you want to become him, you'll be doing that without me."

She waited until I looked at her and nodded.

"Claire, I didn't mean to snap like that ... I would never..."

Claire stopped me mid-sentence, "I know you reacted because you are afraid of losing him." She pointed her thumb toward the back of the house. "But you all but drove him off today. I suspect you know that, too."

Again, I nodded but didn't look her in the eye.

"Let me give you a little advice—if you love him, tell him. He won't admit it, but I think he feels the same. Of course, you have to give him a reason to stay, not a reason to leave, do you understand?"

I nodded and she stood up, came over and kissed me on top of my head. "Damn, you are such a lug nut! Now go out there and make this right with him. Prepare to do some major groveling if you have to!"

I stood up and let her hug me. We held each other for a long time which went a lot further than my verbal apology had.

I walked out to Aiden and sat on the ground next to him.

"Did she tell you, you were just like Jim the old rancher?" Aiden asked.

"Yeah, she did, and she was right. I acted just like him," I replied.

"Good, then you have a good picture of what I saw today. I don't like you a whole lot right now, Devin. I don't usually feel a need for violence, but I really wanted to punch out your lights—not just because you yelled at her, but because I saw the look on her face. That look was one of betrayal. I never wanted to hurt someone as much as I did when I saw that look, Devin."

"You'd have been in your rights to beat me with a two-by-four."

"I'm not going to disagree with you, but I think you feeling the way you do right now, is better than any beating I could give you."

"You'd be right about that, too," I whispered. "So, do you think you'll ever forgive me?"

Aiden sat for a very long time looking out into the distance before he spoke. "It isn't for me to forgive. You need to square things with Claire, then you need to resolve to never let yourself treat her, or anyone for that matter, like that ever again."

Then Aiden turned to me and looked me square in the eye. "I have amazing memories from these past few days, I have come to love this place and Claire and I even feel very strongly about you, but you have to live with the fact that I'll also never forget seeing you attack that wonderful person in there just because you were upset about circumstances between you and me. It doesn't take away how I've come to feel about you, but it does cloud my opinion of you and makes me question whether I have misjudged your character somehow." Aiden turned back away from me and returned his gaze back to the picturesque scene before him.

"I think I feel the same way," I said. "I'm questioning my own character at the moment. I can promise you this, if I'm ever in the situation where I'd take my frustration out on her or anyone else that I care for again, I'll remove myself from the situation before it happens. I've never taken my anger out on someone I've loved, at least not since I've been grown up. And I'll never allow it to happen again."

Aiden didn't look back at me, but said, "I can believe you are telling the truth about that Devin and I am glad to hear you say it."

We sat just as we were for a long time. Finally, I said, "If you're hungry, I brought supper. I figured it was the least I could do to make up for my actions."

Aiden

I nodded and stood up without looking at Devin and headed back toward the house. When we walked in, we saw that Claire had set her table. Devin had baked some kind of casserole. Despite myself, I was impressed and looking at Claire, I saw a glint of pride in her eyes as well.

Claire looked back at me with a smile and said, "At least our boy knows how to grovel."

Pointing a thumb at Devin, I replied, "With that temper, that is a good trait to have."

We all sat down at Claire's table and after the awkward silence finally passed, we slowly began to enjoy our evening although there were still very distinct walls between us.

When we were done eating, Claire sent us both back to the house saying, "The sky looks like rain again and since Aiden doesn't know the terrain very well, it's best that he gets the truck back before the rain hits."

I kissed Claire's cheek before I left, then went out and started the truck to head back before Devin.

Devin

I waited and when Aiden was gone, I asked, "Are we okay?"

"Yeah, we're okay," Claire replied.

"Are *you* okay?" she asked.

"No, not really. When I should have been doing everything in my power to get that man to stay, I fucked up worse than I ever have, and like the old man, pushed both you and him away. I don't know how to take that back."

Shaking her head, she said, "You don't. But you took a lot of good steps forward today when you took responsibility for your actions and made amends with this meal you brought. We all make mistakes, Devin. It is only the strongest of us who can admit those mistakes and try to make things right. You did that, and I believe that registered with him," then she looked in the direction Aiden had left.

"What should I do now?" I asked.

"Let him have his space," she said. "He'll let you know when he's ready to give you another chance."

Then Claire smiled at me and kissed me on the cheek in a way that reminded me of when my mother would pat my head when I'd learned a difficult lesson.

"Thank you, Claire, you know I love you, right?"

"I do," she said and then shooed me out the door.

Aiden

I beat Devin back and went into the main house to collect the things I'd left in Devin's bedroom. I decided during the day with Claire that I'd not be spending the night with him tonight. Too much had happened, and I wanted to have the evening to myself. I grabbed my toothbrush and an extra towel and washcloth off the shelf and walked back to the apartment.

I closed the door behind me just as the rain came pouring down. I hoped Devin would get back before the road became impossible to drive down. Then I was surprised at how fast I'd started worrying about when or how Devin would get home. The rain was surely going to swell the river once again. Damn, I didn't appear to be going anywhere, anytime soon. I put my things on the small table and peered through the door at the rain just as the lights to Devin's ATV pulled into the lane in front of the house. I sighed with relief despite myself. This was really becoming more difficult by the day.

PART THREE
THE
COMMITMENT

Devin

I got out of the truck, looked toward the stables and could see the light on in the apartment, so I'd assumed correctly that Aiden would already be there when I got home. I wanted to go to him, but as Claire had instructed, I knew Aiden needed space; maybe I did too. So, I went into the house, poured myself three fingers of Jack and downed it. I climbed the stairs and went to bed. I knew bed would be useless—despite being exhausted, it was unlikely I'd get any sleep, but I didn't know what else to do.

I lay in bed all night listening to the pounding rain and pondering what I'd say to Aiden that might heal the wounds between us.

As dawn broke, I groggily began dressing and preparing to speak to Aiden. I had rehearsed my speech over and over hoping it would make a difference. My intention was to start with another apology, then reiterate what I'd already promised about never verbally attacking my loved ones again then I'd fling myself at his mercy, lie prostrate if I had to.

I was just pulling my shirt on when I became distracted by a noise ... At first, I didn't recognize the sound; however, as the helicopter got closer, I recognized it for what it was and wondered why the hell it was flying over my property.

I quickly finished dressing and came downstairs then stepped out the front door. The helicopter had begun its descent over the front paddock like it was going to land. Much to my surprise, it did land, and two women and a man jumped out and slogged through the muddy pasture and toward my front door.

The noise of the helicopter was so loud I didn't hear Aiden's voice until he was close enough to me that we were almost touching.

I heard Aiden say, "Mom, Suzie ... *dad*?

Then all four of them ran to each other and embraced. I could hear Aiden's mom tell Suzie to go tell the pilot to power down that they had found Aiden. Then I heard Aiden's mom chastise him for not calling them.

"We were all worried sick," she said.

Then she looked over at me and with both an expression of exasperation and appreciation leaned over to her son and loudly said, "But I can see what held you up."

Aiden looked over at me, but no humor crossed his face. "No, mom it isn't what you think. If..." I could tell Aiden was having a hard time figuring out what to call me, then settled with my formal name. "If Mr. Pierce doesn't mind, I'll fill you in."

Aiden's formality hit me squarely in the gut, and the impact didn't go unnoticed by Aiden's parents who looked at each other quizzically. I knew the way I was looking at their son clearly indicated that something more than formal acquaintance had occurred between us. I was amused when the look they exchanged held the decision not to question their son about it—at least not yet.

I finally regained my senses and invited the rescue party into the house. "I've just gotten up so I'm afraid I don't have anything prepared for breakfast but ..."

At this, Aiden's mom interjected. "Mr. ..."

"Devin, just call me Devin," I said.

"Devin," she continued, "if you'll trust me in your kitchen, I'll throw together some breakfast and make some coffee, if you have any. That will give you a chance to recover from Aiden's family showing up on your property all at once."

Aiden stared at his mom for a moment, then asked, "Where ... why are you here?"

"Because, honey, the last thing we heard was that you were going to traipse across the country to meet a man who could be a serial killer ..." Blushing, she turned to me and said, "Sorry about that."

I couldn't help but blush a little myself. "No, don't be. I'd have worried about the same thing," I said.

She continued, "Then you drop off the earth. I can see the man is handsome," then under her breath, "and built, but you couldn't pick up the phone?"

I took up Aiden's cause, feeling a bit sorry for him, considering it really wasn't his fault.

"Actually, no, he really couldn't. Our phones are out, which means our internet is out and since my mobile only works through the Wi-Fi, that was out, too. Unfortunately, your poor son was stuck here with me unable to communicate with the outside world."

Aiden's mom turned her gaze toward me and looked me up then down.

Aiden

Seeing Devin was about to get the wrath of my mother, I grabbed my mom's arm and turned her toward me. "Mom, the flood waters covered the bridge right after I got across and then my Miata got stuck."

Then it was my dad's turn, "Why the hell did you drive a damned Miata all the way out here?"

I huffed, "Because dad, the rental company didn't have the 4-wheel drive I had reserved. The Miata was all they had left. I thought I'd run in, deliver my card, then, be out by nightfall. Fate had a different idea."

My parents looked at each other in that well-rehearsed way that assessed whether they both believed me. Luckily, I saw the look that said they did, although they thought it was unlikely.

"Well, you'll need to get in touch with that rental company as soon as possible because they contacted us asking if we'd seen you, the car was supposed to have been returned two days ago." my dad said.

Just then the door flew open and Suzie walked in, clearly angry enough to fight. Although Suzie was shorter than me she was a force to be reckoned with when mad.

"Why the hell didn't you get in touch with us? We had to fly halfway across the country chasing your ass and come to find out you're laid up with some Italian looking...hunk." she gestured angrily at Devin and continued her tirade.

"You scared the hell out of me and not to mention our parents and even Margie—who, I might add, is in Spokane waiting to hear if you are alive or dead." I was more than used to being on the receiving end of Suzie's rants, so I waited for the fire to die down before explaining to her the same story I'd just relayed to my parents.

Suzie, not all the fire out of her yet, turned to Devin and said, "What about the...hunky piece of meat over here? Is he a serial killer or what?"

I burst out laughing for the first time since Devin yelled at Claire the day before, "He's an ass, but there's no indication he's a killer."

Devin turned narrowed eyes at me and said, "Let *me* introduce myself. I'm Devin Pierce. I found your brother wandering alone down a desolate road half frozen. So, I may be an ass, but at least I got him into a warm bed before he froze."

At that, the entire room looked at Devin just as he realized what he had said, "No, not like that."

Laughing, and feeling sorry for Devin for the first time, my mother took the heat off him before he could say anything to make the situation more embarrassing.

"Aiden, you and Mr. Pierce go out and talk. I can see you need to. Suzie, you and Bob stay here and help me with breakfast." As usual, my mother was now in charge, so Devin stepped out of the house with me following behind him and we walked toward the stable.

"Aiden," Devin began, "I didn't mean to hurt you ... I..."

I put up a hand and interrupted Devin before he could go on. "You did, and you hurt Claire, but we've said all there is to say about that. I'd already decided we needed to put the skids on before my parents showed up. Not because of yesterday, but because we don't really have a future and pretending like there was would only lead to problems. I'm sorry we fought, but I'm not sorry I met you."

At this, I reached up and gave Devin a gentle kiss. "No matter what happens, I will always be grateful to you for joining *CMTOCM* and I'll never forget the time we spent together. You made me feel things I didn't know I could feel—that will always be with me. Besides, I think I might be crazy in love with your housekeeper...and your horse."   This made Devin smile although it didn't quite reach his eyes.

"Follow me," I commanded and walked into the apartment.   I rushed upstairs and was back down moments later with my carry-on bag in my hand. I unzipped it, pulled a card out, and handed it to him.

"This is the card I wrote to you before I met you. I had second thoughts about giving it to you after we met, then second thoughts for different reasons after we made love, but now it seems appropriate again."

I broke away, then left the apartment and walked toward the house with Devin following behind me. Devin put the unopened card on his entry table then went into the kitchen to join the rest of us. As usual, my mom had turned Devin's kitchen into a gourmet one and the breakfast we ate was delicious.

When Devin bragged on it, all three of us, as well as the pilot, nodded in agreement. "Don't tell Claire, or you'll be in trouble for cheating on her," I smirked.

Devin smiled and the rest of the party looked confused.

"Who is Claire?" My mother asked.

"She's Devin's fiery housekeeper and he's already in the doghouse with her."

Devin once again looked at me with narrowed eyes. "She has never minded if someone was willing to take the cooking chore away from her. I doubt she'll give me much grief about this, but she will be after me with a hot poker if you leave without saying goodbye though."

"I agree, when do you think she'll be here?"

"I doubt she'll come considering the rain. That's her way of punishing me for not putting gravel down. Guess I'll be doing that sooner than later now."

"I guess so," I agreed, smiling at Devin's uncomfortable situation.

I patted Devin's hand and said, "I'll try to get the pilot to do a quick flyover and wave at her as we go by. That is about all we'll be able to do."

Devin nodded but said, "It won't be enough, she won't ever forgive me for letting you go..." he hesitated long enough to garner some interesting looks from the group, then finished his statement, "without saying goodbye."

When we finished eating, Suzie and my father refused to leave before finishing the dishes and cleaning up the kitchen. "We've had a lot of training, young man," was dad's response when Devin told him to leave it. "I don't think I could leave a dirty kitchen if my life depended on it." At that statement, mom chuckled.

The dishes were cleaned and placed in the drainer; I told Devin that I'd send a tow truck to pick up the Miata once the river receded. My parents, as well as Suzie, thanked him for rescuing me and I rolled my eyes. Although, they would never know how lucky I was that he did.

As the helicopter lifted into the sky and the scenery disappeared from view, I thought of how the view would normally cause me to want to paint—to capture the images. Instead, leaving this place, even after only being here a few days, caused something inside me to wither away.

Devin

I almost wished the kitchen was dirty because I couldn't think of what to do with my hands. In less than a week, this amazing man had come into my life, turned it upside down, and then left me to pick up the broken pieces of my heart. He literally flew away in a helicopter. I wondered if it wasn't a strange, devastating dream.

As I walked toward the door, I realized that Aiden had left the painting. The helicopter was long gone. I glanced over at the card and almost opened it, but my heart was too broken to look it just now. Instead, I went outside to work and hopefully get my mind off of the irretrievable, missing pieces of my heart.

Aiden

My return to civilization was anti-climactic. After we got back to Kansas City, I decided to spend some time with my parents before we all went to Paris for the showing. I had over a month to waste, so I decided I'd divide my time between Steve's parent's farm, my friends in Kansas City and my parents.

Jace was busy in New York getting the paintings sent off to the Louvre. My sister, although completely intrigued by my experiences in the mountains of eastern Washington, must have recognized the pain when she had asked me about it. Even though it was completely out of character, she let the subject lie and didn't press me on it.

Unfortunately, nothing lifted my spirits. The animals on the farm reminded me of the ranch which reminded me of Devin. My friends, as usual, were trying to fix me up and even tricked me into a blind date before I knew what they were up to. But, all guys paled in comparison to Devin and I left the dates more depressed than ever. After that, I avoided my friends altogether.

Of course, the exception of that was Margie, who would never tolerate me being in town without spending copious amounts of time with her. It was on one of our visits that Margie cornered me and insisted I spill the beans.

"I've given you plenty of space and now you need to come clean. What was the cowboy like, what happened while you were stranded together and why are you so damned depressed all the time?"

Knowing Margie would never be brushed off, I surrendered to her questions and answered them as best as I could.

When I finished telling the story, she looked at me and said, "That still doesn't explain why you are so damned depressed now, does it?"

"No, but the fact that I was in love with the jackass sure does." I blurted that out before I realized that was how I was feeling.

When had I realized I'd fallen in love? Before my parents had arrived or after we got back home? I wasn't sure, but I knew that since I'd been back, the world had taken on a shade of grey that I hadn't been able to shake. Colors lost their vibrancy and my paintings, the few I attempted, were grey and black and utterly depressing.

"So, you fell in love then," she asked.

"I don't know, Margie. Can you fall in love with someone in a few days?"

Margie sighed, looked at me and replied, "If it had only been the sex, I'd have told you no, it was only infatuation and you just needed to move on, but I've never seen you like this, Aiden. You are literally turning blue," she said, pointing at a slightly blue paint splatter on my arm I'd missed while cleaning up before coming to visit Margie. I chuckled halfheartedly.

"Margie, this guy made it clear there was no future for us. Now, I find out I'm in love with him. What am I supposed to do?"

"Baby, I've been in love several times and there is nothing to do except go on. You will always feel that stab of pain when you think of him, but trust me, eventually you'll be able to function without the pain overwhelming you."

I accepted the hug she offered and let my tears fall on her back.

Margie pulled away and looked me in the eye and said, "You know, I was one of the first female CEOs in the country. To say I had difficulty with men is an understatement, and hell, my social life was no good anyway considering the hours I put in. When I finally wised up and realized that life was too short to be working away at something that didn't fulfill me, I sold the business and focused on my love of art.

What I'm telling you dear one, is you have to figure out what is important to you then go after it. For me it was art but if for you it's this cowboy, then you have to go after him. Don't let anything stand in your way."

I shrugged and said, "It isn't that easy Margie. He lives thousands of miles away, we are so different."

Margie just chuckled, "Who are you trying to convince, Aiden? Aren't you the one who signed up for that website to begin with?" She stood up, grabbed our tea cups and started toward the kitchen. Before she got very far, she turned around and said:

"I've known you most of your life, Aiden Fisher, and the truth is you're scared, and it isn't like you to let fear keep you from going after your dreams." Margie turned to walk back to the kitchen and asked over her shoulder, "So why the hell are you starting now?"

I stared at the coffee table and said out loud, but mostly to myself, "You're probably right."

I should've known the woman would hear me. She responded, "Honey, of course I'm right. Now, let's go over to the Nelson's restaurant for lunch. My treat."

Devin

I didn't need anyone to tell me I'd turned from an asshole to a dragon. At one point, Claire told me if I snapped at her again, she was going to "cut my balls off and fry them." That woman had such a way with words!

My workers all avoided me like the plague and their avoidance had already caused more than one catastrophe. I was either going to have to figure this whole thing out or I was going to become like the asshole previous owner.

After a particularly difficult afternoon with a cow that was losing her calf, a horse who had thrown a shoe and various other incidents where I had yelled at the hands, Claire met me at the door with the card from Aiden in hand.

"I'm not sure what this is, but I'm guessing you'd better read it before your entire crew quits you. At this point, it would be less stressful working in a shipyard hauling shit," she said.

I grumbled at her, but she didn't even blink—no surprise, since she had survived way worse with the old man. I took the card from her and went up to my room, slamming the door like a teenager. God, even I knew I was acting like a child.

I threw the card on the bed, undressed, threw my clothes across the room and went into the shower. Of course, since Aiden, I couldn't take a shower without thinking of those beautiful hands wrapped around my waist; so where a shower should have made things better, it, in fact, made it worse.

I finished off the shower, toweled off, threw my towel on the floor, fully intending for that to piss Claire off, and sat on his bed. I picked up the damned card and tore off the envelope...then hesitantly, I opened it.

Inside was one sentence, "Thank you for the inspiration."

Aiden had drawn an intricate design with a vine twining around the words. In the vines, I saw birds, wildflowers, a deer and various other creatures. The longer I looked at the vines, the more they looked alive and the more details I saw hidden in crevices and spaces you would miss if you just glanced at it.

I had seen trendy art pieces with Irish inspired vines around words, but this was something different, something more—this was Aiden's sincere appreciation for the inspiration given. It was clear the card wasn't done quickly or without thought. Aiden had poured his soul into it, much as he had the painting still sitting on the side table where he'd left it.

I put my head into my hands and let the tears flow.

By the time I came down the stairs, Claire was standing at the front door preparing to leave.

"Well," she huffed, "Did you read it?"

"Yeah," I responded, "I read it."

"So," she asked with frustration, "What did it say?"

"See for yourself," I said and thrust the card into her hand.

"Oh my," was her reaction. "That boy has a natural talent, huh? I'm guessing the painting over there is his, too."

"Yeah, and it wasn't supposed to be here. Aiden left it in his rush to leave."

"So, I would be guessing you need to return that painting, then, right?"

"Sure, I guess," I responded not taking her hint.

This time, the older woman stepped over to me, took my hands and looked me in the eye. "Child," she began, "I liked him, too. He is your soulmate. I'm guessing he misses you as much as you miss him, besides, you have been in the worst temper I've ever seen in a man...well, since the old man died."

She hesitated for a moment until I met her eyes, "That old man, he died of a broken heart. He died knowing he'd pushed everyone he'd ever loved away. Take my word on this one, don't make his same mistakes."

She turned away from me, went to the side table, picked up the painting and brought it to me, "You need to *return this in person!*"

My eyes must have lit up with recognition of what she was insinuating because Claire smiled and nodded in the way she tended to do when she knew she had made her point.

As she left, she said over her shoulder, "I've already told that lot," pointing toward the stables, "that you're going to be gone for a week or so. Not that any of them said they'd miss you." She chuckled to herself as she got into the old pickup and left without another word.

Claire's words echoed in my mind long after she had left. I went outside and sat down on the swing. Unfortunately, even the old swing, no, especially the old swing, brought back memories of Aiden and I'd be damned if I was no longer able to separate this old swing that I'd sat on a thousand times before Aiden arrived from my feelings for him.

I looked over at the apartment entrance, the stables, back in the house at the ugly couch, that I'd never thought ugly before, then into my kitchen and all I could see was Aiden. Somehow, that man had seeped into every crevice of my life and he'd done so in less than a week.

I wanted to get up and turn my life back to before the flood, but then again, I knew there would never be another Aiden for me. I feared Claire had been correct. If I didn't act now, I would grow to be just like the old man—grouchy and angry with the world, letting no one in, alienating everyone, especially those closest to me.

I took the card and put it in the place of Aiden's painting on the side table. I knew that would be its space and I knew I had to return the painting to Aiden...because I needed to see him. I needed to know if there was any way we could have a future together. And when I wanted something, I damned well knew how to fight for it!

So, with a willful purpose, I bought a ticket to New York, did a Google search for Aiden's studio and packed my bags. It was my turn to go on a quest, I chuckled to myself. It was my turn to put everything on the line for Aiden.

Aiden

I decided to fly home to New York and get loose ends tied up with Jace before the exhibition. Suzie met me at the terminal and grabbed me into a big hug.

She pulled back and said, "I'm so glad to see you, little brother," then grabbed me into the hug again.

"Thanks Suzie," I said.

Suzie took one look at me and sighed. "Oh no, Aiden, are you still mooning over that hunky cowboy?"

"Not the time to talk about that, Suzie," I said, looking around the terminal.

She laughed out loud, causing several people to look our way. I missed her so much and she could read me like a book. Maybe I should have come back sooner. Suzie always seemed to know how to make me feel better.

"Okay, point taken," she admitted.

"Let me get you out of here and we'll go to Vinnie's for dinner. Nothing like a little heart burn to take the edge off." She said and laughed out loud again.

I knew better than to argue, and I didn't want to anyway, I needed the kind of comfort only Suzie could give. Once again, I thought I should've sought her out sooner.

Suzie accompanied me to my apartment where I dropped off my crap, then we headed over to Vinnie's.

As usual, there were several open tables at the little dive we frequented, and we had no trouble finding one in a secluded corner where we could talk.

The waitress, long accustomed to our orders, brought me a sweet tea, and a lemonade to Suzie unbidden. I smiled and asked her how she'd been. The older lady didn't bother to smile and said all was still the same since last she'd seen me.

As soon as she left, Suzie reached over and grabbed my hand. "Okay, I should've made you talk before I left Kansas City. So now spill, I want to know all about it," she demanded.

I just sighed. "Suzie, there isn't much to tell. I met him, we had mind blowing sex. I tried every way I could not to have feelings for him then I lost my fucking head and now I think I might be in love...if that's possible in such a short time."

Suzie always had advice, and she always tells you her opinion even if you don't want it, so I was shocked when she just sat back and lowered her head.

"What's up?" I asked, stunned.

Suzie looked up and a tear slipped out of her eye and down her face. "I could tell you were in love when we were there," she admitted. "I didn't want to admit it to myself because the thought of you moving to the other side of the country made my stomach hurt."

I was still in shock because as loud and in your face as Suzie could be with her opinions, she was a rock emotionally. I was the one to cry on her shoulder, and I fully expected to get a lecture one way or another, but I didn't expect her to have emotions about me leaving.

"Suzie, I didn't say I was leaving or going to go chase him or anything like that, I'm just trying to figure out how to get over him."

"Get over him?" she all but yelled. "Why the hell are you trying to get over him?" she asked incredulously.

"Suzie, you just said it—he's on the other side of the country. We don't have anything in common. Why wouldn't I need to get over him?"

"Because you are in love, stupid!" she said. "Besides, this is my time to be mad at you for leaving. I'm not supposed to have to convince you to go after him. Damn it, Aiden, you are supposed to have enough sense to figure that out on your own."

Suzie got up and stomped away toward the bathroom.

"Okay," I said to myself shocked, but then remembered that my sister was the biggest drama queen I knew, so I just smiled and shook my head.

When she came back, she sat down and looked me in the eye. "Okay, Aiden Fisher, I'm going to say this one time, and then we'll get back to *my* well-deserved, self-pity. You are head over heels in love with that rancher dude. Any fool could see that— even a clueless queen like you. If you throw away the chance of finding true love, I'll never forgive you, Aiden. You are the sibling that is supposed to find true love and live happily ever after, making grandkids and all that shit. If nothing else, you owe it to mom and dad!"

If anyone else had said that to me, I'd have gaped at them. But Suzie, well, she was Suzie, and I could always depend on her to put things in perspective.

"Suzie, I knew him for less ... than ... a ... week ...," this time punctuating each word to get my point across. "I'm clearly out of my mind. How can I be in love with him?"

She just shook her head, and said, "I'm not going to buy your shit. Besides, as I already said, this is *my* pity party, not yours!"

I couldn't help but laugh, and the stone that had been sitting in my stomach since I'd left Washington began to dissipate.

"You are ridiculous, sister. Totally ridiculous," I said with a chuckle.

Suzie smiled back at me. "Yeah maybe, but you know I'm right."

"I don't know anything of the sort," I told her. "But, of all the people in my life, you are the only one I know that can make me feel guilty for not letting you feel bad about my life crisis."

"Someone has to help you keep things in perspective, and I'm thinking that is the older sister's responsibility. And besides," she said, with the arrogance of a skilled manipulator, "I'm really damned good at it!"

Suzie was a master at making the world feel better and helping me get out of my own head. No wonder she was such an amazing actress. She seemed to have a sixth-sense about what to say and when to say it.

To stop the argument -- which I would never win -- I said truthfully, "I'm so glad to see you, sis. Thanks for this!"

Suzie smiled at me, but the sadness had returned. "You are welcome, Aiden, so can we go to the bar to celebrate?"

I moaned and she laughed. I should have known she'd manipulate me into going to dance. I just shrugged and accepted the inevitable.

Thank god for my sister. She was one in a million...and thank god for that too!

Margie had booked us all in an exclusive hotel just across the Seine from the Louvre. She assured us all that the place had everything they needed, alleviating a lot of mom's fear of not speaking French in Paris.

She, Suzie and mom, had all taken a trip down to *Halls on the Plaza* to buy Paris-appropriate clothing, which was just an excuse for Margie to spoil my mother a little. They had become close over the years, but mom was a prideful woman and refused to let Margie spend money on her. That was the first time that Margie could convince Beth to let her buy a gown that would be appropriate for her baby's debut.

When the day finally came to board the flight, everyone was excited and ready for the adventure.

The flight attendant had just announced to shut down all electronics when I got a call from Jace. I quickly texted her and said I couldn't answer now but

I'd see her in Paris. Hoping there were no problems, I turned my phone to airplane mode and we were off.

The flight was bumpy and long. Mom was a bit afraid of flying, so Margie had convinced the passenger riding next to trade seats and she began plying Mom with Champagne. If I knew Margie, and I really did know Margie, mom would be well beyond drunk in less than an hour.

Dad eventually came over and took the empty seat next to me, and after stumbling over some nonsense conversation he finally got to the point he was working up to.

"Aiden, son," he began, "you know we love you. You also know we would never have you any other way than you are. You know that, right, son?"

Perplexed where this was going, I looked over at him and said, "Yeah, I know you are there for me."

"You also know you can't go through this life alone, right?"

"I'm not sure what you are getting at, dad," I replied.

"Well, to us, it don't matter if it is a man or a woman, but it does matter that you have someone, *some person* you can wake up next to every morning. I know not everyone needs or wants that, but, son, you aren't just someone—for you, that kind of relationship is important. That man ... Devin, was it? You seemed to have taken a shine to him."

Surprised that my dad would notice such things, I looked over at him and nodded. "So, why didn't you try to make it work with him?"

"Dad," almost in tears again, which I was determined to control, I responded, "I'm not sure it's really love."

With this news, Dad leaned back in his chair and looked ahead for a few moments. "Your mom was in love with another man when I met her. She would argue that wasn't true, but I know what I saw, and she loved him. He was no good. They broke up when he got another girl pregnant, but your mom's heart was still broken. I asked her out six months after they broke up and she refused me saying she wasn't ready to date.

I knew she was saying she wasn't ready to trust a man, but I already believed your mom was the one for me, so I told her, 'Beth, you take your time, but I'm going to ask you again in a few weeks.'

"She laughed, not believing that I would, but I did. I asked her out every month for eight whole months before she agreed to go out with me.

"I was so nervous the first date I spilled my drink all over myself at the theater and she laughed at me. Before I took her home that night, I asked her if she would consider another date even though I was a total klutz.

"Of course, she laughed at me again and confessed she didn't think she would ever date again. If I hadn't been so persistent, she doubted she would have, at least not for several years.

"The long story short here, Aiden, is that she did go out with me, but it took some work on both of our parts. For her, she had to get over her heartbreak, and for me, I had to be patient and kind. If I had pushed her, she would've never given me a chance. I saw how that boy looked at you." Dad looked away again and squirmed a bit in his seat before continuing, "It is hard to see someone look at your children that way, so you need to trust what I'm saying. He may have told you he isn't interested, but you take my word for it, he *is* interested!"

Dad patted my knee and stood up to go. I caught him before he did and asked, "Weren't you afraid she would laugh at you or tell you to get lost?"

"No, son," he smiled, "If she had done that, she wouldn't have been the person I knew her to be. I didn't spend that much time with your young man, but he seemed pretty well put together to me. He runs a large ranch, and from what little I saw, it appears his animals were well taken care of and his property also appeared to be well maintained. I'd be willing to go out on a limb and say that young man is a good one. But, that isn't for me to say. This is all your call. Your mama and I will love you whatever choice you make."

Dad left me with a lot to think about. Should I go after Devin? What if he didn't really want me? Hell, he did join an online dating app, -- even if he was drunk when he did it. Clearly, he was looking for something. We made love that couldn't be faked— not that kind of lovemaking. Sex was sex, but *that* was something more.

As I thought about things, I decided my father might be right. Maybe things weren't right between us now, but we could make them right in the future. My mind was made up. When I got to Paris, I'd sit down and write a postcard to Devin and ask him if he'd mind meeting me at Billie's diner for coffee.

Feeling freer than I'd felt since getting back from Devin's place, I fell asleep thinking about Devin and his beautiful, devilish smile. I could almost feel pieces of his heart mending just at the thought that maybe with time and patience I'd coerce that man into considering a relationship even if it was only friendship.

Devin

When I arrived in New York, it was like hell had descended on my head. Even growing up in Seattle did nothing to prepare me for the insanity that was New York City.

Despite this, I was determined to make amends with Aiden. If I had to move to this hellish place, so be it. Nothing was going to stop me now.

I had downloaded the information about Aiden's exhibition and studio from the web before leaving the ranch. Thank god for that because I would've never figured out how to find him otherwise.

With luggage in hand, I went to the studio first thing. I waltzed into the studio and asked how to reach Aiden Fisher.

The woman that sat at the entry table was naturally unwilling to give me any information. I'm sure I looked like a wild man and it was clear I wasn't from here, so she was certainly right not to give information to me, but I was desperate.

I all but fell into the chair sitting across from her table and buried my head in my hands.

"Sir," she commented. I could hear the panic in her voice. "Are you okay? Do I need to call someone for you?"

"Yeah," I responded, "Call Aiden. Tell him I'm a total idiot and that I would trade everything I own if he'd just give me another chance."

The woman sucked in a breath and asked in a whisper, "Are you the rancher?"

I looked up at the woman, hope filling me for the first time since landing. "Yeah, yes...I'm him. Did he tell you about me?"

The woman, I noticed for the first time, was probably either a high school student or at best a first-year university student, and she flushed like she'd just disclosed a big company secret.

"Um...no," she said. "But it is such a romantic story." The blush deepened as she looked down at her hands.

"Please," I pleaded then, "I fucked up so much when I let him go. I just need to speak to him, beg him..."

I couldn't finish my statement. I could feel tears behind my eyes, and it wouldn't do to lose it, not yet...not until I had Aiden in front of me.

The young woman sighed. "Aiden is already gone," she said. "He left for the airport. His showing in Paris is this week."

"Oh," I said, realization hitting me for the first time. "Damn, I forgot about that," I said.

"You know," I said looking directly at the young woman, "I have a personal invitation to attend that showing. I just need details so I can make it."

There were several emotions that crossed the young woman's face. Luckily, her romantic side apparently won because she turned to the computer sitting next to her, typed a few things and then printed something.

When she came back, she said, "This is Aiden's itinerary while in Paris." She sighed again and said, "This is probably going to get me fired, so if you reconnect, you have to promise to give me credit when you write your memoirs or name your first kid after me or something." Then she sighed again and smiled.

I grabbed the paper from her hand and pulled her across the table into an awkward hug.

"Thank you, thank you!" I all but cried as I ran out of the gallery's front door.

I pulled the app for airline travel up on my phone, found the next trip to Paris and booked it. Thank god, I remembered to bring my passport.

I hailed a taxi and had him drop me off at a men's clothing store on the way to the airport, bought clothes that would be appropriate for the trip, as well as a tux, confident that at the very least, Aiden wouldn't renege on his offer to let me come to the opening.

I made it to the airport and got through security just in time for my flight to be called. I thanked whatever gods were listening that my luck had held out.

Now, how the heck was I going to explain all this to Aiden? I prayed my luck would hold out there as well, because now that I'd started this journey, I couldn't imagine it ending without Aiden in my life, in one way or another.

Aiden

I didn't wake up until the plane hit the tarmac. Once again, my memories turned to the trip to Spokane and I smiled with the similarities of how the two adventures began. I stretched, trying to undo some of the knots my body had acquired while sleeping on a redeye trip to Europe. As we exited the aircraft, all of us gathered together chatting happily, but with travel-weary excitement.

Margie took the lead and the group followed her to the baggage pickup site of the airport. Within half an hour of our arrival, our luggage was picked up and we were all sitting in a limousine—courtesy of the Louvre. The driver took us to their hotel and dropped us off into the hands of a waiting bellboy.

We hugged each other and turned to go to our respective rooms, excited about the upcoming Parisian adventures. As we turned to leave, I heard someone calling my name—first, kind of quiet, then louder. I turned toward the entrance and was surprised to see Devin being forcefully restrained by two bellhops.

"Wait, wait!" I cried out at them before they could haul him out of the entrance.

When I got to the door and assured the bellhops that Devin was with me, they still looked hesitant. "I'm sorry, sir, but this man fits the description of someone we were warned not to let pass."

"Well, it isn't this guy because I invited him to meet me. It must be someone else."

When the bellhops relented, and we were away from them, I turned to Devin with a perplexed look and asked why he was here.

"Because you invited me...didn't you?"

I stared at Devin for a few moments then nodded my head. "Yeah, I ... I did."

Smiling, Devin reached in his carry on and handed me the painting. "My housekeeper told me I needed to return this."

I stared down at the painting and for the first time seeing that I had forgotten the poor painting once again, I began to laugh.

"Remind me to give Claire a big sloppy kiss"

"Listen, Aiden," Devin added, this time more serious, "she also reminded me that when someone comes into your life that makes an impact like you did with me, you don't just let them go, at least not without some effort to see if you are right for each other. Aiden, I'd like that chance."

I was speechless. Just a few hours ago, I'd come to the same conclusion and now this man...this handsome, sensual, beautifully rugged man was here, standing there right in front of me. Without thinking, without responding, I grabbed Devin's face in my hands and kissed him long and hard right in the middle of the lobby.

"God, I love Claire!" I said and Devin's eyebrow cocked in confusion.

I chuckled at the look that crossed his face, "I love her because she is right, when you find what we found with each other, you don't let it go." I looked over at the small group standing at the back of the room and smiled. "It took all of them to get me to realize that very same thing."

The group was staring at us, mesmerized by the events taking place in front of them.

"I guess you better come with me and meet the gang. Where are you staying?" I asked.

"I'm not sure yet. I rushed to your studio in New York only to be told that you were already here in Paris, so, I played on the romantic side of the woman at the front desk of the studio to find out where you were. She gave me this address. I've only been in Paris an hour at the most. I took a taxi here and saw you standing in the lobby and, amazed at my luck, I jumped out to speak to you. The rest you know. I'll have to figure out the rest now that I'm here."

I smiled, looked up at Devin and said, "I have a good recommendation for a hotel room. Only thing is you'll have to share the accommodations."

Understanding what I was hinting at, he responded, "I think we can make that work."

By the time we reached the entourage, the entire group was beaming. Everyone started talking at once. Finally, Margie stepped up and took Devin's hand in hers, and in her eloquent aristocratic way said, "My name is Margie and I can speak for all of us here when I say it is exquisite that you are here!"

I felt my eyebrows go up automatically as the entire group laughed, then took turns introducing or reacquainting themselves with Devin.

Eventually, exhaustion overtook the group and again we parted for our respective rooms. Devin and I were in a luxury suite located on the 4th floor, with a balcony that looked out over the Seine and Louvre.

Devin came up behind me as I was looking out at the scenery and put his arms around me. I lay back enjoying the feeling of being in his arms once again, then after a moment of pure happiness, I turned to face him.

"Why did you come, Devin?"

"Because I'm in love with you." The words hung between us for seconds before Devin added, "And because my staff was threatening mutiny if I didn't stop verbally attacking them. I have plenty to apologize for when I get back."

I looked at Devin with a perplexed look. Devin continued sheepishly, "I have been a bitter ass since you left, Aiden. I don't know how you did it, but you somehow left an impression of yourself in every aspect of my life. When you left, it felt like a chunk of my heart had been removed. It took me weeks to realize that I was angry—not at you or my staff—but that I was angry with myself. I was angry I let you go. At first, I refused to believe I could be so completely taken with you after only a few short days, but I've dated a lot of men and I've never felt like this before."

Turning away from me and resting his back against the balcony's railing, he began to fidget with his cuticles, "I realize you may not feel the same way, hell, I know this is nuts, but if you'll give us a chance, I'd like to see if maybe there is a future for us, together."

I was watching Devin with intensity, "You are sure about this then?" I asked.

"I am sure I want a chance."

"Where would we live, Devin, your ranch? ... my tiny apartment?" Even as I spoke, I could see the sunny room, the warm stables, and rolling hills of his ranch.

Devin shook his head. "Aiden, I don't have an answer. My ranch has become a part of me. It is the first place I felt like I belonged. Being able to touch the animals, ride the horses, everything needing me to tend to them, to make sure things are right for them, all that keeps my soul's light burning. But, the old man before me taught me that a ranch isn't enough without love. You lit the match in my heart, a place I didn't even know was missing the light. I realized, with Claire's help of course, that you were what the old man was missing. If he'd let someone like you into his life, he'd never have become the closed-off block of concrete he was when he died." Devin let his face fall as he said, "So, if I have to choose between the ranch and you, Aiden, I choose you."

I was taken aback. I went to Devin and put my hands to his face feeling the day-old scruff under them. "My heart already belongs to you and it would destroy me to see you lose the part that fills your soul with happiness. I will never ask you to give up the ranch, in fact, I had already decided before I met you that I was leaving New York, but I hadn't decided where I was going yet. It appears that I may be headed further west than I anticipated."

Devin grabbed me into his arms and kissed me passionately. "I will make you happy, Aiden! I will also make you mad and I'll drive you crazy, but I will love you with all my heart for all my life." The warning bells that should have been ringing, saying we were moving too fast, weren't working properly. We both knew we'd found a match in each other and with our locked expressions, we admitted that although this all seemed surreal it also felt very natural.

We fell asleep curled up in each other's arms, both too exhausted from our long travels to do more than reassure the other that our love was real and solid.

When we woke the next morning, we could hear the Paris traffic below us. We lay in each other's arms just stroking and touching one another, comforted by the other's presence. Finally, close to ten am Paris time, the phone rang. Knowing who would be on the other line, I answered, *"Bon jour. Margie. En quoi puis-je vous servir?"* Despite hearing the French and knowing she was being teased, she responded,

"You and the Roman god have exactly thirty minutes to meet us here for brunch if you plan to eat. Then, we need to head over to the museum. In case you forgot why we are here, my love."

Giggling, I responded, "The god and I are just getting ready. We'll see you in half an hour."

I hung up with Margie, swung my leg over Devin and, while rubbing my dick on his, I kissed him lightly on the cheek. "Margie says we gotta get ready."

"Hmm, it feels like you are ready enough now, let's hit the shower and see how quick we can be."

Devin flipped me over and kissed my neck while letting his dick slide over my ass. "You tease like that and we won't be making it to brunch." I laughed as Devin pulled me up and out of bed shoving us both into a cold shower.

By some miracle, we made it down just five minutes later than Margie had requested. There were *beignets, croissants, pain au chocolat,* as well as a variety of other assorted pastries waiting for them in the hotel's breakfast room.

The group was waiting for us to join them and when we did, Devin was assaulted with a hundred questions, the majority of which came from my sister,

"Where did you live before the ranch?"

"I grew up in Seattle,"

"Did you go to the University?"

"Only two years then my dad passed away and I moved to the ranch."

She only hesitated a moment to offer condolence for the loss of his dad. "What was your major?"

"Art Appreciation, if you'd believe it." At this, everyone, especially me, looked at Devin.

"You were an Art major?" I asked.

Devin snickered a bit, "Yeah. I wasn't sure what I wanted to officially do, something between architecture and graphic design, so my advisor recommended I declare a major of art appreciation and I could change when I made up my mind."

I elbowed Devin in the side and said, "I think you are lying."

"Do you now," Devin's reaction undeterred, "I'll have to have my transcripts sent to you then."

"No need," Margie getting into the game, responded, "I can settle this once and for all. So, you said you have two years as an art appreciation major, that would mean you have the basics. Who painted the Mona Lisa?"

"Oh, that is too easy, Leonardo da Vinci."

"Ok, what year did he paint it?"

"Ahh, now you are playing dirty and I remind you I was an Art Appreciation major NOT Art History, but if I remember correctly, it was either 1503 or 1504 and before you ask, it was in Florence that he painted the lovely lady."

Seeing he was beginning to impress the group, he continued. "Some say the Mona Lisa is Lisa Gherardini, the wife of Francesco del Giocondo and that is more likely true than not."

Devin turned to me. "But I believe the mischievous smile belonged to his muse, one of his lovers, Gian Giacomo Caprotti da Oreno. Gian was referred to as the 'little devil' by all of da Vinci's family. That smile on Mona Lisa's face was neither happy nor sad, but it was definitely the smile of someone who had a secret...I believe that is the secret smile of a lover.

We know da Vinci was more interested in men than women, so it is unlikely he had an affair with his patron's wife, but it is also my thought that the smile is the reason he never gave the Mona Lisa to the patron who had commissioned it. I also think we get some insight into the relationship between the painting and the artist's lover by the simple fact that da Vinci bequeathed the Mona Lisa to Gian upon his death. What makes this most impressive is at the time of his death, some estimated that the painting was even then a priceless treasure—some estimates going as high as the equivalent of 200,000 euros today."

Finishing his history lesson, Devin stuck the rest of a *pain au chocolat* into his mouth, winked at me and grinned while chewing.

Dutifully impressed, the inquisition appeared to be stalled for the moment. Clearly approving of his knowledge and his sexualized conspiracy theory, Margie turned to my sister and began a discussion on how they'd convince the guards to give them a quick peek at the Mona Lisa after viewing the exhibit.

I couldn't hear all of the discussion, but I thought I heard something about wearing an off-the-shoulder dress with copious amounts of cleavage showing, combined with the necessary amount of flirting. I assumed they had a chance, considering we were in France and French men seemed exceptionally susceptible to the flirtation of attractive women.

With the attention drawn away from us, I turned to Devin and over another *pain du chocolat*, asked, "When you heard about my art, why didn't you tell me you were an art connoisseur?"

Devin almost choked on his pastry at my question, "Two years in undergraduate school hardly makes me a connoisseur. I didn't think it was consequential. All I have are some history lessons and some pretty outlandish theories about the homosexuality of the greats."

"Yeah," Aiden chuckled, "a theory that kinda turned me on. Remind me to ask about your take on the Sistine Chapel."

"Oh," Devin replied, "If Mona turned you on, we won't get out of the bed for a week after I explain what I see in Michelangelo's paintings..."

"I'm still amazed about how much we don't know about each other. You were an Art major, I'm an artist, shouldn't that be something we both knew?"

Devin chuckled again, "If I remember right, you really just wanted to get away from me the first few hours after meeting, then, you slept like a log, cleaned like no one I've ever met, then attacked me for sex."

It was my turn to choke, "So that is how you see our time together--I'm an obsessive cleaner that just wanted to get into your pants!"

"Yep," Devin tapped his head like he was trying to remember, "that pretty much wraps it up."

"Devin Pierce, you are a total jackass. I never knew I had such a thing for jackasses."

Devin leaned over the table toward me, but before he kissed me, said, "I'm really glad you do."

Margie, true to form, shuffled everyone to our rooms to change for the day. She had the entire day mapped out and checked off the day's agenda with each of us. She told us we would go to the Louvre to check in with the curator and meet up with Jace who had set up a time after the Louvre had closed to see the exhibit.

She and Suzie exchanged sly looks. Clearly neither of them was above seducing a guard into giving them a tourist-free look at the Mona Lisa. Margie continued with her agenda, stating that after leaving the Louvre they'd catch the sites of Paris, come back to dress for the evening, have dinner and then go back to the Louvre for their private showing of the collection.

Confident that Margie's preparations were adequate, the group was off, each of us understanding the sequence of the day's events. When we arrived at the Louvre, Margie had the driver pull around to the designated area where we had been instructed to meet the Louvre's staff. I could see a posse of people waiting for us in the corridor.

I couldn't help but make a comparison of the British nobility returning to their country home with the staff at attention, waiting for us. As each of our party stepped out of the car we were greeted with smiles, which I thought very unusual for the French. When I stepped out there was applause. To say I was taken aback would be a massive understatement and I froze in my tracks at the gesture of appreciation. Devin stepped up behind me, put his hand around my waist, bent down and whispered in my ear, "Imagine they are all naked," which caused me to laugh and undid the shocked state I had been in. I shyly bowed before them and thanked them for their generous reception.

The curator introduced herself as Inez Boutella then introduced the rest of the staff. "These are the people who are in charge of your collection and the display of it here at the Louvre," she said.

After the introductions, she and Jace pulled me ahead of the rest of the group and into her office. She handed me a set of passes and instructions on how to access the building after closing.

The curator first looked at Jace, then me and asked, "We have the press here and they would very much like to meet you. They, of course, know of your collection, but they also heard you and your family were arriving tonight to see the collection before it is opened to the public. They have asked if you would give a brief interview."

My first thought was to decline, then I thought of Margie's and Suzie's plotting to get a private tour and before I could stop myself, I agreed. "Yes," I said, "but only under one condition—before I conduct the interview, I would like my party, including myself, to be given a private tour of the Louvre. We are especially interested in seeing the Mona Lisa."

I turned to the window and winked outside the office at my sister and Margie; then turned to see a terrified look on Jace's face. After only a moment's hesitation, Madame Boutella, a woman who appeared to be in her fifties and whose professional, if not sharp demeanor, clearly kept her staff on a short rope, shrugged and said, "But of course, monsieur, it would be our pleasure. Oh, one more thing, the director wanted me to ask if there were any other paintings in your series or if you thought that you might be planning more paintings?"

Startled and not anticipating the question, Jace jumped into the conversation, "No..."

But before she could finish, I chimed in. "Yes, actually there is still one painting that is part of the collection, but I have kept that one as a gift for someone else." Seeing Jace's alarmed look, I quickly added, "The piece was not included in the sale nor in the contract for the paintings you have purchased."

In French, the curator said almost to herself, *"Je savais qu'il manquait un ..."* She looked back at us and continued in English. "The director and I argued, he was the one who was at the show in New York and he was the one who made the offer. He said he knew this was the entire collection, but I believed one must be missing."

The woman seemed to be struggling to explain how she knew a painting was missing. Finally she said, "Almost every detail in the larger paintings had a matching smaller painting that, how do you say, *démontré le détail*—demonstrated the detail ... the last big painting, it has an obvious detail that I would've thought you'd have, what do you say ... 'accent'."

Dutifully impressed, I looked at the curator and said, "You are correct, the very last painting is the one I kept. It is a small painting that finishes the entire set."

The curator sighed, clearly pleased with herself, "I assume you don't have it with you, would you? It is a shame the entire collection isn't together."

I looked outside the office once again—this time catching Devin's eye. "Actually, you are in luck, Mademoiselle. The painting is in Paris, but it isn't in my possession. It belongs to one of the people I have brought with me. You will have to convince him to part with it."

The curator was beside herself with excitement, and now speaking only in French, too excited to translate, asked to speak with the owner, begging for the piece to be loaned to the museum for the showing. I agreed to speak with the owner and to get back with her.

Later, after Madame Boutella bid us farewell and asking again to see if the last piece could be loaned to the exhibition, Jace and I stood in the small corridor the group had entered into upon arriving.

Jace reached over and punched me in the arm saying, "Why the hell didn't you tell me there was another piece? God, I spent three days negotiating the contract and had I not been your best advocate ever, you could have been held liable for holding a piece back. The Louvre's original contract demanded that any current or future projects associated with this collection would be given to them to purchase. I had to negotiate with the director to have the language deleted and they only did so because I threatened to pull out of the deal and sell to individuals, telling them others had offered more than their bid."

I shrugged and said, "I forgot. I had some stuff draped over the easel when your men came to the house to pick up the final paintings, and by the time I found the painting, you were ready for the show. I didn't dare bring another piece into the gallery after you'd changed it around for the millionth time."

"Aiden, I have a mind to skin you here and now, but I'm afraid of the iron lady curator. I've been terrified of her since we met. I thought she was going to tell you to go to hell ... *Alenz en enfer!*" Jace said waiving her hands in the air in almost perfect impersonation of the intimidating curator.

I laughed at her before responding, "No, not with her staff watching. They are making a show of me. I'm guessing my interview, and now even the tour will help justify the purchase and make the work and showing of a little-known artist's work seem more legit. I wonder if they are having buyer's remorse."

"No, I think not," Jace commented. "Your name has been passed around the art world a lot lately. In fact, I didn't plan to tell you this until after tonight, but since you brought it up, you've been asked to give a number of interviews, mostly by art magazines, but some from larger magazines and news outlets as well. You, my boy, are becoming famous."

I shrugged that off. "At the moment, I just want to enjoy Paris and not worry about being famous. Mostly I just wanted to be with Devin."

"Oh, that reminds me, I will be firing a certain wench when I get back to New York. She called me after she gave that man your itinerary, feeling guilty and concerned he might be a deranged admirer. I called ahead to your hotel and asked that they keep whoever was showing up from getting to you until we sorted it all out. In fact, I tried to call you to tell you he was coming, but you were on the plane, and after texting me, you disappeared." Jace shifted, looked back over to me and added, "So, I'm hoping he isn't dangerous. Well, I'm hoping he isn't a serial killer ... I can see he is dangerous. Those eyes and sexy body are more than a little dangerous, I'm sure. So, what's the scoop, why is he with you? More important, why is he touching you and whispering in your ear? Yeah," she looked at me with knowing eyes, "I noticed that!"

On a sigh, I responded, "He is the muse. He is what sparked the inspiration for all this. Long story short, he is why I went to Spokane, why I disappeared for a while. Because of his importance to this project, I invited him to the showing. Our last conversation didn't go so well, so I didn't think he was coming. Obviously, he had a change of heart and here he is."

"Obviously," she responded, "I want a lot more details before this is done, but for now, promise me he isn't going to kill you or rob the Louvre or anything."

"I promise nothing, Jace. Absolutely nothing."

"You know how to make a gal feel better, Aiden," she said with a huff. "So, he has the painting? When did you give it to him?"

"I haven't yet. I accidentally left it at his home while there. I took it to prove I was a real artist and not a pervert trying to get into his pants. My story was a bit outlandish ... My parents showed up and whisked me away and I left it in his living room. His excuse for coming all this way was to return it to me."

"So, you are going to give him the painting now, then take it away from him?"

"Nope," I replied, "I am going to give it to him then he'll decide what to do with it."

"This guy is the reason why you were a bitch for the last month?"

"I wasn't a bitch," I said feeling wounded. "But he was the reason why my heart was broken. I now get the chance to see if he is the man I think I'm in love with."

Jace sighed, "I do enjoy a good love story ... but this one had better get a move on. *Dame de Fer* will not wait for a decision about that painting and I'm sure it'll end up being my hide that is beaten if she doesn't get her answer soon."

"I'll have an answer for you this evening," I replied.

"That will work, now go away so I can go back and make arrangements with the lady of iron!"

Devin

I watched Aiden during his conversation with the curator and the woman he introduced as Jace. All the time I watched him, I had to dodge questions from Suzie and Margie. The inquisition had begun again during the lag time waiting for Aiden to finish his interview.

It seemed the group had appointed the two women to conduct the interrogation, but everyone within earshot was listening intently. Once or twice, Steve would chime in with a question or two but that was mostly to ensure I knew Aiden had back-up.

I both recognized and appreciated the gesture. I was sure Steve would be someone I could, at the very least, respect if not come to really like in the future.

At one point in their conversation, I saw Aiden's face freeze with a look of terror. I felt cold alarm, like ice water being poured over a fire. I stood up to go to Aiden when the look switched from terror to mischievous, followed by a wink at his sister and

Margie. I wasn't totally sure what Aiden was planning, but he was up to something clever.

When I stood up, the entire group turned their attention toward the conversation in the office, and just as I was about to sit back down, Aiden turned toward me, but not entirely seeing me. I knew the conversation had somehow involved me, but I wasn't quite sure how or why. I guessed I'd find out soon enough.

Aiden's father, with his super dad skills, continued to watch me like he had the first time we met on the ranch, and since arriving the previous night. I could tell he was assessing whether I measured up to the standards he knew his son deserved. I must have passed the test because when I stood up in a protective way, it seemed to trigger both his approval and support, so with the authority only a loving father could have, Bob ended the interrogation with, "Let's *all* take a walk outside and give the boy a rest for a moment. There'll be plenty of time for questions later."

Clearly, Bob wasn't one to be disobeyed since the group did as he instructed. I walked into the corridor and admired some of the pieces reserved for the private walls of administration. There were no ancient works of art, no, these pieces had been painted recently and I suspected by the employees who worked at the museum. Although there were no plaques speaking to such a probability, it was clear that each painting had been done by people who admired art maybe more than they had the talent to paint it.

I had circled the office corridor and came into the main room just as Aiden and Jace were finishing their conversation.

Jace turned to me, smiled and said, "Speaking of the god, here he is now." Aiden watched my expression and laughed at Jace's statement. Aiden took my arm and led me toward the door before I could respond.

"We'll see you this evening," he said to Jace and then drew me out the door before she had a chance to respond.

Of course, I had a hundred questions, but Aiden put me off, saying, "I'll fill you in later, but first I need to get rid of my family."

When we reached the group, who were standing next to a rather modern piece of sculpture all either ignoring, admiring or blankly staring at the piece, he said, "I hate to do this, but I need to have some time alone with Devin, we have something rather important to discuss. Would you mind if we let you tour the sites and Devin and I will catch up to you at dinner?"

Steve looked over and said, "Man, you can have sex later. You dragged us here, now you gotta play host." It was Steve's turn to get Aiden's stern look.

"This isn't about sex—it is about the exhibit and it has something to do with Devin. I promised the curator and Jace that I'd discuss this with him before tonight."

Again, Aiden's dad came to his rescue, "Son, if it is important, then, you go with Devin." He looked over at Steve with an expression that clearly meant that was the end of the discussion. With that, Aiden and I took our leave of the group.

Aiden took my hand and led me toward the river. "Do you mind walking, Devin?" He asked. "I need to talk to you about something."

"Sure," I responded, "But for the life of me, I have no idea what I have to do with your exhibit."

"Well," Aiden began, "The painting you brought back with you, I intended to give that to you after having some pretty spectacular Parisian sex. Then, after you got it, you were supposed to be so impressed that we'd have more spectacular sex, but the curator threw a wrench into my plans and really screwed up my scheme to get more out of you. They want to exhibit it with the rest of the collection. I've already told them it was yours, so the decision had to be yours to make."

As Aiden said he was giving the painting to me, shock stopped me in my tracks. "You want to give me your painting? The one you left at my home and that I brought halfway across the world to return to you?"

"Yes," Aiden chuckled at my response, "I think I had always intended to give it to you. I'd even go so far as to admit, I may have deliberately forgotten to give it to the gallery and forgot to mention it to Jace. Then, I might have deliberately forgotten to bring it back with me when we left the ranch. I think this painting belongs to you and I think in some metaphysical way, it wants to be yours, as well."

I stood dumbfounded, staring at the Seine. "That painting speaks to me ... I won't pretend that I almost didn't return it. There is part of my soul that selfishly wanted to hide it away and never let another person see it, but owning it was nothing like having its creator in my life. To have the chance of having you and it ... I don't actually know what to say."

"So," responded Aiden, "Can we still have the spectacular sex?"

I grabbed Aiden in a hug, lifting him up into the air, kissing him long and hard on the lips, "Oh baby, we are going to have some *spectacular sex!*"

The moment we got to the hotel room, clothing hit the floor as the door closed, and I pushed Aiden onto the bed with an assurance that I was going to show him just how much I appreciated my gift.

My desperate kisses started at Aiden's mouth and then gently flowed down his chest and stomach until my lips wrapped around his glorious penis. I slipped

Aiden's cock in and out of my mouth until he pushed me away saying I was going to force him to come too soon.

With this revelation, I forced Aiden's legs into the air and began to lick the recesses of his ass, pulling the moans of pleasure out of my love. I warmed him up, reaching up for his cock as I loosened up his ass. Aiden squirmed under me, and then with a quick move, I flipped him onto his knees then slipped on the condom. I dug my hands into his hips, slowly allowing my cock's head to begin penetration. Aiden moaned and thrust himself toward me to get deeper, but I'd be damned if I was going to pass up the opportunity to squeeze every ounce of delight out of the act. I wanted it slow, pushing my head in then pulling it out over and over each time a little deeper, but maybe a bit cruelly, not giving into Aiden, who was now begging me to move faster and fuck him deeper. I kept my grip firmly on him, teasing him with how much I let him push back into me, until I could feel his muscles coiling desperately under my fingers.

When Aiden was lost to a state of ecstasy, it was then that I thrust himself fully into him. He screamed my name and each thrust brought the man closer to the edge. Finally, with sheer force, Aiden came with a final thrust of my dick inside him.

I still hadn't come so I laid Aiden gently on his back, pulled the condom off and jacked off into Aiden's mouth. Aiden gladly accepted my cock, mouth damp and gaping, as I both fucked Aiden's mouth and jacked off at the same time.

My moans alerted Aiden that I was about to cum and Aiden wrapped his lips around the head of my cock to accept the entirety of what I had to offer. I doubled over with a soft cry, and caught my breath as he shuddered under me. Aiden swallowed just in time for me to lean down and kiss him.

We both fell into each other's arms and relaxed in the afterglow of our love.

When we began to regain consciousness, I looked over at Aiden and asked, "Do I have to leave the painting here?"

"No, of course not. It belongs to you and you can do with it as you please."

"Then I don't want to leave it here. I want it ... need it to be with me in the home I hope to share with you." Aiden nodded and told me he'd let the curator know that night.

Kissing and holding onto each other as if at any moment the other could be lost, we stepped into the shower.

I wrapped my arms around Aiden. Now that the demand to have him had been satiated, I wanted to show him how much I loved him. How much I'd missed him.

I got soap and began to wash him, first his back, then letting my hands roam across his beautiful chest and stomach. Aiden moaned when my soapy hands found his groin, and began to lather him there.

"Thank you, Aiden," I said fighting back tears of gratitude that he'd let me back in his life.

"For the painting?" he asked.

I chuckled despite myself, "Yes, and for giving me another chance, for not kicking me out of the hotel when you first saw me."

Aiden turned to me, filling his hands with soap and washing me now as well.

"You brought daylight back to my life by coming here, Devin. I should be thanking you."

We both wrapped ourselves around the other and let the shower wash over us, content to be in each other's arms.

When the moment had passed, I pulled Aiden away so I could look at his face and smiled asking, "Was the sex spectacular enough?"

Aiden looked back at me with a mischievous look and said, "It was pretty good, but what I had in mind required a lot more time than we have to spare."

"I'll keep that in mind, my love. I'll make sure to schedule you in for a day or two to properly pay you back for your gift."

"That is what I'd hoped you'd say," Aiden responded.

Finally, after getting dressed for the evening, Aiden and I went down to the lobby and grabbed a taxi to take us to the restaurant Margie had chosen for us. Dinner was a pleasure and the interrogating questions had ceased. I guessed Aiden's dad had stepped in to save us from an evening of unending inquiry.

I struggled not to monopolize Aiden knowing the event was about family and friends, so I begrudgingly pulled back and enjoyed the camaraderie of the group.

Margie and Suzie sat companionably with Aiden's parents discussing a myriad of subjects that ranged from Broadway to Greek literature. Steve, however, spoke mostly with Aiden. Aiden would bring up something from their childhood and he and Steve would laugh, then Steve would bring the conversation back to me, continuously keeping me in the loop.

Aiden often reached over and grabbed my hand in an unpracticed, even unconscious effort that endeared me to him even more. When the meal was over, the group was in high spirits. Margie demanded that the meal was on her, refusing to allow any other discussion, then whisked us all off toward the Louvre. The museum closed at 9:45 and Madame Boutella had asked us to be at the museum doors at 9:30.

We were to have a small reception with the director and some VIP guests, then they would be taken to view the collection.

True to her word, the curator was in the great hall waiting for us when we arrived. We were escorted to the VIP room. I didn't spend much time looking at world news, but I had enough to recognize several dignitaries, including the current, as well as one of the past French presidents.

The curator introduced everyone to Aiden. She escorted him first to a very old man who stood alone at the edge of the room. He was the one who donated the money for the Louvre to purchase Aiden's collection. "Your beautiful art was exactly what I had in mind when I gave the donation," the man said in an Italian accent. "You have made me very proud to be a part of this."

The curator then took Aiden over to the U.S. Ambassador to France. I watched the Ambassador shake his hand vigorously, and say he wished he'd been able to keep the collection in the U.S., but if it were to be displayed outside the country, the Louvre was the place.

I could see Aiden was feeling a bit like Cinderella at the ball. He watched his friends and family hobnob with the government elite.

I came up behind him and whispered, "Are you okay?"

He turned to me, smiling. "I don't think I'll ever forget the image of my father laughing with the French president over canapes. I would have traded my ability to paint just for the memory of this event," he said.

I leaned over and kissed him and said, "It is a remarkable evening."

After *hor 'd oeuvres* were finished, the Louvre's director clanged his glass for attention then announced that the family would, as agreed in the contract, be given the opportunity to view the collection in private first. When they were done, the rest of the congregants would be allowed into the gallery, he then announced that a private tour would be given to the family, and if anyone wished to follow along, that would be permissible. I could hear Margie and Suzie moan, frustrated that their private tour could be taken over with dignitaries.

Aiden

My family took our leave, escorted by Madame Boutella who left us at the gallery's entrance to explore on our own. The paintings had been hung in almost the exact placement as Jace had hung them— a point that hadn't escaped her and I could see her beaming with pride.

I watched my family and friends take in my exhibit for the first time. Emotion welled in their eyes and I noticed my father put his arm around mom and kiss her on the cheek, whispering something that made her cry and cough at the same time.

Margie grabbed Suzie's hand and they walked around the room together. Steve stood spellbound in the middle of the room turning circles and staring at each of the paintings in turn.

When I finally laid eyes on Devin, I was shocked to see the giant of a man standing and staring at the art like a child. His hands were at his side and his mouth was open and slightly askew. Although I was not the best at deciphering human emotions, I could see that Devin was impressed. I was a little ashamed that more than anyone else in the room, his reaction brought me the greatest satisfaction.

The group, not unlike the New York crowd, took in the exhibit in silence. Eventually, mother came up behind me and hugged me tightly. "You have made your mother proud, sweet boy. Your dad and I have always known you had talent, but we didn't know you painted for the gods."

My father put a rough hand on my shoulder, squeezed tight and said, "You are a master now, never forget that." Both of them walked away with tears in their eyes.

Margie took their place. "I knew you had talent, Aiden, but to be honest, I sponsored you all those years because I liked you. Then, I fell in love with you and we became close friends. But, honey, I never expected you had this in you. This art, no, these *masterpieces*, they will go down in history with the greats ... I'm spellbound ... the first time in a very long time, honey, I don't know what else to say."

We both laughed at the thought she was without words. I hugged her then hugged my sister who confirmed how proud she was of me, and they both wandered over to where my parents were studying a particularly detailed monarch butterfly painting.

Before I knew what was happening, Steve grabbed me into a bear hug, "You can actually paint," he said, shocked. "I just thought you were full of yourself."

Admiring a best friend's ability to both complement and bring me back to earth, I laughed and returned his hug.

After what seemed like an eternity, the group reluctantly left the room. Devin came up behind me and simply said, "I had no idea ... the little painting is beautiful and now that I've seen the entire collection, I understand it better now but ... I had no idea."

I reached over and pressed a gentle kiss on his lips. "Now you do," I said as chipper as I could and walked toward my parents.

I heard the curator behind me ask Devin, "So, you are the one who owns the final piece of this collection, I presume?"

"Apparently, I am," he said and crossed over to her. I assumed they were hashing out the future of his piece as the others wandered the halls of the prestigious Louvre museum.

When the tour was done, I reluctantly walked toward the press room. Before entering, I looked for Devin, and smiled when I saw him standing next to the door—the closest place he could be without actually standing next to me. The protective and loving gesture warmed my heart and I was very happy to have him standing close enough that if things got tough, I could simply look over at my lover for reassurance.

The press conference was simple, and the press were not pushy nor flashy like I'd seen so often on television. Most of the questions were about the collection or about how I felt with my fresh notoriety.

As I suspected, I was eventually pressed about the inspiration for the piece and looking at Devin, allowing him to squirm a moment before answering, I looked at the reporter who asked the question and simply replied, "My inspiration came from someone who loves the land, nature and America's western landscapes as much as I." The reporter looked at Devin and hesitated as if she wanted to ask something further, but quickly backed off when she caught a glance from the curator.

The press conference ended quicker than I had expected, and I stepped to Devin's side and was preparing to leave when he whispered, "Hold up just one moment." I was surprised, but not nearly as much as when Madame Boutella announced that there was a final piece that would be added to the gallery tonight and would only be with the collection for one year before it was returned to its owner.

Then with a smile, she said in French, "Et dans la plus pure tradition française, la pièce finale se joindra chaque année à la collection pour marquer l'anniversaire de l'amour du peintre et du

350

propriétaire de la peinture." She turned to Devin and her smile broadened as she interpreted what she'd just said in English. "And in true French style, each year the final piece will join the collection for a week marking the anniversary of the love of the painter and the painting's owner."

Devin then conspicuously took my hand in his and led us out of the press room. The room was literally writhing with anticipation and from his smug look, I could tell Devin knew he had started a windstorm that was bound to ripple for years to come.

As we left, I whispered, "So, I see you changed your mind."

Devilishly, Devin responded, "You see correctly."

"So, what brought that on?" I asked.

When we rounded the corner and out of earshot of the reporters, Devin told me, "The second I saw the complete collection, I knew I couldn't be so selfish to keep even a small part of it from the public, at least not all the time. So, I compromised.

The museum agreed to place a monument in place of the missing piece that read:

'Love is life. All, everything that I understand, I understand only because I love. Everything is, everything exists, only because I love. Everything is united by it alone. Love is God, and to die means that I, a particle of love, shall return to the general and eternal source.'

"It is from Tolstoy," Devin concluded. "Once a year, on the anniversary of our meeting, the original painting will be sent to the Louvre to be hung in the place of that quote, but for one week only, then it is to be returned to me so that I am not separated from it but for a short time.

"The curator agreed to this?" I asked surprised.

"She agreed or the collection would never be complete. I also agreed to allow the painting to stay with them for exactly one year before it has to be returned to me. I told her I would be too busy with the painter to enjoy it properly for at least that long."

I laughed at Devin's antics and scolded him, "You seem pretty sure of yourself."

Devin nodded and said, "Oh, I have many plans for this year. I'm *very* sure. Aren't you?"

I nodded snuggling closer to Devin as we walked toward the waiting car.

EPILO GUE

Aiden

Arriving back to the States, we spent some time first in New York, collecting my things and closing my apartment. What couldn't be shipped, I sold or donated.

Devin constantly asked me if I was okay with such an abrupt change. Apparently, he was very concerned that I would back out, but he had no reason, my home was with him.

I kept reassuring him by saying although I was sad about leaving friends, I could always stay with Jace or Suzie if I needed a New York fix.

It only took a week to get things ready for my move and Devin was clearly happy to leave New York. Right before we left, Devin told me, even though he loved me, he hoped he wouldn't be required to spend much time in the city.

From New York, we flew straight to Spokane. Claire met us at the airport and seeing us at the gate, she grabbed me in a huge bear hug and told me how much she missed me.

Then, she playfully elbowed my tummy and said, "Don't ever leave me again without a proper goodbye. Hell, if Devin hadn't got some sense when he did, I was going to come find you myself."

I promised her I wouldn't and hugged her again. I was so happy to be back with the two of them again. After all the proper hugs were out of the way, Claire rushed us to her old truck.

"What's the hurry?" Devin asked.

Claire mischievously responded, "I have a date tonight and I need to get back in time to spruce up." Aiden smiled, and Devin cocked an eyebrow.

"In all the years we've known each other, this is the first time I've known you to have a date, Claire McDane. Why is it I'm just hearing of this?"

"Well, first," she said, "it isn't any of your damned business, and second, because I was testing him out before I made a fuss about him."

I chimed in before Devin ended up going too far and pushing where his overly protective nose didn't belong. "So, tell us the details ... is he hot?"

Claire burst out laughing, "For an old man, he is pretty hot."

"How did you meet him?" I asked.

"Well, after you left, I figured if Devin had been so lucky with his online thing, I should try it out myself.

I met him on a dating site for country folks—straight ones, that is."

"Oh, this is getting tastier by the minute," I exclaimed.

Claire elbowed me again and climbed into her truck and we climbed in beside her. I sat in the middle, saying I wanted to be closer to Claire so we could get to the juicy details quicker than if we had the stick-in-the-mud between us and I gestured toward Devin.

As we merged into traffic, Devin asked, "What do you know about him, is he safe? Are you sure he isn't trying to rob you or something?"

Both Claire and I looked crossly at Devin, and Claire said, "No, he is very responsible. In fact, he is a retired Agribusiness professor from Eastern Oregon University where he has a daughter about to graduate with that very same degree."

"Does that mean she is going to be trying to get me to hire her?" Devin asked irritably.

"I doubt it," Claire said, "considering her father just bought a vineyard."

We both looked at her and she returned our look with a smile.

"Which vineyard?" Devin asked.

"Oh," Claire said nonchalantly, "You know, the one we stole the wine from."

I couldn't help myself and laughed heartily at the coincidence, then laughed harder when I turned and saw Devin's expression.

"Claire, you are something else," I said, and we side hugged as she drove down the road.

"What happens if it doesn't work out?" Devin asked.

"Oh, hush," I chided. "If it doesn't work out then it won't be nearly as uncomfortable as it could've been us living next to your pervert ex-boyfriend's family."

Devin couldn't argue with that and we drove the long way from Spokane to the ranch chatting about everything from the new neighbor/hot new boyfriend to the Paris show.

"I wish you could've been there, Claire. It was something else."

"Next time, you'll be inviting me to the soiree," she said.

I answered with an unequivocal yes. She would always be a part of his family from then on. I also knew I'd want her with me from now on when life's big events happened.

Life on the ranch was filled with joy, as well as the expected hiccups anyone would expect from a couple who fell in love and then moved in together after less than two weeks of romance. I required that I be able to keep the stable apartment in case I needed to get away from Devin, and getting my wish, I went to work updating and renovating it.

When I was done, the little apartment was a mix of western and shabby chic. When my family came to visit, they usually fought over who'd get to stay there—everyone with the exception of Margie, of course, who 'refused to sleep in a barn', as she put it.

The little room behind the stairs became my favorite place on the ranch. Just as Claire had predicted, it fit me perfectly with just the right amount of coziness and perfect lighting. I painted the walls a stark white, so they would be neutral enough for my paintings, but I also added warmth in cream-colored sheers which I loved to watch flow with the breezes on warm afternoons and evenings when I could leave the windows open.

The first-floor bedroom, which was the house's original master, became an extension of my studio and the place where I hung my art between shows. Of course, this was the room Margie claimed as her own, and as such, I fitted it with a small crystal chandelier and antique four-poster bed I found when Devin and I were exploring the small towns in eastern Oregon and Washington that surrounded our ranch.

Devin and I worked together to renovate the rest of the first floor of the home, debating paint colors and kitchen designs which led to numerous arguments and just as many delightful make-up sessions. As we had with the small room cleanup, we enjoyed working side by side on the house renovations. As promised, one of the first things I did was to send the ugly, but remarkably comfortable sofa to an upholsterer I found in Walla Walla. When Devin argued about the cost and travel to have the thing redone, I told him that was one thing which was non-negotiable. If he wanted me to live in Eastern Washington, miles from civilization, I would *not* be living in the same house as that ugly upholstery.

Naturally, I got my way and when the sofa returned, it sat proudly and beautifully as a focal point in the room. The warm creams with accents of black and brown perfectly accented the turn of the century dark woodwork in the room. Even Devin had to admit it was a very adequate improvement over the 1980's fabric it once had.

The days went by fast and there were plenty of rain storms that kept us in place—times we learned to love, knowing we would be cooped up together like we were when we first fell in love.

After a year of life on the ranch together, we formally got engaged and were married a few months later in Claire's beautiful bungalow garden overlooking the river and pastures. Everyone, from Devin's Seattle friends to my New York friends, and of course, my family from Kansas City, converged on the ranch.

We rented yurts that the ranch hands helped to construct around the stable where there was plenty of access to restrooms and showers.

Of course, no one would've expected a large wedding party out in the middle of nowhere, but our love affair had become quite the thing among our friends.

Suzie, Margie, and my mother flew out to assist with decorating for the wedding. Both Devin and I were firm that we wanted the décor to be minimal so that we could accent the natural beauty of the place. Despite that, Claire and the others ganged up on us and brought in flowers, and streamed lights. The effect was simple, but breathtakingly beautiful.

The experience was a festival in and of itself, and as such, a new tradition was formed that occurred every year around our wedding anniversary.

The event became so popular with our friends and family that Devin eventually had an old derelict workers' quarters that hadn't been used since World War Two, rebuilt into a lodge with big shower rooms and toilets for the occasion.

As Claire had indicated, calving time was wicked busy, and I did what I could to be a useful part of the ranch life. Although I made damned sure my husband understood I was never going to be one of his ranch hands, when needed, I loved working alongside the men.

One evening after having too much to drink, I disclosed Claire's secret about her inheritance and the fact that she didn't need the job to Devin, which of course, made her angry.

"Well," I responded, "now that *I'm* the mistress of the place, I can do most of the heavy lifting and there is no need for you to be traipsing over here unless you want to."

After a week of being mad, she forgave me and took to the new arrangement like a fish to water. Unless it rained, or she was helping her new man-toy at the winery, she showed up for a few hours each day to help me feed the troops or more often, just to shoot the bull with me—her new best friend.

Needless to say, Claire and I were keen on our monthly trips to Walla Walla, Kennewick or even Spokane to get in our treasured shopping spree. We would always spend the night at a posh hotel, at Devin's expense, of course, get a massage if it were available, and of course, what shopping spree was complete without a mani-pedi?

Claire's new man built a nice bridge between the winery and the ranch and put down gravel between his home and her little bungalow. It took some convincing to get Devin to go along with it, but Claire reminded him that the bungalow was hers and that she needed a way to get off the ranch when the floods hit.

"I hate depending on the Wickerman Bridge that floods every damned year. This way, we always have a way out," she argued.

As time went on, she and her man had become fairly inseparable and preferring her bungalow over the monster mansion on the ranch, she wanted a way for him to be able to get back and forth to the winery even when the flood waters were up. He never complained about the cost and secretly, I thought the bridge was his way of giving Claire her independence while still keeping her close.

When they finally got married, they continued to live in two separate homes, although I doubt they ever spent more than a couple nights apart. deLisha the drag queen came to the wedding and stood as Claire's maid of honor. The two had become intensely close, which was amusing, considering that Claire was a backwoods country woman and deLisha was a six foot three African American drag queen who wore remarkable red wigs and strutted a beautiful figure most women would die for. As fate would have it, deLisha found her a man while at the wedding ... but that was another story.

I never knew if Claire ever disclosed their heist involving the wine with her new man, but over the years, his wine improved significantly. Within five years, they were beginning to receive awards for excellence. I sort of guessed the heisted wine became the standard the new owners strived toward, but since I swore never to disclose their secret, and it was never brought up, I never knew for sure.

Claire and Suzie hit it off like champions. When she came to visit, Claire would insist that she stay at the bungalow with her. Many years later, when Claire and her husband went to live at a senior living facility in Milton-Freewater, Oregon, Suzie bought the bungalow from her saying that she would eventually retire there. Of course, Suzie's husband and children would have a say about that, but again, that too is another story.

I continued to paint and my work improved as my relationship with Devin deepened. Jace told me more than once what the missing ingredient must have been was love.

I knew she was right. Even I could admit that my earlier work missed the warmth and reflection that my paintings had now. Jace would tease me about my pieces calling them BD or AD—before Devin or after Devin. I swore if she ever made that a thing, I'd write about her as a nasty, needy gallery owner if I ever wrote an autobiography. Jace, of course, laughed and said she didn't mind me telling the world the truth about her.

I continued to have pieces that received acclaim. To my surprise and delight, my art continued to be sought after throughout the world. Instead of making me feel like I'd accomplished something, it humbled me knowing that even after I'd trained most of my life in the skills of art, it was love and the intense support of my lover that made me a real artist.

I made a distinct effort not to be stingy with my art, but when a piece needed to stay at home, I used it to decorate the homestead with scenes I captured on or around the ranch. I also gave several strategic paintings of the gardens around the cute little bungalow to Claire which she relished her entire life.

Devin seemed to be my number one admirer, and he guarded the first piece I gave him like a dragon guarded a diamond. I loved how much he admired and cherished his gift.

Devin and I were solid and lifelong lovers, each giving and taking, learning to love and cherish the other while enriching our lives with friends and family, as well as a host of family dogs. Those who say love that occurs like a wildfire can't last don't take into consideration that with the right amounts of support, passion, respect, and just a little bit of stubborn determination, few things could stop a love affair like ours.

THE END

CPSIA information can be obtained
at www.ICGtesting.com
Printed in the USA
FSHW012037190519
58279FS

9 781091 846678